holding on

The Haven, Montana Series

JILL
SANDERS

Summary

Trey McGowan is no stranger to the inside of a jail cell, but this time it really wasn't his fault. Well... maybe a little. What's worse is that the gorgeous hottie he was defending didn't even notice. But make no mistake, the jerk she was with really had it coming. Now she has the nerve to show up, looking for work. And not just for her! She wants him to hire the a-hole who was pushing her around, too. And with the legs on this one, he was tempted to consider it, just to keep her around.

Dylan has had a run of bad luck. After losing both parents to a tragic accident, she was left in the care of older brother, Brent, who hasn't exactly been a model parent. He'd started off okay, but in the last few years she'd felt like she was babysitting him. Now, he's dragged her to Haven, Montana, in a last-ditch effort to find work. To make matters worse, he just punched Trey McGowan, one of the only men in town who could guarantee work for both of them. This may require a little persuasion.

holding on

JILL SANDERS

GRAYTON
PRESS

Jill Sanders

*Remember to look up at the stars
and not down at your feet.*

Stephen Hawking

Text copyright © 2018 Jill Sanders

Printed in the United States of America

Published by Grayton Press

DIGITAL ISBN: 978-1-942896-97-5

PRINT ISBN: 978-1718675-13-1

Chapter One

*Y*ou know those feel-good movies that start with the heroine driving down a long highway in a convertible, the wind blowing her long hair while dark sunglasses shade her eyes from the bright sunlight as iconic music plays loudly in the background? Yeah, Dylan's life was nothing like that.

Once again, she was sitting in the police station waiting for her brother's paperwork to be filed so she could use the rest of their small savings to bail him out. This would be the last time, she told herself, and this time she really meant it.

Glancing at her watch, she groaned when she realized only five minutes had passed since the last time she'd checked the time.

Leaning her head back against the wall, she closed her eyes and dreamed of a different life. One where she could have a small patch of land of her

7

own, a horse, maybe two, a solid job that didn't require her to wear short skirts and earn tips based on how big her tits looked that night. Maybe even a good man by her side, one that she wasn't having to bail out at least once a month.

"McCaw," someone shouted. Dylan bolted awake.

"Yes." She rushed to the window.

"Your brother has been processed," the clerk said from behind the thick glass. "How would you like to post his bail?"

"Can I write a check?" she asked, pulling out her checkbook. *There goes what little future I'd hoped for*, she thought as she wrote a check for almost every dime she'd saved over the past several years.

Had it really been almost four years since their parents had died in the boating accident off the coast of Mexico? What would become their last family vacation had turned tragic on just the second day of their trip to Cancun.

It had been their parents' twenty-second anniversary and, a week later, her brother's twenty-first birthday. Her dad had splurged on an all-inclusive deal for the whole family—snorkeling, sight-seeing, you name it. They had planned on doing it all together.

The first day had been wonderful, with the exception of Brent complaining that he had to spend his birthday with his family instead of his girlfriend-at-the-moment, Tilly.

But on day two, Brent was actually excited about snorkeling. They'd taken a boat to the snorkeling site, and the guides had set each of them up with the gear they needed. They had all jumped into the water eagerly.

They'd taken a break around lunchtime and enjoyed sandwiches with the other people who'd been booked on the same tour.

After lunch, her mother hadn't been feeling well, and the group had agreed to return to shore early. Dylan and Brent had been sitting near the front of the boat, and Brent had been pestering her about a text message she'd received from Jax, her boyfriend at the time.

She remembered the sound of the engine starting and vaguely remembered hearing her father say that something didn't sound right just before a loud explosion threw both her and her brother more than fifty feet into the water.

She had hit the water hard and had inhaled more than a mouthful of salt water.

Brent had gripped her wrist and pulled her to the surface. Then he'd wrapped his arms around her and swum towards the destruction. The boat had still been engulfed in flames, and she'd screamed for her brother to stay away from it.

"Mom and Dad are in there," he'd screamed at her.

Her mind had gone blank for the rest of her time in the water. It had almost been like watching a horror movie. She couldn't do anything but watch the boat burn and sink. By the time she had regained herself, she and her brother were being hoisted into another boat. Blankets were wrapped around her shoulders. She remembered laughing at this. It was strange since it was so hot outside, and she'd actually still felt sticky from the heat.

But her teeth had been chattering and she couldn't control the shaking. Her brother had wrapped his arms around her and cried as she stared blankly at the water where the boat had gone down.

She and Brent had been the lucky ones that day. Two more people had been pulled out of the water, but both had needed multiple surgeries. She'd heard that one of them had lost his leg in the explosion.

For the first year after their parents' death, Brent had taken complete control of everything and she'd blindly allowed him to. Then a little over a year later, he'd been arrested at a bar.

She'd been a month away from graduation when she'd gotten the call. She'd had to drive down to the police station and learn all about posting bail. It had been humiliating. And it had kept her up all night. By the time her brother walked out of the building, she was late for first period and had to go to school in the yoga pants and sweatshirt she'd been wearing the night before.

From that day on, Dylan had taken over the role

of provider while her brother threw his life away.

She had found out that, over the course of that year, he'd blown almost every dime of their parents' money.

Within three months of Dylan's graduation, they'd had to put the house up for sale. Before it could sell, the bank had repossessed it, taking any money they would have gained from the sale away from them.

They had sold all the family's possessions in a hasty garage sale, and Dylan had hidden half of the money away from her brother in a checking account under her name only. She'd gotten a job waiting tables, then had gotten another job at a car wash.

By the time she'd turned twenty-one, she was working three full-time jobs while her brother bounced from small job to small job, occasionally being hauled into the jailhouse for public intoxication or bar fights.

A month before her birthday, she had found out that Brent had emptied her checking account. She'd made her car payment on time but her check had bounced.

She'd rushed to the bank and had found out that her account was overdrawn. When she'd confronted her brother, he'd yelled at her and told her that she didn't understand the pressure he was under.

A week later, her car had been repossessed, and she'd been kicked out of her apartment when she couldn't pay the rent.

She'd saved her money until she could afford a two-hundred-dollar piece of tin that would get her to and from her many jobs. Brent's truck had been a graduation gift from their parents, and he still drove around in the shiny massive beast that was decked out like some spoiled country boy's toy.

The next big chunk of her money had gone to move them into an apartment on the south side of Seattle, the part of town where you locked your car doors and tried to avoid eye contact with other drivers.

The one-bedroom place had only allowed her to sign a three-month lease, since her credit scores were so low, and she'd had to pay the three months in advance along with a security deposit.

Brent didn't seem to mind sleeping on the old pull-out sofa or sharing the tiny bathroom with her. Actually, about the only thing her brother did mind was talking about money or about him getting a full-time job.

"McCaw." Once again, her name was yelled out, and it echoed in the sterile waiting area.

She rushed over to the window. "Your brother is being released. You can head down to the east exit. He'll be there."

"Thank you." She tucked her purse close to her side and walked down the long hallway. As she went, she planned out her speech. She was going to force Brent out of her place. She simply couldn't afford to be his sister any longer. He was dragging her so far down, they were both drowning, and she needed to start thinking about her own future.

"Hey, sis." Brent looked to be in good spirits as he walked out, and she wondered what sort of scheme he'd try to talk her into next. He wrapped his arm around her shoulders. "Have I got an opportunity for us."

"What?" she asked, feeling her entire body tense.

"I met some guys last night, and they're heading over to Montana later this week. They say there are high paying jobs up there for guys like me."

She raised her eyebrows. "Guys like..." She let the rest hang.

"You know." He flexed his muscle. There was only one aspect of her brother's life that he truly cared about. Lifting weights. Their little living area was full of weights. She couldn't even walk to the kitchen without stubbing her toe on a dumbbell.

"Okay." She held her breath. This was the first time he'd shown any interest in getting a good job. If he didn't change his mind, this could be a godsend.

"Don't worry about a thing, I'll make all the arrangements," Brent said as he climbed into her small car.

She inwardly groaned at the thought of her brother arranging anything on his own, but at least he was finally taking the initiative. Maybe this would be good for them both. He could head to Montana and make some money, and she could get on with her own life. She would hate not being close to him, but part of her was looking forward to being on her own for the first time in her life.

"They say there's good work up there for you, as well."

"Who is they?" she asked.

"Two guys I met last night at the bar."

"The same two that you say jumped you?" she asked.

"Huh?" He glanced over at her, then chuckled. "Naw, two different guys." He crossed his arms over his chest and seemed to take a nap as she drove them across town.

Glancing at her watch again, she groaned when she realized she wouldn't have enough time to shower before heading into work.

"I'm going to drop you off here. I have to get to work." She pulled to a stop in front of their building.

"Huh?" Her brother jolted awake. "Oh, sure, just leave everything to me." He smiled. "See you tonight."

"Right," she said before driving away.

Ten hours later, after being on her feet for most of it, every part of her body hurt. She'd had to swallow a couple aspirins halfway through the day.

Normally, she could make it through the workday on one soda, but today had been a three-soda kind of day. That told her it was past time for a day off.

As she was clocking out, Darian, the manager at Roco's Diner, waved her towards the back.

"I won't keep you long, but I thought it best to give you your final check." He handed her an envelope.

"Final…" She felt her heart miss an entire beat.

"We're sad to see you go, but I understand you and your brother have new jobs already lined up."

"Me and…" She felt her knees go weak. "Who?" She shook her head.

Darian smiled. "You look exhausted. You'd better get some rest before the big move."

"I…" She took a deep breath and blinked like someone had just throw water in her face.

Just then Darian's phone rang. "I've got to take this." He held out his hand for her to shake. "If you need anything…"

She left the building, unsure of what had just happened. She was halfway across the parking lot when she realized that her car wasn't where she'd parked it. Turning a full circle, she frowned as she hunted her bag for her keys, as if they could magically make her car reappear.

She dug to the bottom of her purse and frowned. She sat down on the curb behind the diner and dumped the contents of her purse out. Her keys should have been there. She always put them in her purse, which was stored in the back office along with all the other waitresses' things.

Just then, she heard a horn and jumped. Her brother drove up in his truck, a huge smile on his face. "Ready?" he called out to her through the open window.

"Brent, someone stole my car," she said, approaching the truck.

"Stole?" Brent frowned. "You mean sold." He smiled. "Get in. We've got lots of miles to go if we plan on making it."

"Sold?" She felt her headache return full steam. It was then that she noticed the boxes in the back seat of the truck. "What's all this?" She pointed to the back as he drove out of the parking lot.

"Our stuff. I think I got everything." He shrugged.

"Everything of what?" She glared at him.

"Our stuff." He chuckled as she climbed into his truck. She was almost on autopilot at this point. She'd gone almost two full days without sleep. Her entire body heated with anger as realization sunk in.

"You sold my car and packed up my stuff?" Her eyes narrowed. "Did you tell Darian I was quitting?"

Brent frowned over at her. "Well, sure, how else

are we going to move to Montana? You can't take the job with you and that old piece of shit car you drove would've never made it. Besides, we needed gas money."

"You sold my car!" Her mind refused to focus.

"I told you I'd take care of everything." He smiled over at her. "I have."

"Brent, I don't want to move to Montana!" She practically screamed it.

He was silent for a while. "I've already got a nice secretary job lined up for you."

"I don't care." She crossed her arms over her chest. "You don't get to make these kinds of decisions for me."

"But you'd be making more than you do now working three jobs."

Her eyes narrowed. "How do you know what I make?"

He smiled. "I took a guess. Besides, you'd have health benefits. You don't get those working three part-time jobs."

"Three full-time jobs," she corrected. "And yes, I had—"

"Besides," he interrupted. "I have a job working the oil fields. It's just what I've always wanted to do. It pays more than double what you'd be making."

She opened her mouth, then shut it and slowly let the breath out of her lungs. "How much?"

"Five figures a year."

"Minimum wage is five figures a year." She rolled her eyes. "How much?"

"Eighty-thousand," he said, but it sounded like he was just throwing a number out.

"You already have the job?" she asked slowly.

"Yes." He smiled.

She glanced back at all the boxes. "You packed up our stuff, sold my car, quit my job—"

"Jobs," he corrected with a smile.

"You did all this in one day?" she asked, feeling a little light-headed.

"It wasn't hard." He shrugged.

Her brother had never shown this much interest in anything in his life. The only thing he'd ever worked hard at was his physique.

"I'm too tired to think." She rolled her shoulders.

"Then don't. I'll take the first shift driving."

"We're leaving now?" She sat up a little straighter.

Brent chuckled. "Well, yeah." He nodded to all the boxes shoved in the back seat. She glanced behind and saw more boxes in the bed of the truck. "Work starts bright and early Monday morning."

Feeling a little hijacked, she wanted to argue, but she was far too tired to try and come up with a good debate. If he was telling the truth and they both had jobs waiting for them, then why fight it?

Montana or Seattle, the fact was, she didn't care either way. And she didn't have the energy to argue.

She rested her head against the glass. Her brother had dragged her around for the past few years, so what was once more? She drifted off to sleep as she thought about a new future in Montana. The possibility of working one job instead of three lifted so much weight off her shoulders that, for the first time in years, she slept like a baby.

***

Thurston McGowan the third, Trey to his family and friends and pretty much everyone else in the world, was drunk. And why not? He was celebrating the birth of his first nephew, Timothy Jack McGowan. A good name for a beautiful baby.

He'd spent the morning at the hospital with his brother Tyler and his wife, Kristen, along with the rest of his family. After everyone had been kicked out so that the new family could have some quiet time, he and his other brother, Trent, had hit the local bars along with several of their buddies.

One bar had turned into two, which had snowballed into hitting every single bar in the small town of Haven, Montana, before closing time, which was less than three hours away. They still had the biggest hole-in-the-wall bar, Carrie Ann's, to go.

The place was full of the lowest of the low. Trey and his brothers hardly ever stepped foot in the place, unless they were looking for a fight. But tonight, Trey could honestly say he wasn't. He doubted anything could get him off the high he was on.

He'd lived in Haven all of his life, except when he'd taken off to Miami for a year shortly after graduation. He'd rushed home after his father passed away suddenly.

If he had to be honest with himself, he'd hated Miami. It had been too hot and full of too many people. He'd felt like he would suffocate if he stayed any longer.

Losing his dad had been tragic, but the family had bounced back after learning to lean on and rely on one another. It had taken some time for the three brothers to get the hang of running the family business, but in the end, McGowan Enterprises had flourished.

"I'm buying this round," one of the guys called out as they walked into Carrie Ann's. Trey wobbled his way across the sticky dance floor and made his way down the short hallway towards the bathroom. He was thankful Mason, one of his buddies, had been picked as designated driver that night. Usually they drew straws, but tonight Mason had volunteered since he was trying to cut down on the calories and drop some weight for his girlfriend.

Swinging the door wide open, he almost toppled over a muscular guy standing just inside the door. The man looked familiar, but that wasn't surprising; Trey knew everyone in Haven.

"Sorry," he mumbled. He moved past the guy, heading for a urinal.

"Jackass," the man said to his back.

Trey smiled. "Sure, buddy." He finished doing his business and turned around to face the guy, who was still glaring in his direction.

"You've got a problem," the man said, taking a step closer to him.

Trey took in the guy's size and quickly shook his head. "Don't think so." He smiled. "Just had to piss." The man easily outweighed him by at least thirty pounds, and Trey bet most of it was muscle.

Moving slowly, Trey walked over to the sink. His mother had taught him right, so he proceeded to wash his hands thoroughly.

The man continued to hover just inside the doorway. Trey turned towards him and the door, but the guy moved slightly and blocked it. The man still looked familiar, but since Trey was too far into the festivities of the evening to place where he'd seen the guy before.

"Do I know you?" Trey asked, trying to get his eyes to focus.

"You won't forget my fist..." The man lifted his arm at the same time the bathroom door swung open, causing him to fall off balance. Trey took that moment to make a quick escape. He chuckled about the entire ordeal as he crossed the room to find his buddies.

He was halfway across the dance floor when he bumped into someone else. This someone, however, was a lot softer and a hell of a lot prettier than the man lurking in the bathroom.

"Scuse me," he said, reaching out to steady the woman. His hands gripped her shoulders to make sure she wouldn't fall over. Upon seeing the sexy raven-haired beauty, his fingers tightened slightly. "Well, hello there." His smile turned from apologetic to one of his well-practiced flirty smiles.

Her dark eyes narrowed slightly. "Excuse me, I have to find someone." Her eyes traveled past his shoulders and he saw heat and anger take over.

She pushed past him, and he turned to watch her walk away. The fact that she was wearing tight black leather shorts in the dead of winter in Montana made him smile. Then his foggy brain registered the long sexy legs that she used to make her way across the dance floor. He watched her hips sway and was almost hypnotized by the motion.

He must have stood there in the middle of the dance floor grinning like a fool in her direction for several seconds before he finally registered what was going on. The raven-haired beauty was arguing with angry bathroom man. His feet were rooted to the spot on the dance floor as he watched the couple arguing. The woman moved her hands and arms around as if she was trying to make a point. The man, for his part, looked at her with the same look he'd given Trey moments ago in the bathroom.

Trey was just about to turn around and go find his buddies when bathroom man reached out and pushed the woman. Trey was across the floor in a flash, his fists swinging, before he remembered that the guy outweighed him. His first blow caught the man off guard, thankfully, sending him flailing back towards the wall. He didn't think he'd try for another swing, but the man came at him, knocking the pair of them to the dance floor.

Trey face was pushed up against the sticky floor. He bucked and kicked until the man's grip on him finally loosened. He swung his elbow out, catching the man under the chin. The next blow went to angry bathroom man, who clocked Trey in the left eye, sending his head backwards and knocking it into the hard dance floor.

The guy had just set up residence above him, and Trey had braced for the repetitive blows that he knew were coming, when the man was yanked from him.

Ethan and Mason held the man back as Trey pulled himself off the floor. His two friends were equal matches for the other man. Both men worked for him, Mason as a motorhand and Ethan as a derrick worker. Both jobs required strong muscles.

"Are you okay?" Trey turned to the pretty raven-haired beauty, just as several other people stepped into the mix.

Trey groaned when he saw two of Haven's finest police, Tom and Dale rush over to them. He wiped the blood from his lip and held his hands out.

"Everything's okay," he tried.

"Trey McGowan." Tom shook his head. "You know better than this."

Trey smiled but turned when the raven-haired beauty gasped. Her eyes got bigger as she looked him up and down. He felt a little nervous as she assessed him. What did she see? He thought about it and groaned inwardly. He was probably a mess at this point. His T-shirt was hanging half off his shoulders since the man had ripped it in the fall. He knew he had blood dripping down his lip and would probably have a fat lip and a black eye soon. He was drunk, disorderly, and for some reason, for the first time in his life, he felt ashamed for it.

"We'll have to haul you both in," Dale said, taking the other man from Ethan and Mason. The man jerked his arm, causing both Ethan and Mason to grip him tighter.

"Just try it, buddy," Mason added.

"Trey didn't do…" Ethan started, earning him a stern look from Tom. His friend wasn't dumb and shut his mouth quickly.

24

"We'll take them both in," Tom repeated. He turned to the other man and narrowed his eyes. "We aren't going to have a problem, are we?"

The other man grunted and rolled his eyes.

"No, he won't cause any more problems." Everyone turned towards the beauty as she stepped forward. Trey's eyes moved down to her legs one last time.

Hell, he didn't know how long he'd be in the drunk tank and the memory of those legs would help him through the next few hours.

The woman turned to the other man and glared at him. "Go."

Trey was ushered outside, while the other man was cuffed. Dale opened the back door and Trey slid into the back seat and rested his head against the leather. His head was spinning slightly, and he could feel his lip and eye start stinging.

The other man was put in the seat beside him, his hands cuffed behind his back. When the doors were shut, he glanced at the bar as they drove away. The raven-haired beauty was standing outside in the fresh snow, her arms wrapped around herself, biting her bottom lip with worry as she watched them drive away.

"Lucky," Trey said under his breath.

"What?" the man sitting next to him asked. Trey gave him his full attention and turned towards him.

"I said you're lucky to have someone like that. You don't deserve her," he said clearly.

The man frowned at him. "She's a pain in the ass," he grunted in response, and Trey thought about punching the man again.

Chapter Two

Dylan watched the police cruiser drive away and cursed under her breath. Her brother had assaulted Trey McGowan. Trey McGowan! The man was their last hope in getting a decent job in this town.

Shivering, she turned back towards the building and thought about packing up her small bag and leaving her brother to rot in the jail cell. But then a pair of piercing blue eyes popped into her mind.

The man was so different than his brothers. Different, but the same in many ways. She'd seen his brothers around the small town. How could she not? After all, it wasn't as if Haven, Montana, was the sprawling metropolis her brother had led her to believe.

Upon arrival, they had taken up residence in a

small hotel that was equivalent to their last apartment. Her brother had had an interview with the McGowans the first week and, no surprise to her, he'd come back empty-handed.

That was when he'd told her that he'd been misinformed about the secretary job she was supposed to apply for. Since they were down to their last few dollars, she'd taken the first job she could find.

Dressing for the job in short skirts, high heels, and busty tops was nothing new—it all went to making her a bigger tip in the end. What was different was the number and amount of tips she got. She'd been shocked at how much more she made here than she had in the big city.

Angie, one of the other waitresses, had told her that oil money ran free and that if she gave the men what they wanted, she could be sitting pretty and possibly buying her own place in a year. Angie herself had just paid off her little house in downtown Haven after working at the bar for only ten years.

Ten years. Dylan thought she'd go mad before then, if she hadn't killed her brother and gone to jail for it. Walking to the back office, she knocked on Ricky's door. Ricky had, at one point, been married to Carrie Ann, who'd died a few years back of cancer. The man was nice enough to work for. He wasn't handsy like some of the bosses she'd had. Plus, he'd agreed to pay her first paycheck in advance, since they had needed to pay for their hotel room up front.

"Come in," he called out.

"Ricky, I need the rest of the night off." She shut the door behind her and leaned against the frame.

"What for?" He frowned up at her.

"My..." she started, then sighed. "Woman issues," she lied.

The man's eyes narrowed. "You'll have to work a double shift tomorrow," he warned. "We're supposed to have bands playing all day."

"Fine." She held in a groan.

When she parked in front of the police station, she sat in the car for a few minutes, debating how to handle the lack of funds to spring her brother.

She felt like banging her head on the steering wheel. Instead, she pulled herself together and stepped out of the truck. Her boots sank in the snow, and she shivered at the cold as she made her way into the building. Even her thick jacket couldn't keep the cold from reaching her bones.

"Can I help you?" the woman behind the counter asked immediately when she stepped inside. The place was pretty much empty, which surprised her.

Walking over to the desk, she straightened her shoulders. "Yes, my brother was just brought in. I need to post bail for him." She held in her emotions and tried to fight back the tears that stung behind her eyes.

The woman tilted her head and instead of looking down at the computer or paperwork asked, "Brent McCaw?"

"Yes."

"He's in holding. If you want, I can call you when he's ready, so you don't have to stick around here and wait."

Dylan swallowed slowly. "Um, that would be okay."

"What's your number?" The woman took out a sticky note pad and wrote down the number at the hotel.

"My name is Carol. I'll give you a call. It should be around eight."

"In the morning?" she asked, glancing at the clock on the wall. Five hours from now. Dylan doubted she could wait that long to know how much Brent had cost this time.

"Yeah, we want to make sure they're sober before we let them out." Carol smiled at her. "Go get some rest, sweetie. I'll call you when we open the gates and let them out." The woman chuckled.

Driving back to the hotel without her brother was both rewarding and nerve-wracking.

The room was quiet, too quiet. She decided on a long hot bath to try to shut off her mind.

Closing her eyes, she rested back and cleared her mind of her troubles. She wasn't surprised when a pair of blue eyes surfaced in her mind. Blonde curly hair, a sexy chin full of stubble, and lips that she imagined would feel perfectly wonderful rubbing up against any part of her body. Trey McGowan was the opposite of her type of man, and she couldn't understand why her body had instantly reacted to his gaze. He'd run those sexy blue eyes up and down her like he knew what she was wearing under her shorts and tank top.

Her type leaned towards beefcake bad boys in all leather, muscle-bound men who in the end revealed their true inner jerk. She had fallen for four of them so far in her life.

Her first long-term boyfriend, Jax, had been a tattoo artist. Her many tattoos, which she loved, were the only good things to come out of that relationship. Then there had been Chet. What had made her date a man named Chet was beyond rational thinking. That relationship had only lasted two weeks. She'd called it off when the bromance between Chet and Brent had grown stronger than their relationship. Lee had been a blip on her radar. She'd worked with him and for almost three months they had been friends with benefits. That was until she found out that he had similar arrangements with several other women.

Corey, the last man who'd gotten her interest, had taught her a valuable lesson and had, she hoped, turned her completely away from the muscular type.

31

She had a fresh scar along her hairline to prove that men with bulging muscles were not a good idea. Even her brother should have proven that to her, but she was still allowing him to drive their lives forward. Living in a shit-hole hotel and working one of the most humiliating jobs around were just a couple of the products of her brother's handling of their lives.

Still, she had to admit, working one job was a lot better than three. And the money was good. She even found herself liking the little town and dreaming about what it would be like to have a little house somewhere in the hills. She'd driven by the school once and had imagined dropping her kids off, making sure they had their lunches before they raced through the snow towards class.

Still, they were just dreams. Unless Brent suddenly got his shit together, Dylan was doomed.

When the hotel phone finally rang, she had drifted off to sleep. The shrill ring woke her up and startled her.

Carol was just as nice over the phone as she had been in person.

"We're getting ready to release your brother. He'll be ready for pickup in half an hour."

"Thank you." She had hung up without asking how much his bail was going to cost. She would find out soon enough.

Driving her brother's truck through town, she

was surprised at how many people were out already. The sun was at least an hour from rising and yet the town of Haven was awake. People were out shoveling the fresh snow from the sidewalks and driveways.

The grocery store was open, and the parking lot was slowly filling. When she pulled into the police station, the parking lot was almost full.

This time when she walked in, the lobby was packed, no doubt with people waiting for their loved ones to be released. She approached Carol as she was opening a box of donuts. When the smell of the baked goods hit Dylan, she felt her stomach growl loudly.

"Morning." Carol smiled at her. "Want one?" She held out the box for Dylan. Dylan paused a moment, then grabbed up a glazed donut and held it. Coveted it, drooled over it.

"I need to post bail for my brother." She felt her stomach roll and decided that she probably wouldn't be able to stomach the donut after she found out how much it was going to cost her.

"Oh, sweetie, your brother was just put in the drunk tank," Carol answered.

"Oh?" She waited. "So, what does that mean?"

"Well, since Trey didn't press charges, once we open up the doors, he's free to go."

"He's…" She almost dropped her donut. "You mean… I don't have to…" She swallowed the sour

33

taste in her throat.

Carol smiled and shook her head. "No charge." She leaned forward. "This time."

Dylan nodded, as the reality sunk in.

"Why don't you go have a seat. Tony should be in in a few minutes. He'll open up the tank and let everyone go."

Dylan went over to stand by the front door with the rest of the group, the donut almost forgotten until her stomach growled again.

How had she lucked out this time? Then Carol's words hit her. Trey hadn't pressed charges. Her brother was free to go, and it was all thanks to the man who had come to her defense.

Brent had never hit her, but when he got drunk, and she complained about it, he had pushed her before, much like he'd done last night.

She'd never had someone come to her defense before though. Maybe that was why she had found herself dreaming about Trey last night. Whatever the reason, there was no way a man like him would be interested in someone like her, especially after he'd found out that it was her brother's fault he'd ended up sitting in a jail cell all night.

∗∗∗

"You're the asshole who wouldn't hire me. McGowan?" the man sitting across from him in the drunk tank said, causing Trey's eyes to snap open.

It had been almost five hours since they had been shoved in the small holding area with all the other town drunks.

It was a Friday evening, two weeks after Christmas, and half of the town's local drunks were still deep into celebrating the holidays, with no signs of slowing down.

"I'm Trey McGowan." He frowned at the man who'd given him the bloody lip. "But I don't think we've met."

The man tilted his head. "You were there, with the other brother."

Trey tried to remember. He knew he'd seen the man before but hadn't been able to place it. Then the man flipped his head, pushing his hair back, and suddenly Trey remembered where he'd seen the guy before.

"You applied for the motorhand job. The one we gave to Mason," he added. "Brian?"

"Brent," the man corrected. "We came up here with the promise of that job. We left everything we had behind. Then we get here, and you hire someone else."

"I'm sorry about that, but I don't know who promised you the position. It was open, and we hired the best man for the job." He leaned his head back and tried to let his head settle. He was already enjoying the effects of the hangover.

His answer didn't seem to satisfy the guy.

35

"We had everything planned. Now, because of you, Dylan has to work at that shit-hole place."

Dylan, Trey thought. Was that the raven hair's name? It suited her. Jet-black hair with cropped bangs that hung over dark eyes, tattoos along her shoulders, beautiful body, and killer legs. Legs he'd been dreaming of since he'd been shoved in the tank. Dylan. He ran the name over in his mind again.

"What about you?" Trey asked.

"What about me?" The man looked at him like he didn't understand.

"Why haven't you found a job? There's plenty of work here besides working for us," Trey supplied.

The man cursed under his breath. "Dylan makes enough for us, for now. If I know her, she'll be looking for a second job soon enough."

Trey's anger spiked again. The bastard sitting across from him was a slacker, letting his girlfriend work two jobs just to keep him satisfied. He'd known plenty of men like that in his lifetime. Hell, half the women working in the many strip clubs in Haven had men sitting at home drinking away their hard-earned money.

Trey glared at the man. "You're a real piece of work."

Just then the cell door opened. Trey stood up, as did everyone else in the cell who was awake and alert.

Haven was a small town, and the police station was one of the busiest buildings at this time of morning since Tony usually came in at eight and released all the people who'd been held in the drunk tank for the night.

Stepping out, he wasn't surprised to see Tony shaking his head in his direction.

"Don't start," he mumbled.

"What will your mother think?" The man had been seeing his mother for almost three months now. Trey still wasn't sure about it but figured that his mother had a right to find happiness after losing his dad suddenly almost two years ago.

"Need a ride?" Tony asked.

Trey glanced around the room and, upon spotting the sexy beauty, Dylan, leaning against the front doors, his scan for his brothers halted. She had changed from the shorts and push-up top to more practical jeans and a black leather coat with a hoody underneath. She fit in to the small town of Haven like a nun fit in at a strip club.

He continued looking at her and realized everyone in the room was eyeing her. He watched Brent cross the room and start talking to Dylan. The woman's eyes moved over to him, and Trey could have sworn he saw heat flash behind them as her cheeks heated.

"Sure, I'll be back in a moment." He walked towards the doorway, catching the pair before they left.

"Hey," he said, getting the man's attention. They both turned towards him. "If you're serious about a job, we still have a few rig jobs open. Why don't you come in tomorrow and see me?"

The man's eyes turned from agitated to shocked. "Really?"

Trey's eyes moved to Dylan's. "Sure."

"We were hoping, that is…" Dylan stepped forward. "I am looking for work as well."

An image of the petite woman as a derrick worker flashed in his mind and he almost laughed. Then he remembered that Rea was trying to retire, and Kristen, who had been filling in for her, would now be home with the new baby. They were out a secretary.

"Can you type and answer calls?" he asked.

She tilted her head and narrowed her eyes. "Can't everyone?"

He smiled quickly and her eyes flashed to his lips. Damn, was she flirting with him in front of her boyfriend? He was fixing to get punched again. Turning away from her, he held out his hand towards Brent. "Both of you swing by. I think we might have something."

"Ready?" Tony asked behind him.

"Sure." He threw over his shoulder, "Tomorrow around eight. We're in the old brick building…"

"We know where it's at," Brent said. Dylan lightly slapped his side. "Thanks."

Trey nodded and followed Tony out. He desperately wanted to look back to see if Dylan was watching him, but she was taken so he had to try to cleanse his mind of her.

Jill Sanders

Chapter Three

"Don't screw this up." Dylan shoved her brother into the bathroom. "You promised me you wouldn't drink last night." She pushed harder, but her brother's big form didn't budge.

"Aww, come on. It was three beers." Brent finally moved.

"Shower, dress. And hurry, we're going to be late." When her brother didn't move, she pinched his side until he howled.

"Damn it, Dylan!" He turned on her. She raised her eyebrows in challenge. "Don't do that."

"Go, now." She pointed to the shower. "I will not let you mess up our last chance at decent jobs in this town."

"Man, you're bossy all of a sudden." Brent turned and pulled off his shirt.

41

When he started to step out of his shorts, she retreated to the bedroom and slammed the bathroom door between them. "Five minutes," she called out to the door. "Or I'm leaving without you."

Fifteen minutes later, they walked into the old brick building downtown that housed McGowan Enterprises.

She had on her best outfit, while her brother wore a pair of worn jeans and a clean polo. Still, at least he'd shaved and showered.

When they walked in, she was surprised to find the front desk empty.

"Last time there was a pregnant woman behind the desk," Brent added as he took a seat.

Dylan stood at the desk and checked her watch. They were five minutes late. She groaned and glared at her brother as he started flipping through a magazine.

"Hello?" she called out down the long hallway. When the phone started ringing, she jumped slightly and glanced around. Biting her lip, she waited until the phone stopped ringing before she started down the hallway. When the phone started up again, she sighed and rushed to pick it up.

"McGowan Enterprises, this is Dylan, can I help you?" she answered while her brother watched her.

"Dylan?" The voice on the other end sounded familiar. "You're hired. I'm the last door on the left. Please send Brent back my way." The line went dead, and she blinked at the receiver for a full minute before she realized what had happened.

"You're supposed to go on back. Last door on the left," she told her brother.

"Who was that?" he asked, moving towards her.

"Trey McGowan, I think. He told me I'm hired and said to send you back." She leaned closer. "Don't screw this up." She motioned towards the hallway as she sat behind the desk.

For the next half hour, she waited patiently, answering the phone when it rang. She took messages, gave help where she could, or simply told the caller that she didn't have access to the computer yet, which was locked with a password. She took notes and told them she would return their call once she was in the system, which she hoped would be after Trey was done with her brother, since it appeared neither of the other brothers were in the office at the moment.

When the mailman arrived, he leaned on her desk and chatted, asking her when she had been hired and if Rea was every going to return.

She found out from Gary, the postman, that Kristen McGowan had had her baby two days ago, a boy by the name of Timothy Jack. The man gossiped a lot and in the ten minutes she spent chatting with him, she found out more about the brothers than she had in the month they'd lived in Haven.

Trey was the youngest of the three boys. Tyler, the oldest, was married to Kristen. Trent, the middle boy, was married to Addy.

By the time her brother walked out of Trey's office, she was feeling a little more comfortable with the situation. It seemed that Rea had officially retired a few months back, and Kristen had taken over temporarily until they could find someone full time, which it appeared they had.

"He wants to see you." Brent nodded towards the back. "I start a week from today. I have to have a physical and some paperwork done first." He held up a piece of paper. "I'm heading over to the clinic now to get the blood work." Her brother smiled and for the first time in years, he looked happy. "I'll pick you up around five."

She smiled and hugged him. "We did it," she whispered to him.

"You did it." He leaned down and placed a brotherly kiss on her cheek.

When she heard someone clear his throat, she glanced over and smiled, seeing Trey at the end of the hallway. He was dressed in a dark grey suit and leaning against the door frame. He looked even sexier in the suit than he had in the worn jeans and black shirt the night before. It was funny, but he looked like he was comfortable in both.

"Coming," she called out. She quickly gathered the stack of messages before waving to Brent as he walked out. "I have some messages—"

"I expect that won't happen too often in the workplace." Trey motioned for her to enter his office.

She stopped and frowned. "What won't?"

"The PDA." He motioned for her to sit across from him as he took the spot behind the massive glass and wood desk. There were large windows behind him that looked out over a small creek. She wondered why his desk didn't face the view instead of the doorway. If it was up to her, she'd turn the desk around and... probably not get a thing done all day long. His words registered finally.

"PD..." She almost laughed, but then she nodded quickly. "Of course." She straightened her shoulders. "I have some messages here." She handed them over. "If I can get access to the computer, I can start to learn your system better."

He pulled out a piece of paper. "Rea's notes are here. Everything you need to know about the job." He handed it over. "I'll need you to fill out some standard paperwork for your paychecks, health benefits, retirement." He pulled out a file and handed it to her. "Take some time and get these back to me before you leave today."

"Sure." She leaned across and took the folder. "I can't thank you enough for everything you've done for Brent and me."

Trey nodded. "I'm expecting a few other

meetings today, since my brothers are out. Tyler won't be in for a full month. His wife—"

"Just had a baby," she filled in. His eyebrows rose. "Gary, the mailman, filled me in. Trent is on the job site, filling in for Tyler." She nodded.

"Right." Trey sighed. "Which leaves me stuck in the office for the next month." He practically groaned it.

"I'll show them back when they arrive. I assume there is a calendar of these meetings?"

"Yes, it's all there." He nodded to Rea's notes. "Lunch is from noon to one. You can take it in the break room or feel free to go off site."

She frowned. "Brent won't be back until five. I... didn't pack a lunch."

"I can drive you somewhere if you need. I was planning on hitting the Dancing Moose. You're welcome to tag along."

"Thank you." She smiled. "That would be fine." She stood up and smiled when Trey stood up quickly.

"No, thank you. You came at the right time. Without you, I'd be stuck out front trying to do my job while I answered phones."

She smiled. "I'll..." She heard the phone ring and he nodded. "Thanks," she said, rushing to answer it.

Over the next two hours, she familiarized herself

with their system. It wasn't hard and by the time noon rolled around, she was confident with most of it.

She answered the phone with assurance and when the folks showed up for Trey's meetings, she showed them to the back and happily got coffee and drinks for everyone.

She had to admit, it felt wonderful being off her feet most of the day and working a real job. She filled out the personnel paperwork and, just before noon, knocked on Trey's door to turn it in.

"Come in," he called out.

"I have my paperwork all ready." She handed him the folder.

He motioned for her to sit as he glanced through it. "You and Brent have the same last name?" He glanced up with a frown. His eye zeroed in on the many rings on her fingers. "Married?" he asked.

She laughed quickly. "God no, Brent is my brother."

She noticed the change in him right away. It was as if Trey totally relaxed around her and, for the first time, she realized why he'd been a little icy with her.

"You thought…" She took a deep breath trying to hide the humor she felt about the entire situation. "Our parents died a few years back. Since then, we're all we have. We've stuck together through thick and thin."

Trey nodded slowly. "Our dad died almost two years back. My brothers and I had to step up our game to save this place." He leaned back, glancing around. "Course, we were lucky we had this."

"Yes." She smiled as she looked around. "Our father was a banker. You would think he would have put some money away himself, but when they died, we were strapped and, less than a year later, we lost everything."

"I'm sorry." Trey leaned forward.

"Don't be. This is the first time something has gone right for us." She smiled. "We can't thank you enough for giving us a chance. Especially after the other night."

Trey's blue eyes turned down slightly. "I kind of egged your brother on in the bathroom." He stood and leaned on the edge of the desk in front of her.

"You don't have to lie," she broke in. "Brent can be a jerk when he drinks. That's one of the reasons he'll be staying sober from here on out."

"Your brother doesn't have to turn into a saint. Half the men in the hold with us the other night work for us." He chuckled. "Hell, what else is there to do around here but drink, fight and..." He cleared his throat. "Sorry."

She smiled. "What? Fuck?" She laughed. "For most of the last four years, I've been around my brother twenty-four seven. Nothing you can say will shock me."

"I doubt that," he said softly.

She stood up suddenly and then realized too late how close the move put them.

"The only reason I gave your brother another chance was the need to see you again." He moved closer. His hand reached out to touch her elbow.

***

Dylan's eyes darkened. For the first time, he was seeing them clearly and up close. He'd imagined they were a dark mocha color, but there was a light ring of hazel along the iris that turned slightly green when he touched her. Her cheeks flushed, and he wondered how her skin would feel next to his.

Suddenly, he broke contact and stepped back as he realized they were standing in the middle of his office and he'd just officially hired her.

"How about lunch?" He turned and flipped his computer off. "I'm starving," he said, trying to hide what being so close to her had done to him.

"Sure, let me grab my coat." She rushed from the room and he took his time pulling on his own jacket and gloves. The weather called for more snow today and he knew better than to ignore the predictions.

He had been pleasantly surprised that she was wearing nice black slacks with a cream top and a thick sweater jacket over it. The outfit was business-like but warm enough for winter in Montana. She'd pulled her jet-black hair up into two small clips above her ears, and he had found himself wishing she'd left the short tresses down.

When he figured he'd waited long enough, he headed down the hallway. She was standing at the desk, a large black bag in her arms, watching him.

Suddenly, he felt like he was on a runway, being assessed by the best fashion critics.

He'd worn a standard suit he and his brothers had purchased together. Since all of them hated shopping, they had made a trip into Helena and gotten the deed done at the same time.

Since they no longer lived under one roof together, they had purchased identical items and quickly gotten out of the shops.

Still, he had enough sense to add his own style to each outfit. He hated ties but left one balled up in the top drawer of his desk, in case he ever absolutely needed one.

As it was, her eyes were soaking him up, and he felt his body instantly react to the heat coming off her gaze.

"Ready?" he asked, trying to swallow the desire that had built up.

She nodded quickly and turned away from him.

He walked over to his car and opened the passenger door for her.

"This is yours?" she asked, standing on the curb

beside his BMW.

"Yeah, I usually don't drive it in the winter, but…" He waited until she slid into the seat. "My truck's in the shop getting new brakes." He shut the door gently behind her, then crossed over to climb behind the wheel.

He hated driving his baby in the snow, but the truck hadn't come back from Ed's, the local auto repair shop, yet. The truck was for snow and work, the Beemer was for fun. It was the first item he'd purchased on his own and the most expensive by far. But it made his occasional trip to the city more than an hour away pleasurable.

He pulled into a parking spot at the Dancing Moose and opened his door.

"Why is it called the Dancing Moose?" she asked, looking up at the sign.

He smiled. "The story goes that a moose broke in during a wedding party. He made a mess of the place before finally walking out the front door."

When she chuckled and glanced out the windshield at the building, he climbed out but before he could race around and open her door like he'd been taught, she was already shutting the car door and standing on the sidewalk.

When they entered the diner, he inwardly groaned when he recognized every single person in the place. He knew by the end of the day they would be the hottest subject in Haven. He could just imagine the conversations.

"Did you see who Trey took to lunch?"

"Who was the woman Trey McGowan was having lunch with down at the Dancing Moose?"

"Is this Trey's latest catch?"

Thankfully, the list of possibilities was interrupted when Rumi, the owner of the diner, greeted them.

"Hey, Trey." She smiled up at him. "If you can find an empty spot, grab it," she said as she rushed past them. "The lunch rush is in full swing."

He leaned over to Dylan. "Don't let Rumi's small stature fool you. She's an ex-marine and can probably kick the ass of everyone in here." He chuckled as he took Dylan's arm and guided her towards the back where a table was just being cleared. "She and her husband Neal bought this place a few years back from her parents. The Dancing Moose has been in her family for almost four generations." He pulled out the chair for Dylan.

Once she was seated, he sat across from her. He could feel every eye on them but chose to ignore the stares.

Kristy, one of his favorite waitresses, came over and set two menus on the table. "I'll be just a moment," she said before making her way across the room quickly.

"Have you eaten here before?" Trey asked,

pushing his menu away, since he knew it by heart.

Dylan picked up the large menu and scanned it.

"Not yet." She bit her bottom lip as she looked over the items.

He leaned in. "Don't worry, McGowan Enterprises is picking up the tab today," he said in a low voice so everyone sitting next to them wouldn't overhear. "My father always said, when two employees got together, it's a meeting."

He'd meant his words to be lighthearted, but he noticed that her slight frown grew.

"I'm not looking for a handout," she said in a clear voice as she laid down her menu.

Now he was the one frowning.

"You aren't getting a handout. After saving my butt today, it's the least I can do to pay you back." He leaned back in his chair and ran his eyes over her. "Why don't we consider this an official interview, that way there won't be any... questions."

"But I've still got the job?" she asked.

He let out a quick breath of relief. "Yes. I don't know if you know this, but the pool of professionals in Haven is very..." He thought for a second. "Limited."

She thought about it for a moment, then nodded. "Fine."

He watched with amusement as she straightened her shoulders and prepared herself for the interview.

"So, it's just you and your brother?" He could tell the personal question threw her off balance.

"Yes." She nodded.

"Since?" he asked. "You said your folks died?"

"Yes, in a boating accident in Mexico a few years back."

"I'm sorry," he said. Her eyes turned sad. Reaching across the table, he brushed the back of her hand, then tucked his hands under the table. "It's hard losing one parent, I can't imagine losing both at the same time."

"Your mother is still alive?" she asked.

"Yes." He glanced around the room. "I'm surprised she's not having lunch here today. I thought…" His eyes zoned in on the far corner and nodded. "There she is. She and Tony have been seeing one another for a few months now."

Dylan glanced over to where his mother and the police officer, who'd busted him more times than he remembered, were quietly eating lunch together. He leaned across the table. "If we don't bother them, they won't bother us." He smiled. "As I mentioned, my brothers are usually in here too, but Tyler and his wife just had a kid."

"Yes, I heard. Congratulations." She smiled, and he watched as she transformed. She had been beautiful before but seeing the first real smile on her was like seeing light for the first time.

"Thanks. So, why move to Haven? Your brother mentioned you'd been in Seattle before."

"It really wasn't my choice." She relaxed slightly. "When Brent gets something in his mind…" She took a deep breath, then opened her mouth to speak again, but Kristy was back.

"Have you decided yet?" she asked.

He motioned for Dylan to go ahead. She ordered a small side salad and a cup of soup. He thought about telling her to order some real food, but instead told Kristy to bring a basket of fries before their meal.

Kristy smiled at him. "Will do." After she walked away, he continued with his questioning.

"Where are you living?" he asked, "I didn't have a chance to look at your paperwork."

"We've got a room at the hotel just down the street." She motioned towards the front of the place and he winced.

"You're staying there?" He shook his head and thought about it.

"It was the only place we could afford." She sighed. "Now that we both have jobs, we'll be looking for something more permanent."

"I know of a few places that are for rent." He thought about the small house in town that he'd

55

rented from his mother's best friend after returning home when his father had died. Shortly after he'd moved in, his mother had purchased the place as an investment property. Since he was living on his own land now in a double-wide his brother Trent had finished with, the place on Main Street was sitting empty.

Trent had finished building his own house a few months back and since his two brothers were now on McGowan land, he felt it was only fitting he move out to his plot of land as well. So, instead of his brother hauling the double-wide away, he'd parked it on the plot of land his father had willed to him.

It was, in Trey's opinion, the best plot of land out of the three brothers. Tyler's new home was on the hill side, overlooking the valley. Trent's was halfway up a small hill, overlooking the stream that ran through the flatlands. Trey had tucked the two-thousand-square-foot trailer back in the trees right along the brook. He figured when he got around to building his own home, he'd do it right there, hidden away from the rest of the world.

The hot fries were delivered, and he nudged the basket her way and smiled when she nibbled on a few.

"Any more personal questions for me or are we going to keep pretending this is a job interview?" she asked.

Chapter Four

*D*ylan didn't know what had caused her to ask the question. Maybe it was the fact that she was feeling full for the first time in months. Trey had pushed the basket of fries her way and the smell of them had called to her. It had been too long since she'd eaten so much, and her salad and soup hadn't even arrived yet.

It stung, knowing she only had two dollars in her purse, hidden from her brother for emergencies. She'd expected to buy just a cup of coffee or maybe a basket of fries and was thankful she would be getting a full meal instead.

She had a job, a real job, she reminded herself. Instead of putting in a few hours here and there at Carrie Ann's when the owner felt like calling her. Sure, tips were great, but the job sucked. More nights than not, there were fights, and she was usually stuck in the middle of them, fending for and fearing for her own safety. It hadn't gone unnoticed by her that every time her brother showed up, fights were inevitable.

Feeling the need to apologize ahead of time for anything Brent was going to do in the future, she glanced around and wondered how to go about it.

"About my brother..." She leaned in slightly. She wanted to make sure her job didn't hinge on his. "I'm not... he's..." She shook her head, at a loss for words.

"Hey," Trey broke in, "I understand how siblings are. Half the town judges me by what my older brothers do or have done. Do you know, I walked into my freshmen year at high school with a bad-boy reputation already firmly in place?" He sighed. "Teachers would call out roll call and once they saw McGowan behind my name, they would groan and say, *'We aren't going to have problems are we, McGowan?'* It was almost like they didn't know my first name or care to know it. I was just another McGowan to them."

She'd watched him talk. He had gotten very animated when he was lost in the story, and she found it almost hypnotic to watch. His blue eyes turned slightly darker as his emotions spiked.

"I'm not my brother," she said softly.

"And I'm not mine." He smiled. "So, we're in agreement. You won't judge me for being a

McGowan and I won't judge you for anything Brent might say or do." He held out his hand for hers. She reached out and took it easily. Instead of shaking it, he held it firmly. "But, know this, if I ever see him push you around again, I have no problem living up to the McGowan name and kicking the shit out of him."

Her smile grew. "Agreed."

For the rest of their lunch, they talked about family. She heard all about his brothers and their new wives, along with small details about his mother, Gail. He'd warned her that she and her new beau Tony might swing by their table when they left, and they had. Trey had quickly introduced her as his savior, who had taken over Rea's job at McGowan Enterprises. She'd been happily surprised at her title of office manager. Not that she had anyone to manage, but it sounded better than secretary.

She'd liked Trey's mother instantly when the woman asked about her tattoos and had been sincerely interested instead of judgy like a lot of older people tended to be.

"Trey has several tattoos," Gail had nodded towards her son. "Of course, he's not the only one." She'd winked at her.

"What?" Trey had broken in. "Who?"

Gail smiled and tugged on Tony's arm to get him moving out of the diner.

"Mom?" Trey had called after her. "Who else has a tattoo?"

The woman had just chuckled as she waved and walked out.

"I think your mom has a tattoo." She smiled as she finished her soda.

Trey was frowning into his empty plate. He'd eaten an entire steak, a baked potato, and a massive helping of broccoli, and he'd ordered a large slice of chocolate pie on top of it. She was surprised that he didn't weigh three hundred pounds. "She can't. I would know about it."

Dylan just laughed. "Are you really upset about this?"

He frowned at her as the waitress set the massive slice of cake in front of him. "No, of course not. She was probably just messing around."

"What tattoos do you have?" She couldn't remember seeing any the other night, and since he was dressed in a long-sleeved button-up shirt, she didn't see any now.

She could tell that she'd gotten his mind off his mother. He smiled at her and slowly bit into the cake. He handed her an extra fork. "Dig in." He nodded to the dessert.

She chuckled. "Not going to tell?" she asked.

"With someone like you, I might have tattoo envy," he answered.

She smiled. "It helped that I dated a tattooist for almost a full year."

He nodded. "I dated one in Miami. Rainah worked at Tatts and played in an all-girl punk band." He sighed heavily. "Good times."

She took a nibble of the chocolate cake and held in a groan. It was hot and melted in her mouth. She quite possibly could orgasm right there in the middle of the diner with everyone watching. It had been almost two months since she'd been able to afford a chocolate fix.

"Jax had his own shop and played bongos on the streets of Seattle when he needed extra money," she added between bites.

"Sounds like a real winner." Trey smiled over at her as they finished off the cake. "What kind of name is Jax anyway?"

"What kind of name is Trey?" she countered.

His blonde eyebrows shot up. "It's a nickname. I doubt if one person other than my family knows my real name at this point."

"Oh?" She smiled. "What is your real name?"

He chuckled. "Not going to happen." He waved the waitress over and handed her a credit card, then glanced down at his watch. "We'd better get back. I'd hate to be late for my meetings. Tyler gets pissy when I do."

They drove back to the brick building that

housed his family's business.

When Trey parked in his spot, she noticed him frowning at an older truck parked near the doors.

"Are we late?" she asked.

"No." He shut the car off and she missed the warmth from the seat warmers almost instantly. "I'll warn you about this part of the job as well. Dealing with my uncle."

She turned back towards the truck as an older man climbed out. She was surprised at how much the man looked like Trey's father, whom she'd seen in a family picture. She had studied the family painting in the waiting area while Trey had interviewed her brother.

Out of the three boys, Trey had gotten his father's blonde hair and blue eyes. The other two boys had darker hair and brown eyes like their mother.

"Carl McGowan is a drunk. Anytime he shows up here," Trey said quickly, "call the police." He handed her his cell phone. "It's in speed dial under PD." He got out of the car, but before walking away, he leaned in. "Stay put."

She found and dialed the number in his phone as she watched Trey move across the parking lot. The man sure knew how to wear a suit, she thought as she waited for someone to answer the phone.

"What's up, Trey?" a woman answered in a sweet voice. She guessed it was the same woman from the other night but didn't want to make assumptions.

"Hi, this is Dylan. I'm calling for Mr. McGowan. It appears that his uncle is here—"

"I'll send Mike on over. Are you at the office?" the woman broke in.

"Yes," she answered. There was a slight pause and Dylan could hear the woman talking to someone.

"Okay, they're on the way. Who is this?"

"My name is Dylan…"

"From the other night? Your brother is Brent?"

"Yes, I'm the new office manager here." She felt a slight twinge about throwing the fake title around.

"Oh, wonderful. They found someone to fill Kristen and Rea's shoes. Well, don't worry, Mike and Tom are on the way over. Just keep Trey from killing his uncle before they get over there."

The line when dead and Dylan tucked his phone into her coat pocket and got out of the car.

"I don't give a shit what you think, there's nothing here for you," Trey was saying in a clear voice.

"You know as well as I do, that's shit. I'm due…" Just then his uncle's eyes moved past him and landed on her. She thought about retreating for a moment, but then held her ground. She'd never backed out of a fight.

"They're on their way," she said, stopping next to Trey.

"Thanks." He turned back to his uncle and she noticed that he moved slightly putting his body between her and the older man.

"Who?" his uncle asked her, ignoring Trey. "You call the cops on me?" His eyes narrowed at her. She raised her chin slightly and didn't answer. She knew the signs of someone far gone into the drink and didn't care what he said. By the looks of it, alcohol wasn't the only thing pulsing through the man's bloodstream.

"You never could fight like a man. Always running away to get your brothers or making your bitch call for help." The older man swung out, missing Trey as he easily ducked.

"Easy, old man." Trey held onto his shoulders, stopping him from falling over.

"Let go of me you son of a…"

Trey moved so quickly, Dylan didn't have time to respond. One moment his uncle was standing and, the next, he was sprawled face first on the ground with Trey standing over him. All Trey had done was let go of the man's shoulders and his uncle had fallen into the freshly fallen slow in the parking lot.

"You'll need to be careful how you treat our employees from here on out," Trey warned, as he pulled the man back to his feet. "And you'll want to be extra careful. The parking lot is slippery," Trey said as the man gained his feet again.

Dylan noticed the older man's face was bright red. He swung out, catching Trey unaware. The man's thick fist slammed directly into Trey's nose. Blood splattered over her as she gasped, and Trey cursed under his breath.

The fight between her brother and Trey had left marks on both men. For his part, Trey was sporting a swollen eye and lip. Her brother had a matching swollen eye and a cut across his bottom lip. Now, however, looking at the amount of blood flowing from Trey's nose, she wondered if he'd broken it.

"Son of a..." Trey said, swiping his nose. His hand came away covered in blood. Instead of releasing his uncle, he gripped him tighter and pushed him towards the front doors.

She followed and when they reached the doorway, the police cruiser pulled in and stopped a few feet away.

"Damn it," the officer said as he climbed out of the cruiser. "Did you have to hit him?"

"I didn't touch the man," Trey said, holding his hands up as his nose continued to bleed all over his white shirt.

"Trey didn't hit him," she jumped in. "He hit Trey." She pointed to his uncle.

By now there were two officers there. One of

65

them had Trey's uncle and was holding him up.

"The boy attacked me," his uncle was saying.

"That's not—" she started, but Trey glanced at her and shook his head.

"It's okay, they know," he said softly.

She sighed and nodded. Trey reached into his pocket. "Why don't you head in? It's freezing out here." He gave her the keys to the door. "I'll handle this."

She decided it was easier to retreat inside than argue. And she could grab some tissue to help stop Trey's nosebleed. Besides, she hated dealing with cops. She'd had enough of them over the last four years to last a lifetime.

***

Trey stood in the cold and ran over the last five minutes with Mike Taters, the chief of police. The man had been around long before Trey had, and he knew that the chances of Trey starting a fight with his uncle were slim. He was guaranteed not to be put in cuffs.

His uncle, however, was cuffed and shoved in the back of the police cruiser.

"We'll call and get his truck towed," Mike added, writing something down in his book. "You'd better get that looked at." He nodded to his nose. "It might be broken."

"It's not." He sighed. "I know the difference."

He dabbed his nose with the towel Dylan had rushed out to him.

"Looks like he ruined your shirt." Mike nodded to his chest.

Trey glanced down and cursed. "I've got a meeting in an hour."

Mike chuckled as he walked away. "You boys always did look funny in suits anyway."

He tried not to slam the front door as he walked in. Dylan was on the phone as he walked by. Stepping into his office, he threw his jacket on the sofa and pulled off his ruined shirt. His nose had stopped bleeding moments ago, so he was clear to pull on the backup shirt he always kept in the closet.

When he heard a funny sound, he turned around to see Dylan standing in the doorway. Her dark eyebrows were raised as her eyes scanned over his chest. When he started to put the shirt on, she rushed forward.

"Don't." She reached out and stopped him.

He couldn't help but smile. "Why? Seeing me half-naked is making you swoon?"

Her eyes narrowed. "No." She pointed to a spot on his chest. "I was just stopping you from ruining a second shirt."

He followed her gaze to where her fingertip was touching his chest. There, on his skin, was a dark blob of blood that would have soaked into his backup shirt.

"But, if you're so vain as to think that every woman who sees you without a shirt would swoon at your feet…" She turned on her heels and waltzed out of the room. "Who swoons anymore, anyway?" she threw over her shoulder as he chuckled and wiped the blood from his skin.

Slipping on the new shirt, he wiped the rest of the blood from his face with water from the small bar area in his office. He checked to make sure his nose had stopped bleeding before cleaning his face. He texted his brothers to let them know what had happened and called his mother as well. He finished up with his family just as Dylan buzzed his meeting in and for the next hour, he listened to them drone on and on about the benefits of the latest computer system for locating oil and mineral deposits. He and his brothers had already agreed to purchase the new system.

He ended one meeting and had less than five minutes before his next one. This meeting, however, was a lot different. Local boys flooded their conference room as he began going over the slides of their new school facility.

The ground breaking was set for some time in the spring, but Trey was having a hard time waiting that long. Just looking at the graphics and drawings for the Thurston McGowan Flathead Drilling Training Center got him excited. More than one hundred acres of prime Montana land was all theirs for this project.

There were going to be three large buildings for housing employees and families along with seven larger buildings for classrooms. Future plans included a daycare and even a general store.

If all went well, there was plenty of space around town for new home sites, which they hoped would be a big plus, since they were looking at some pretty big contracts from in-state colleges that wanted to expand environmental studies at their facilities.

His father had put it in motion and all they needed to do was see it through. All three of them were determined to do so, even as their uncle fought it.

Tyler had received a call a week prior from a lawyer out of Helena. The man claimed to represent their uncle in the case against them. The man claimed that their uncle had proof that their father's patents on his drilling and extracting methods were the sole property of Carl McGowan.

Less than an hour later, after Tyler faxed the man all the legal documents where Carl had signed away his rights to the patents for cold hard cash that he had spent years ago, the lawyer quickly withdrew his claims and they had not heard from him since. But, if Trey knew anything about his uncle, they hadn't heard the last of it yet.

He spent almost two hours going over every detail of what he and his brothers were starting to think of as the 'A Team.' They were a bunch of men who were the best of the best at what they did. They knew all the ins and outs of the oil refining business and knew what equipment was needed, how much space, how much power, and most important, what would be needed to protect from any incidents and accidents.

He had hoped his brothers would be available for the meeting, but with Tyler at home enjoying the new baby and Trent filling in for Tyler in South Dakota at a meeting with suppliers, he was in charge. A scary thought.

When the conference room was empty, he sat alone looking over the proposed changes on his laptop screen. His stomach growled, and he desperately wished for a cup of coffee. There were a few more hours of work to do before he headed home to a frozen meal and more work. Maybe he'd swing by his mother's place for a home-cooked meal instead.

"Coffee?"

He'd forgotten that he wasn't alone. Glancing up, he smiled at Dylan as she walked in with a cup in her hands. "I didn't know how you like it, so I kept it black."

"Just the way I need it now." He took the mug from her.

"What's that?" She nodded to the projected screen on the wall.

He had forgotten to shut the thing off, so everything he'd been doing was showing up on the screen.

"Our proposed site changes for the school." He tilted his head. Seeing it bigger helped him make his mind up about what he'd been toiling over for the past ten minutes on the smaller screen.

"What school?" she asked, walking closer to the wall and crossing her arms in front of herself as she gave the image all of her attention.

He took a large gulp of coffee and went to stand next to her.

"The Thurston McGowan Flathead Drilling Training Center." He smiled every time he said it out loud.

She narrowed her eyes at him as she glanced his way. "The…"

"Thurston McGowan Flathead Drilling Training Center." He chuckled. "It's a mouthful. Basically, it's a drilling school and an environmental study site."

"Okay," she said slowly. "Why are you opening something like this?" She motioned to the screen. "I thought you guys were in business to make money drilling for oil yourselves."

"Well, we are, right now. But this was my father's dream before he died." He motioned towards the screen.

71

"A school to teach everyone else how to do what you do?" He heard the sarcasm in her voice and chuckled.

"It sounds crazy, we know." He shifted slightly, turning towards her. "Our father was... a visionary." He decided he liked the word and nodded.

"Like Disney?" she asked.

He frowned. "No, more like Nikola Tesla."

She tilted her head. "The guy who makes the cars?" Her eyes were glued to his.

"Okay, a serious gap in your education," he murmured as he turned towards the white board and picked up a marker. He drew out the plans as his father had laid them out so many years ago.

"See?" He stood back and let her take it all in.

Once she was done looking at it, she turned to him. "So, in essence, you're getting paid for others to le teach them everything you know, while they help you reinvent the industry, so that once they're done, you have the leading edge in methods?"

He nodded. "Okay, you just redeemed yourself for the Nikola Tesla remark."

She smiled and slowly turned and lifted the hem of her shirt. He got excited at the amount of skin she was showing him, but then he laughed.

There, in delicate print along her ribs, was a tattoo. He leaned closer to read the fine print.

'Be alone. That is when ideas are born.'

He smiled, remembering the quote. *"Be alone, that is the secret of invention; be alone, that is when ideas are born,* Nikola Tesla." He smiled. "One of my favorite quotes from him. You had me there." He wanted to reach out and run his finger over the quote but stepped back. "Why this quote?" he asked her, suddenly wishing he knew a lot more about the woman standing before him.

"Because, *'I don't think you can name many great inventions that have been made by married men,'* was a little too long." She smiled as she laid her shirt hem back in place.

He laughed, really laughed. "There's more to you than first meets the eye."

"I have my secrets." She shrugged. "I didn't always want to be a waitress, you know." She walked over and glanced down at his computer screen. "Your calculations are wrong here." She pointed to a section of the drawings.

He frowned. "What?" He moved over and glanced at what she was looking at. He didn't see anything wrong at first, but then she showed him the correct math while he looked over her shoulder.

For the next hour, he was schooled by their new secretary and wondered if they should have hired her as chief engineer of the project instead. He'd thought she was sexy as hell before, but knowing that there was a big brain underneath those dark

73

locks of hers made her even more so.

He couldn't deny his attraction for her anymore and wondered what the hell he was going to do about it.

Chapter Five

*I*t felt so good to be using her brain again. Challenging problems, focusing on tasks. Even if, for the time being, they were simple things like answering phones and sending contracts or emails.

When she'd spotted a simple error in Trey's calculations, he'd listened to her, actually listened, and had even taken her advice. It had been years since a man had given her respect when it came to technical things.

When five o'clock rolled around, she felt a little anxious and excited to end her first day of work. Wishing for the following day to arrive too soon could make her look pathetic. Still, it was hard not to want to dive into something else exciting.

Trey had packed up his laptop and started shutting off lights. She followed him around to see what was involved with closing the office down each day.

"Normally, we're out of here on time, but there are nights Tyler has to work late." He showed her how to set the alarm, gave her the code and, to her surprise, handed her a set of keys. "We're usually here at eight sharp. On Fridays, we pick up donuts and coffee at Belle's Bakery. We have an account with them, so if you want to take that task on..."

"Sure." She nodded eagerly.

"Wonderful. We also have an account at Grangers Market for office items and the grocery store for milk, coffee, kitchen supplies, and anything else we need. I'll make sure to let them know to add you to the list."

She nodded and thought about where his company was going. It was an exciting field, on the verge of new technology, something she'd always dreamed of diving into further.

While her brother had been caught up in sports and being popular, Dylan had buried her head in the books. Anything and everything science was her calling. She loved spending hours with test tubes and beakers or scanning the microscope until her eyes turned fuzzy.

It was one of the reasons she'd gone dateless until her senior year, when she'd gone in to get her first tattoo and met Jax. She'd hidden her brain from him and their relationship had grown. From then on, she'd found that if you played dumb, there was always a line of men waiting.

Now, however, with Trey, she didn't feel like she had to hide that part of herself. She'd first spoken out about his calculation mistake without thinking.

Before the accident, she'd been looking at attending Stanford, but with her parents' death, her dreams had died as well.

Even though being a glorified secretary for the McGowans was a step up from waitress at a dive bar, it was a far cry from her dreams. Still, it was a step and one that would hopefully pay enough to get them out of the small hotel.

She watched Trey lock up and then glanced around. Her shoulders slumped when her brother's truck wasn't in sight.

"He's late," Trey said beside her.

"Yeah." She pulled her jacket closer to her and cursed the fact that the coat wasn't thicker. She had hoped, but in her heart, she'd known he'd either be late or forget all about her and hit the bar instead. "It's not that far..."

"Stop right there." He held up his hand. "You may not know this yet, but Kristen, my sister-in-law, said the same thing once. She was kidnapped on the way back to the same hotel." He shook his head. "Come on, I'll drive you there myself. Tomorrow, you can check out the sedan we use for corporate business."

She followed him. "What happen to her?"

He glanced over as he pulled open her door. "Kirsten?" She nodded. "We found her. The bastard had stashed her in a cave." He nodded towards the hills that surrounded the small town. Currently, it was too dark to see anything other than soft snow falling. "We found her just in time."

"That's good." She relaxed into his car and waited until he got behind the wheel. "Who kidnapped her?"

Trey's eyes turned dark.

"Dennis Rodgers. You'll want to watch out for that one." He started the car.

"Watch out... Isn't he rotting in jail by now?" she asked as he pulled out of the parking lot.

"No proof other than Kirsten's shoe, which Tyler found in the back of Dennis' truck. He claims Tyler planted it. He denied anything to do with Kristen's kidnapping, but confessed to a bunch of other stuff, like siphoning funds from his employer. He ended up going free shortly after though, since NewField's, his ex-employer, whom he'd swindled out of thousands of dollars, burned down, and the proof they had against him went up in smoke." He motioned to an empty lot. "Shortly after, he was walking around town like nothing happened. Other than losing his job and his wife in a messy divorce."

"It must be hard on Kristen and Tyler," she said as the snow started falling more heavily. It was going to be a cold night and she hated that the hotel room's heater couldn't be set past seventy-one.

"Yeah, but we upped our security." He shrugged. "There isn't much more we can do but keep an eye out for our own." He pulled into the parking lot and stopped in front of her door. She wondered briefly if he knew which room was theirs. "Which is why, until you can get a car of your own, you'll have full access to the corporate car. We need to know you can get to and from places safely, especially in this weather."

"I'm not in any danger?" she asked.

"No." He shook his head. "Everything's been quite since..." She could tell that he caught himself.

"Since?"

He sighed and leaned back in the seat. "Okay, there was an incident with Addy's Jeep, but we're pretty sure that was Darla, another one you'll want to watch out for. She works down at the Wet Spot." He motioned down the street. "Anyway, she's been quiet for a while too. Ever since Tyler and Kristen's wedding, things have been quiet."

"Too quiet?" she added.

He glanced at her. "I'm sure they just moved on. It's not like the entire town of Haven has it out for us." He smiled. "We've just learned to be a little more... cautious."

She nodded. "Okay, sounds good." She reached for the door handle, but he stopped her.

"I'll pick you up tomorrow morning. A quarter till eight."

She smiled. "I'll be here."

"Night." He reached across and slid open her door. "Stay warm, it's supposed to get cold tonight."

"It's Montana in January," she said dryly. "It's always cold."

He laughed as she got out of the car.

***

It was so nice having a set schedule, knowing exactly where you should be and who you were meeting, having all your paperwork where it belonged. Not to mention seeing Dylan every day. They fell into a nice pattern, working around one another, with one another. He had even asked her into his office to help with some calculations.

Sure, he could have used the computer or Googled how to solve the problems, but he enjoyed watching her do the math herself. Not to mention that for almost an entire hour after she'd leave his office, he could still smell her sexy perfume in the air.

Each day she came into the office and he tried to figure out how to keep her there. He had to admit, she'd been right about everything he'd asked her about. Each calculation she'd done for him was spot on. And even more impressive, she had been quick at solving each problem.

"You were a total geek in school," he said, looking over her shoulder as she helped him calculate how much pipe they needed for a certain job. He had a little cheat sheet he'd made up to help with calculations, but at the moment, he couldn't find it.

She smiled over her shoulder at him. "Don't hold it against me."

"Are you kidding, it's a huge turn on," he'd joked, but he saw her eyes change. Quickly, he changed subjects. "So, I have a house you and your brother might look at renting."

Her dark eyebrows shot up. "Oh?"

"Sure, I can drive you by the place during lunch break, if you want to look at it."

She bit her bottom lip. "Any clue what rent is?"

"What's your price range?" he asked.

She sighed. "Well, with just my paycheck, I was hoping to stay under half of my monthly income."

"Not calculating your brothers in?" he asked.

She frowned. "Not that I don't believe he'll stick, but I've learned to not rely on him forking over anything himself."

"Nice brother," he said sarcastically.

She shrugged. "He was there when no one else was. My father's parents, my grandparents, couldn't be bothered during their own grief over losing their

81

son to deal with two teenage grandchildren." She rolled her shoulders. "Sorry, still a little bitter."

"No, it's totally understandable." He moved over and sat on the edge of the desk, next to her. "After my father passed away, we had family members we had never heard of coming out of the woodwork, asking for handouts or insisting they were due something."

She nodded. "It was the opposite for us. My grandparents didn't want to be responsible for us. We've been on our own since then."

"What did you do?" he asked.

She leaned back in the chair, looking very relaxed behind his desk. Something clicked in his mind that she belonged there, in a position of power. Even with her jet-black hair, her cropped bangs, and the many colorful tattoos showing, she was the smartest woman he'd ever met.

"I went out and worked two jobs while I finished school. I took accelerated classes my senior year. Then I worked three full-time jobs to support us."

He frowned. "What about your brother?"

"Oh, he had a few jobs here and there. He couldn't keep any one for too long. There were a few DUIs. At one point, he ended up staying at a halfway house. It was the best three months of my life." When she talked, he could tell she'd lost herself and spoke her mind. Upon her last words, she shook free of the spell and sat up a little.

"Sounds like you could use a break from your brother," he hinted.

She cleared her throat. "Yeah, well, we can't choose family." She stood up slowly. He followed her, their bodies close. She blinked as she looked up at him. *"We are afraid to care too much, for fear that the other person does not care at all."* She almost whispered it.

He nodded in agreement. "Gandhi?"

She smiled, and her entire face changed. Her eyes sparkled in the daylight streaming in through the window behind him, and he felt like he could lose himself in her eyes. He could spend the rest of the day, happily standing there, discovering every curve, every freckle, every inch of her skin.

"Eleanor Roosevelt," she corrected. "One of my favorites. Did you know that both of her parents died when she was young? She went on to attend one of the best academies in London and she has done more for human rights than almost anyone. Not to mention that she singlehandedly changed the role of First Lady." She took a deep breath and he was pretty sure she could have gone on further, but something changed in her and she once again bit her bottom lip.

"Why do you do that?" he asked, curiously.

"What?" Her eyes dipped to her own hands in front of her.

Using his finger, he nudged her chin up, until

83

their eyes met again. "Stop yourself, hold yourself back?" He shook his head.

She was silent for a moment. "It's just... people aren't always happy around smart people. I tend to have a lot of useless knowledge moving around in my head. Sometimes it spills out and I have to catch myself from boring people too much."

"You don't have to worry about that with me. I find your knowledge, and you, extremely fascinating." His fingers spread out and, suddenly, he was cupping her face. He didn't know who leaned in first, but slowly, the gap between them closed. Just before their lips touched, his office door opened.

"I thought you said you hired..." Trent walked in and stopped dead in his tracks. His confused look turned instantly to humor. "Oh, now I see..." He chuckled as he backed out of the room.

Dylan, for her part, jumped away from him, almost tipping over his chair. He'd reached out to steady her, but she'd pushed him away and quickly rushed from the room while making some excuses about filing something.

"You have great timing," he said sarcastically to his brother.

"How was I supposed to know you'd be in here making out with our new secretary?" Trent joked after tactfully shutting the door behind him, gaining him a glare from Trey.

"What are you doing back so early? I thought you were coming in tomorrow."

"Well, I wound things up early so I could get home." Trent sat down on the sofa across from Trey's desk.

"You were just missing Addy." He sat down and glanced at his computer screen, still impressed at Dylan's abilities. "I bet you stopped off at the house for a quickie before coming in here."

His brother sighed heavily and looked mighty pleased with himself. "You're just jealous I have someone to go home to tonight and all you have is Dopey."

"Don't knock Dopey." Trey came to the defense of his almost year-old puppy, brother to his mother's dog Doc, Tyler and Kristen's dog Bashful, and Trent and Abby's dog, Happy. "Dopey is a hell of a lot smarter than any of his siblings." Trey smiled. "Kind of like me."

Trent laughed. "In your dreams."

"Speaking of smart siblings." Trey shifted the conversation. "You'll have to let me know your take on Dylan."

Trent nodded towards the door. "The new secretary?"

"Office manager," he corrected. "Yeah, there's a lot of unused hidden talent. She's blown me—" His brother's chuckle stopped him and he glared in his direction as he continued. "She's blown me away

85

with her knowledge of everything science-y, the kinds of things Dad always easily picked up."

"Science-y?" Trent laughed.

"Sure, I mean, hell, we grew up around this shit, and half of it we still don't understand."

"That's what Tyler's good for." Trent crossed his legs as he leaned back on the sofa, looking like he was going to take a nap.

Trey stood up, getting his brother's attention. "You know those figures I sent you for our order?"

"Sure." Trent shrugged. "You saved our butt with those new numbers."

"I had nothing to do with it." He nodded towards the door.

Trent's eyebrows shot up. "The secretary?"

"Office manager," he corrected again. "And her name is Dylan."

Trent chuckled. "Geeze, don't get your panties in a bind." His brother stood up and stretched his arms above his head. "It was a long drive back, so I'm heading home. I just came to get a few things."

"Yeah." Trey followed him out of his office. "I'll introduce you, officially."

Trent smiled and wrapped his arm around him. "Then come on and make it official."

He playfully slugged his brother in the gut, and he faked being hurt. In truth, the three brothers were physically almost identical. The only exception was that Tyler and Trent had their mother's straight dark hair and brown eyes, while Trey took after their father with curly blonde hair and blueish-silver eyes.

It had taken him years to catch up to Tyler in the weight department. He'd spent countless hours in the garage using his father's old weight set to gain the extra inches on his biceps. In the end, he'd finally caught up with the other two. Now, most people in town had a hard time telling them apart if they were bundled up for winter. He couldn't count the number of times he'd been mistaken for one of his brothers.

"Dylan, this is my brother Trent," Trey said when they entered the front area.

"Sorry about barging in." Trent offered her his hand.

"Nothing happened," Dylan added quickly. She blushed slightly.

"No, of course not." Trent cleared his throat. "Trey was telling me that you're the one who saved our butts on that last pipe order."

Dylan nodded. "Math comes easily for me."

Trent laughed and slapped Trey on the back. "Not for my little brother here. Did you know Trey failed algebra, twice?"

"Shut up," Trey said under his breath. Trent wrapped an arm around him playfully.

87

Jill Sanders

Chapter Six

A wave of jealousy spread through Dylan at seeing how the brothers interacted with one another. Here was the family dynamic she'd desired her entire life. There had been a point, long ago, when Brent had acted like a big brother. That was long before her parents had stopped acting like parents and started acting like older siblings.

The last trip to Mexico had been one of many trips their parents had gone on in a four-year span, and the only time they'd taken her and Brent along.

"Trent is leaving now," Trey said clearly, disengaging himself from his brother. "I've got a meeting to prepare for."

"Right." Trent straightened his brother's tie. He was wearing worn jeans and a sweater so she had figured he wouldn't be sticking around for the rest of the day. "I'll leave you two alone." Trent smiled and winked at her as he walked towards the front door.

"See, that's something else we have in common," Trey said, clearly.

"What?" she asked.

"My brother can be an ass too." He made sure to say it before Trent had left the building. His brother just chuckled as he walked out. "I need to apologize to you," Trey said once they were alone.

"You've nothing to apologize for." She tried to keep her mind off what had almost happened in his office moments ago. "Your conference call isn't—"

"Dylan." Trey's tone of voice stopped her. "Not about my brother. Everyone in town knows he's an idiot. Once you've worked here for a few days you'll understand there will be plenty more instances like that." He nodded towards the doorway. "I'm sorry about earlier. In my office. I shouldn't have pushed... things."

"You didn't push," she corrected, trying not to fidget under his gaze. Even after four boyfriends, she still wasn't any good at this sort of thing. Who was she kidding? She could have had a million boyfriends and Trey McGowan would still make her feel nervous when he looked at her like he was now.

Over the past few days working with him, she'd tried to tell herself that she was being overly dramatic, that she was reading more into what was there between them than really was. Until what had happened in his office, that almost kiss. Now, she was wondering *when* they would kiss, not *if*.

He moved closer to her desk, and she was thankful she was sitting down. She didn't think her knees would hold her up at this point.

"You two are great together." She decided avoidance was the best way to deal with her embarrassment. "I bet you never fought with your brothers."

Trey walked over behind her desk and leaned against the side of it. The desk was raised so she was eye to eye with anyone who came in, so his hip rested against the edge of the desk.

"We fought like a group of baboons, or so my mother always said." His eyes ran over her face slowly. She held perfectly still when he reached up and slid out the pen she'd pushed behind her ear. "Do you wear glasses?" he asked, frowning down at the pen. It was an old habit, one kids in school had always made fun of her for. She'd slide a pen behind her ear and forget it was there, then spend five minutes looking for it.

"Contacts," she said, frowning slightly at how breathless she sounded. The fact was, she'd been wearing the same disposable contacts for more than two weeks. The things itched and irritated her eyes. But she couldn't afford new ones and hated wearing her glasses, so she kept refreshing them with drops all day long. Small price for beauty, or so her mother used to tell her all the time.

Of course, her mother had had more than a dozen plastic surgeries that Dylan could remember. In the end, neither the price nor the pain had been worth it, none of it had really mattered.

"Hmmm." Trey nodded. "Eye care is included in our health package. There's a good eye doctor about half an hour from here."

"Included..." She'd forgotten all about the health insurance, even though she'd been the one to fill out and fax the forms in for her and Brent. She'd been too excited about the idea of a real paycheck to look over the health packet. "Right." She nodded slowly. "I'll make sure to set something up."

He tilted his head a little, and she wondered what it would be like to have him watch her as he slowly undressed her. Which reminder her that her undergarments were not... top of the line. Who was she kidding? She was lucky she had one bra and the underwear she was wearing. The elastic had gone out on both and she was dying to spend some of her first check at the little boutique she'd driven by downtown.

"Are they colored?" Trey asked, breaking into her thoughts.

"What?" She almost choked out the question. She had thought at first he was asking about her panties and her cheeks flushed.

When he smiled, she guessed he'd understood where her thoughts were.

"Your contacts?" he said slowly.

"Oh." She took a deep breath. "No, just disposable." He nodded. "Why all the questions about my vision?" she asked, suddenly curious.

He chuckled. "Just curious. I guess it's my way of saying you have nice eyes." He stood up when the front door opened and glanced over his shoulder. "Looks like my next meeting is early."

For the hour Trey was in the meeting, her entire body vibrated from his compliment. She tried to focus on her work, but each time she thought about his words, her body would react again. What was going on? The guy wasn't even her type.

Sure, he was tall, sexy, and full of lean muscles. Those blue eyes of his seemed to bore directly into her soul, and she was pretty sure that if he ever touched her, she would melt or combust.

By the time he walked out of the office again, she was back under full control. That was, until she got a call from her brother. She was a little surprised that he knew the office number, but after hearing where he was, she realized what had happened.

"I'm at the police station. You'll have to—"

"What did you do now?" she hissed into the phone, hoping Trey couldn't hear her from down the hallway. His door was open, so she spoke quietly.

"Nothing, it's just a misunderstanding. Can you come? They impounded my truck."

"What?" It had come out louder than she'd intended and she glanced down the hallway.

"I'll explain when you get here." Her brother hung up the phone quickly, leaving her no choice but to make an excuse as to why she couldn't see the rental house during her lunch break.

Straightening her shoulders, she pulled out her purse and the keys to the company sedan she'd enjoyed having all to herself and made her way down the hallway.

Knocking on the open door, she waited for Trey to look up from his computer screen. Her breath stuck in her throat when she noticed the black wire frames sitting on the bridge of his nose.

He turned towards her and she felt her heart actually skip a beat. She'd never fallen for a man in glasses, but wow. Trey McGowan wasn't your normal man in reading glasses.

"Yes?" he asked, pulling off the glasses and giving her a slight frown when he noticed her bag.

"I... something has come up and I need to go check on my brother during my break. I really wanted to see the rental, but..."

"It's okay." He set the glasses on the table and waved her inside the office. She moved automatically. "Is everything alright?" he asked.

"Yes, no." She shook her head. "I'm not sure. But he needs me and..."

"I understand." He smiled. "If you want, we can swing by the place after work."

Instantly, she cheered up. "That would be great." She'd been dreaming of getting out of the hotel and having a real house again since he'd mentioned it earlier. At least when she wasn't fantasizing about his hands running all over her body.

"Great." He turned back to the screen. "Can you lock the front door behind you? I'm going to work through lunch."

"Oh, sure." She instantly felt guilty. Maybe he'd been looking forward to taking off for lunch. There wasn't anything to eat at the office, and she thought about stopping at Frankie's Deli on the way back and picking something up for him. Turning back towards him, she watched him slip on the glasses again and held in a sigh. "Mustard?" she blurted out. His eyebrows shot up with humor.

"I'm sorry?" he asked.

She rolled her eyes. "My mouth just acts on its own sometimes." She sighed. "I can stop and get you a sandwich at Frankie's on my way back. Do you like mustard?"

He chuckled. "That would be great. Yes, the works. If you tell Frankie it's for me, he'll know how I like it."

"Great." She smiled. "Thanks, again." She rushed from the room before she could blurt out anything else stupid.

***

Why was it that the week his brothers decide to leave him alone at the office, it was so busy he didn't have time to breathe, let alone give the attention he wanted to Dylan? Still, he made his way through the rest of the day with the help of his favorite sandwich from Frankie's Deli. When Gary knocked on his office door, he waved him in.

"I've got that special order you were asking after." Gary held up the box.

"Great." Trey stood up and met the man halfway across the room. He signed for the box and tried to avoid small talk, but with Gary, it wasn't likely to work. He nodded towards his computer. "Sorry, can't chat now, I've got to get back at it."

"Oh, sure, I bet you're swamped with Tyler and Trent out this week."

"Yeah." He waited until he heard the guy leave the building before making his way down the hallway to where Dylan sat behind the desk.

"I've got something for you." He set the box down in front of her. She looked at it for a moment, then opened it.

"What is it?" she asked as she opened the box.

"Since it's important that we can get ahold of our office manager at any given time, and since I noticed you don't have a cell phone…" He shook his head. "Seriously, who nowadays doesn't have a cell phone?" He smiled as she pulled the new phone from the box. She set it on the table like it was made of glass and she was afraid it would shatter in her hands. "It's a company phone," he added, feeling the need to talk her into the idea of carrying it around.

"I..." She shook her head. "I can't accept this."

He laughed. "Sure, you can. Like I said, it's a company phone. We all have them." He held up his matching phone. "It's a little hard to call the hotel phone when we need to reach you."

She didn't touch it again, so he picked it up and flipped it on. "I've already texted my brothers your number, as well as the site managers." He watched as the new phone booted up. "All that's left is for you to program all the phone numbers into it. You can just log in to your corporate email and your contacts should sync." He handed her the phone. "Then everyone will be in your phone automatically."

"I..." She shook her head. He could see she wanted to say more, but she just swallowed and started the process of entering her login information into the phone.

He helped for a few minutes, then had to go finish his work. When an alarm popped up on his screen, he smiled and pulled out his phone and texted her.

-Five minutes left before we can get out of here.

He waited and when the reply came back, he

smiled.

-Four now.

When he walked out of his office, she was still bent over the new phone. Seeing him, she frowned.

"I can't get the accounting software app to work on this."

"We have an app for our accounting program?" He moved over behind her desk.

She nodded. "Yes, their website shows it. I've downloaded it, see?" She held out her phone for him to see. Sure enough, there was the logo and login screen for the app.

"Maybe it needs the admin user name and password instead of yours." He punched in the access and smiled when it logged in. "Well, I'll be…" He shook his head. "Here you go." He handed her the phone.

"I shouldn't have access to the admin login." She started to delete the app.

"No, it's okay. I can officially say your trial period is over."

"Why would you say that?" She was still frowning up at him.

"Trent liked you." He chuckled.

"But…" She continued to look down at her screen.

He could tell she was having a hard time with it,

so he changed the subject.

"Come on, let's go look at the house." He stepped back, allowing her to close down for the night.

He was locking up the front door when they heard a car pull into the parking lot. Glancing back, he groaned.

"You're about to meet Darla, the woman I warned you about."

"The one who set fire to your sister-in-law's car?" she asked quickly.

"Yup," he said as the woman climbed out of her old clunker. The car had seen better days ten years ago. Now it was just waiting for a reason to die.

"I heard congratulations are in order," Darla said as she approached them on the sidewalk.

She wasn't wearing a jacket even though there was a light dusting of snow covering the ground, so he figured she'd probably just gotten off work. From the smell of her, he estimated she was too drunk to be driving and reached in his pocket for his cell phone.

He didn't respond to her but asked his own question instead. "Darla, should you be driving yourself home?"

"Oh, I only live a block away." She leaned closer to him, almost falling over. His hand reached out automatically to steady her. What could he say?

He'd been raised to help a woman in need, no matter who that woman was. "So, your brother and that... woman had a child." She ran her hands over her flat belly. "I was pregnant once." She said this to Dylan as her eyes raced up and down her.

Dylan, for her part, was wrapped in a jacket. Not the thickest one, but at least it would keep most of the cold out. She'd worn black leggings with a long grey sweater skirt and ankle-high boots. Her hair was tucked under a black cap and she was wearing black gloves that had seen better days but would keep her digits warm. All in all, Dylan looked a lot sexier than the stripper trying to rub her double Ds against his arm.

Setting her away from him, he cleared his throat and pulled out his phone. "I'll get you a ride home."

"Don't bother," she purred as she walked back to her car. "Tell Tyler I stopped by." She waved as she pulled out of the parking lot.

"Wow," Dylan said under her breath, "were those natural?"

He stopped texting Tony and glanced up at Dylan. Then he laughed and hit send. He knew Tony would have someone drive by and make sure Darla didn't hit anything or anyone on the way home.

"Come on." He took Dylan's gloved hand and walked her to his car. "I'm driving."

He'd gotten his truck back from the shop and was happy that the thing would now stop when he hit the brakes. It was an older truck, but it was paid off and reliable enough.

"Nice. This is a better version of my brother's truck," she supplied.

He glanced over at her as he drove out of the parking lot. "I heard that your brother's truck was towed for the tags being expired. Two years expired."

She sighed. "Small towns."

"Yup, you can't escape gossip." He turned down the street the little home sat at the end of.

"I wrote them a check, but I'm hoping they won't cash it until I get my first paycheck." She turned slightly towards him. "And then that will leave me dreaming about moving out of the hotel but having no money for a deposit until my second paycheck."

"We can probably work something out with the landlord. The place is empty now. I'm sure they'll want someone in it now, rather than later." He turned into the cul-de-sac and nodded. "There she is." She glanced out the windshield and her eyes went huge.

Jill Sanders

Chapter Seven

*T*his couldn't be the house Trey had been talking about. The place was a fairy-tale cottage. It was painted dark brown with cream trim surrounding all the windows and doors. The front door was half glass, and there was a light on inside, making the place feel welcoming.

"This is it?" She turned slightly to Trey, who was watching her closely.

"Yup,"

"For the rent you mentioned?" She turned and looked at the house again. A small covered porch ran from the front door around to the left side of the house. A cobblestone driveway led to the back of the place.

"Yup," Trey said again, slowly letting the truck roll down the driveway. He stopped at another set of stairs on the side of the house.

"There's a side entrance here that enters into a mud room. I used that in the winter. The garage is back there." He pointed to a separate building that was as cute as the house. "There's a makeshift apartment above the garage. Basically a room with a bathroom, a small kitchen area. If your brother pisses you off, you can shove him up there." He chuckled. "There are two bedrooms, two baths in the main house. Small, but I'd wager bigger than the hotel room."

He helped her out and, since the snow was falling again, they rushed to the covered wraparound porch. He pulled a set of keys from his pocket.

"You have the keys?" she asked, watching him open the door.

"Yeah, the owner dropped them off while you were at lunch." He opened the door and she tried not to sigh at how wonderful the house was. He leaned in and flipped on the light. "I texted the owner about you. He is willing to work with you to get you in here. He doesn't like it sitting empty for security reasons."

"It's furnished," she said, stepping into the stone-tiled mud room. On the left wall was a long bench with spots for shoes and jackets next to it. The washer and dryer sat across from the space. There was a wall of white box containers with wicker baskets as you made your way out of the room, with enough storage for hats, gloves, or whatever other winter wear one would want to store.

They walked into the kitchen and she instantly could see herself here. She'd really missed cooking. An L-shaped black granite countertop stretched along the right side of the kitchen. There were white paneled appliances that matched the cabinets and a wood chop-block island with a small sink in the middle. There were red bar stools on the other side for seating.

Over the island hung pans of every size and color. She turned to Trey.

"Fully furnished?" she asked.

"Yeah, it's one of the perks." He smiled. "I lived here when I came back into town, before I moved into my current place." He chuckled. "I had to buy everything myself. Actually, I'm still buying stuff."

She walked past the kitchen into the dining room. It appeared that at one point the space had been a back patio area, since there were windows on all three sides, with large French doors leading out to the backyard. An oval table with six chairs sat in the space. She could just imagine sitting in here having dinner on a warm summer night with all the windows and doors open to the cool breeze.

Her heels clicked on the gleaming oak floors, only silenced by the thick rugs in several areas.

Turning back around, she turned the corner and walked into the living room. There was a beautiful stone fireplace with an oak mantel on the side wall. Huge reclaimed wood ceiling beams hung

105

overhead, making the entire place feel warm. Comfortable-looking dark brown chairs and sofa and sturdy wood furniture made the space cozy. Huge windows overlooked the front yard and street.

"It's a real wood fireplace. There are several places in town that can deliver firewood by the week, if you want," Trey said as he walked over to the fireplace. "I'll get a fire started since it's chilly in here. Go on and take a look around. I hope it's okay, but I ordered pizza." He smiled. "It's one thing I miss at my place. They won't deliver since my driveway hasn't been graded yet."

She nodded as she continued to scan the space. There was a narrow hallway with a sliding barn door. She moved into what she figured would become her favorite room in the house.

The space was small, but there were bookcases on every wall. The small library was tucked behind the living room fireplace, and she imagined its warmth would spread there first. Instead of another sofa, the end wall was a wide window seat with more than a dozen thick throw pillows.

Turning back, she passed through the living room and headed towards the front door. The staircase was across from the massive wood doorway with its long windows on either side. Down a small hallway sat a powder room and another coat closet.

She climbed the stairs and found a small loft area with another window seat at the top. The bedrooms sat on opposite sides of the house. The room and bathroom to the back of the house instantly piqued her attention. The comforter was a pale blue, while the bathroom walls were a brighter blue, making it very cheerful.

Each of the bathrooms had a sunken bathtub with a wood ledge, giving plenty of space to sit along the outside of the tub.

The bedroom windows overlooked the backyard, where she could see fresh snow falling on what she assumed was a grassy area. There were flower beds and several benches outside.

Before heading downstairs, she took several deep breaths. She wanted the place. Really wanted it. But she had to be reasonable. She couldn't afford it. Not now. Not until after she'd paid for the towing and for updating the tags on her brother's truck.

She didn't know what next month held for her, but she was pretty sure Brent would do something else to use up the deposit and rent she'd need for the beautiful home.

Making up her mind, she straightened her shoulders and made her way back down the stairs. Trey was at the front door, talking to the pizza delivery person about football when they both spotted her coming down the stairs.

"I'll see you later, Kenny." Trey nudged the kid out the door when he gave out a low whistle.

"Yeah, sure," the boy said as Trey shut the door

in his face.

"Did you at least tip the kid?" she asked.

Trey chuckled. "Yeah," He followed her into the kitchen area.

"It's kind of strange, eating dinner in someone else's house." She glanced around again and, for a split second, dreamed.

"It's not someone else's. You'll be moving in Saturday." He opened the cupboard and pulled out two plates like he lived there. Then she remembered he had.

"Trey, I can't. I just can't make the numbers work." She sat down at the bar area and rested her chin in her hands. "No matter how much I want it…"

"It's all set, then." Trey set the plate down in front of her and poured her some soda. "The deposit and rent will come out of your paychecks—both of yours, not just you—so you can move in." He sat next to her and clinked his glass against hers. "Welcome home."

She set her glass down and stood up. "Trey, I appreciate everything, really I do—"

"I didn't want to have to bring out the big guns, but"—he took a deep breath— "your landlord is my mother. She's actually on her way over here right now to meet you again, officially. But rest assured, everything is already set in stone. She agreed to rent it to you, with your brother as a side occupant. And tomorrow we'll arrange it so that rent will be taken out of your paychecks, equally."

She felt her stomach roll and suddenly was more nervous than she'd been in a long time.

"Your mother owns this place?" She looked around.

"Yeah. When I moved back into town, I was renting the place. The owner and my mom were best friends in school. She happened to mention to my mother she was thinking of selling. When my father died, my mom had come into some money she didn't know what to do with, so she jumped on the house as an investment." He smiled.

Just then, the side door opened.

"Wow, it's really coming down out there," a woman called from the mud room. "I hope you saved me some of that pizza."

When Gail McGowan walked into the kitchen, Dylan couldn't instantly see a resemblance. She'd met her at the diner that first day on the job, but she'd been so overwhelmed, she hadn't paid much attention to her. However, after spending half an hour watching Trey with his mother, she noticed how much alike they were in personality.

She was surprised at how much Trent had taken after their mother in looks. From the painting in the main lobby, it appeared Trey was the only one who resembled his father.

"Trey tells me you and your brother have started

working for him," Gail said over pizza. They had moved into the dining room and Dylan sat with her back to the fire, watching the snow fall outside in the floodlights.

"Yes, although my brother, Brent, doesn't officially start until this Monday. His medical forms were just turned in this afternoon."

"That's good. Trey tells me you've got a science background," she said, sipping some coffee Trey had made for her.

"Um, well, I was top of my science class in high school. I had wanted to go on to college, but after my parents died, there just wasn't enough money."

"Have you thought of online classes? My late husband was a firm believer in higher education. He even implemented a benefit program where the company would pay if the classes have anything to do with the job."

"Yeah," Trey jumped in. "I'm sure we can make something work for you. Not that any of the classes you'd be interested in have anything to do with being an office manager. But I'm sure we can work something out."

For the first time in almost four years, happiness felt within her reach. Could she really have it all? Living in a beautiful home, having a wonderful job, the possibility of college? Not to mention working for some of the sexiest, rugged men in all of Montana.

She was just waiting for the moment when everything came crashing down on her again.

Gail glanced down at her watch and stood up. "Well, I'm sorry to bug out on you two, but it's game night and I'm hosting. I still have to swing by the store for some more bean dip." She took her plate to the sink and rinsed it, dried it, and put it away.

Then she walked back over to Dylan and held out her hand. "I'm happy that this place was available for you and your brother. I look forward to seeing someone back in it." Her eyes traveled to Trey. "Now if he'd just get some of his junk out of our garage, I'd be even happier." She smiled as Dylan shook her hand. "If you need anything, let Trey know. He knows this place inside and out and can arrange for anything that needs to be done." Gail shocked Dylan by pulling her in for a hug. It felt good, the contact from a mother figure. It had been years, ages really, since she'd been embraced by someone she trusted and looked up to. Her mind flashed to all the lost moments with her own mother, moments that couldn't be made up.

She didn't realize tears were sliding down her cheek as she watched the woman leave the house until Trey walked over and gently pulled her into his arms.

***

He didn't know where Dylan's tears were coming from, but he knew how to handle them.

Years of being the youngest in a nearly all-male family had taught him to let his mother lean on him when she needed. He didn't know why she'd picked him out of the three boys, but he always seemed to be the one who was around when his mother's eyes turned wet.

"Feel better?" he asked as he gently rubbed his hands over her hair.

"I'm sorry." She pulled back and wiped her eyes with her sleeve. "I haven't done that in years."

"What?" He frowned. "Cry?"

When she nodded, he shook his head. "That's not normal. People should get their frustrations out regularly."

"Do you?" Suddenly, her sadness was replaced with interest.

"Men get their frustration out differently than women."

When she laughed, he couldn't help but smile. "What's so funny?" he asked.

"You. I didn't take you for the kind of guy to believe in stereotypes." She moved closer to the fire and stood with her hands reached towards the flames. He moved closer to her.

"I'm not. But living with three brothers in a house ruled by the woman who just left, I learned quickly." He chuckled.

"How do you get your... frustrations out?" She

glanced over her shoulder at him.

He shrugged. "Lots of different ways. Running, working, chopping wood, sex." He smiled. "Haven't used that one in a while though."

Her eyebrows arched slightly. "Sex can be a great outlet, if done right."

Damn, was she teasing him? Whether she was or not, his body was responding just the same.

He moved slightly closer. "Oh, I've never had any complaints."

She turned towards him, her eyes raking over him. "No, you wouldn't."

This time, it was his eyebrows that shot up. "Doubt me?"

She shook her head as she chuckled and held up her hands. "I know when to back down from a challenge." She turned back to the fire.

"Why the tears?" he asked after a moment of silence.

She took a deep breath before answering him.

"I guess it just really hit me that I never felt comfortable hugging my mother."

"She wasn't a hugger?" he asked. He'd always gotten affection from his parents. They hadn't been a perfect family, but when it mattered, they had always been there for one another.

"No, none of us are." He noticed the face she was

113

making and closed the space between them.

"Now what?" he asked softly.

Her eyes traveled up to his. "I was just wondering how awkward it would be to get a hug from Brent."

He chuckled. "Yeah, Tyler, Trent, and I don't hug one another much, either."

She smiled and, once again, the sadness was replaced with humor. "Thanks."

"For?" His hands had moved up to her shoulders and her softness was intoxicating.

Her eyes moved past him. "All this." She shrugged. "The job, the car, the house, listening to me. Need I go on?" She chuckled.

"A man's ego is something to be stroked, and often." He smiled. "You're welcome. I did have some selfish motives, though."

"Oh?" It came out as a whisper as her smile fell away.

Instead of answering her, he leaned in and placed his lips softly over hers. He couldn't have expected how that simple first touch would rock him. Instantly, his fingers tightened and he pulled her closer. Once again, she was in his arms, only this time, he wasn't thinking of comforting her.

Dylan melted against him, causing his body to react even more.

"I didn't plan this," he said after nibbling on her bottom lip.

"Course you did." She chuckled. She pulled back slightly. "We both did from the moment we saw each other."

"Okay, true, but not this, here, tonight." He glanced around and realized that from an outsider's perspective, the place was set up for a romantic evening.

Running his hands through his hair, he wondered why he'd thought he'd hadn't planned it. Just then, his cell phone rang. Seeing Tony's number, he knew he couldn't miss the call.

"Hold that thought." He took a step away from her and answered the phone. "Yo?" It was a stupid way of answering, but it was a tradition with his friends.

"Trey, you'd better get to your new site."

Trey's stomach sank. "What?"

"It's not bad, but I called your other brothers first. Sorry, you're low man on the totem pole."

"Be there"—he glanced at his watch and calculated—"in fifteen."

"I'll keep an eye out for you." Tony hung up and he turned back to Dylan.

"Care to go for a ride?" He walked over and stifled the fire, shutting the glass doors to the fireplace so no embers would break out.

115

"What's happened?" She rinsed their plates off quickly and set them in the drying rack.

"I'm not sure, but they called in the big guns. Both my brothers are already on their way up to our new site."

"New…" She looked confused.

"The land we purchased for the school." His stomach sank again at the thought of something happening, but then he remembered they didn't even have a generator up there yet.

"Oh." She pulled on her gloves and when she reached for her coat, he beat her to it and helped her slip it on.

"Not how I wanted the evening to end, but…"

She turned around and, to his surprise, kissed him again.

"Thank you, again."

He wished he could go on for the rest of the night, enjoying her next to him, but there was a fifteen minute drive up the hill.

"I could take you home." He silently hoped she'd say no.

"Why? So, I can watch my brother watch sports on the TV and drink beer he bought with the money he stole from my purse?" She rolled her eyes. "No, thank you. You'd be saving me, actually." She took his hand. "Let's go."

Chapter Eight

As Trey drove through the snow, he told her all about the drama his family had suffered the previous year. She already knew about Kristen's kidnapping, but he filled her in on the details, as well as telling her what Addy had gone through.

"So, is it a theme? The women the McGowan men fall for are always in jeopardy?" She meant it as a tease but could tell that worry flooded him when he thought about it.

He turned slightly towards her, frowning. "No, I… hadn't looked at it like that before." He drove in silence for a while. "I'm sure it's just a coincidence. It's not like Addy's issues were directly tied to us. I mean, her father's death had more to do with Darla than anything."

Dylan shivered. "I can't believe that woman faked being pregnant just to spite Addy. I haven't met Addy yet, but no one deserves that."

"Especially her," Trey said, pulling off the main road. They had been driving up into the hills for almost ten minutes straight. Now, there was a heavy gate that sat open in front of them. "It's normally locked. We've been paying the local police to make nightly visits to various sites to check up on them since... well, since everything started."

They bumped up the dirt path. "Better hold on," he said, pulling the truck to a stop. "Switching into four-wheel drive." He reached down and flipped a lever and then looked over at her. "Do you like mudding?"

She chuckled. "I should, I've been enough times with Brent when he took a wrong turn." She held onto the dash as he started. Unlike her brother, Trey went slow and avoided the bigger holes in the path.

He pulled in behind two other trucks and a police SUV. She had been wondering how a cruiser would make the trek up the hill.

"You can stay in the truck if..."

"I'll go." She started to open the door, but he stopped her.

"Then at least pull these on." He pulled out a pair of rubber boots from the back seat. "I'd hate to wreck those pretty ones."

She glanced down at her boots and nodded. "Thanks." It took her a minute to pull her boots off and put on the rubber boots, which were much too big for her.

Still, when she jumped out of the truck and sunk about an inch in the muddy snow-covered ground, she was thankful.

"How can it be so muddy when it's been snowing for days?" She reached for his arm as she started walking. She lifted her right foot and squealed when the boot pulled right off her foot.

Chuckling, Trey helped her stick her foot back in it, then quickly hoisted her up into his arms. She had to admit, it felt wonderful to be carried. His coat was thick, so she couldn't really feel his shoulders, but she could imagine what they were like under there while he made his way towards the lights.

As they rounded the second truck, they heard voices and Trey called out.

"Over here," someone responded. Trey walked towards the sound.

A bright light shone in their eyes and Trey cursed. "Get that damn light out of our eyes." There wasn't any real anger behind his words.

They were met with laughter. "Now why does that look familiar?"

She knew from the photo at the office that it was Tyler who'd spoken. All four men standing in the mud were looking at them, smiling.

Trey set her down gently in a high spot. She was thankful when she didn't sink into more mud.

"Hi," she said nervously.

119

"Dylan, this is my other brother, Tyler." She reached out and shook his hand.

"As nice as it was for you to bring our new secretary…" Tyler started, but Trent jumped in.

"Office manager."

Tyler rolled his eyes. "Whatever title you want to give out, I don't think this is a good place for her to get her feet wet, so to speak." He glanced down at her boots. "With this sort of thing."

"What's happened?" Trey ignored his brother.

There were two officers dressed in large rubber boots and heavy black jackets. The older man stepped forward. She'd met him before, at the diner. His name was Tony, and he was dating Trey's mother.

The man was as tall as the three brothers but had a head full of grey hair and a day's growth on his face that matched it. He reminded her of the actor Sam Elliott. He and Gail made a very cute couple.

"It's strapped to the inside fence." Tony's eyes moved to her. "She'd better stay here."

She didn't know why, but she was even more determined to go along. "I'm fine." She smiled.

"No offense, ma'am, but you're wearing a dress." Tony nodded to her outfit.

"I'm wearing a sweater and leggings," she corrected. "And I'll be fine." She started walking to where the lights from the trucks were shining. When she slipped on the mud, she was thankful Trey was there to grip her elbow.

"Easy, you don't want to prove them right," he said softly.

"Men." She sighed, and then her eyes landed on what they were there to see. She gasped and covered her face. Instantly, her stomach rolled, and the pizza threatened to surface.

"Take her back to the truck," one of his brothers said quickly.

"I'm fine." She dropped her hands. "I just hadn't expected…" She narrowed her eyes. "What is that?"

"From the looks of it, several different animals," Tony said. "Normally, I wouldn't have bothered, but seeing as it's strapped to the fence…"

"Yeah." The two older brothers moved closer to the tortured creature that had been hung up for display, while Trey stayed next to her.

"Are you okay?" he asked her softly.

"Yes, go." She nudged him. "I'm fine." She took several deep breaths and the chill in the air helped soothe her stomach. Still, she avoided looking at the thing hanging up.

"It's all the shit parts of kills, strapped together," someone said. Without looking, she had a hard time telling which brother was speaking since they sounded so much alike.

"Coyote, bear, moose, hell, I think there's even some parts of a beaver in here."

"The question is, why strap it up?"

"Well..." This time she knew it was Tony speaking. "The Indians have power animals. The bear could mean aggression, the moose for someone who's headstrong, the coyote is stealth or mistakes, the beaver..."

"We don't need a full school lesson. I got enough of those as a kid," the other cop said, breaking in. "It's obvious by the way it's strapped up that it's a warning. Some people around here don't like what your family has planned for up here."

It was then that Dylan noticed that the other police officer was of Native American descent. Every eye turned to him.

"Have something to say to us, Dale?" Tyler asked. She could see the humor in his eyes from where she stood.

Dale chuckled. "If I did, I'm man enough to say it to your face. After you buy me a round of beers."

"Damn right." Tyler reached out his hand and the other man took it easily.

"Still, I'm smart enough to read between the lines," Dale added. "It's meant as a warning. Mark my words, it won't stop here. We'd better spend the rest of the night checking your other sites." He turned to head back to the truck.

"What about this… thing?" Trent asked, motioning to the symbol.

"We'll take it down and bag it," Tony offered. "There might be something left behind that will lead us to whoever did this. Besides, it's not bear season, so whoever did this broke more than one law tonight."

"We can each take a site," Tyler said, eyeing Dylan before turning to Trey. "You can take the two on the other side of town, so you can drop Dylan off at home first."

Dylan almost told them that she didn't want to go back home but decided everyone else didn't need to know her problems. Besides, she was pretty sure Trey would let her ride along.

As they made their way back to his truck, he once again lifted her easily in his arms and carried her through the thickest of the mud.

"You want to ride along with me?" he asked.

"God yes." She sighed as he set her down comfortably in the passenger seat of his truck.

He smiled and nodded. "I figured you might."

***

He tried to keep his excitement hidden, but the truth was, he was hoping that Dylan wanted to ride along with him for more reasons than not wanting to spend another evening locked in a small hotel room with her brother.

Still, they rode in silence back to town. "Why are there so many strip clubs in Haven?" she asked as they drove through the back streets.

He chuckled. "It started more than three decades ago, or so the story goes."

"Okay, I've got time, tell me the story." She shifted and looked like she was getting comfortable, so he started the story his father had told him more than half a dozen times growing up. The town had been failing until oil was discovered. There was influx of men who came to work, and there were so many fights that the town almost failed once again. Until the first strip club opened. After that, more and more opened and the town became what it is today, a peaceful town that a lot of good people happily call home.

"We're down to only a dozen clubs now. With more and more closing every day." He finished the story as he came to a stop outside the first site's gate. He shut off the engine and looked at the gate. "Everything looks good here, but we'll drive up to the trailer and check it all out."

He jumped out, used the code to unlock the gate, and swung it wide. He was a little surprised when the truck rolled slowly through the gate. Dylan was behind the wheel. He could barely see her over the steering wheel.

Shutting the gate behind the truck, he climbed back up into the driver seat, chuckling. "I don't know how you even touched the gas pedal."

She smiled. "I didn't really, I just threw it in gear and let it roll."

The snow was falling faster now as they made their way to the trailer half a mile up the hillside. The land was vacant, but there were old outbuildings sporadically placed on the nearly twenty acres of land.

"Is that your trailer?" She pointed to the lone light in the darkness.

"Yeah. We've got cameras installed here, but no internet, so I have to be close to log in on my phone. He pulled to a stop in front of the small trailer and used his phone to log in. "You can download the app." He showed her. "We use it for all our security cameras. If we have internet access on site, you can log in from anywhere and check out what's going on. Sites like this, where we're lucky to have power, you'll need to be within one hundred yards."

He showed her the screen where the truck was sitting in front of the camera. She glanced over to where the camera was.

"It's in the tree. I would have thought you'd put it on the trailer."

"Yeah, we're hoping everyone else would think that too." He smiled. "If they don't see a camera…"

She nodded. "Smart."

He ran the camera back a few hours until the time the crew left for the night and was satisfied everything was untouched. "Let's roll to the next location." He turned the truck around and headed back down the hill.

This time, he was ready when Dylan rolled the truck through the open gate. Locking up behind him, he jumped back in the truck and headed towards the other site on this side of town.

"How many sites do you have?" she asked.

"Currently eight. Normally there's more, but we've pulled back slightly while we're ramping up for the ground breaking."

"Have any of the other sites been tampered with lately?" she asked.

"No, not since last spring."

"Then maybe it's just the site where your school is going to sit," she suggested as he drove. He thought about it and agreed with her. Whoever was doing this opposed the school site only. Only one name came to mind.

"Your uncle didn't seem too keen on the school." Dylan broke into his thoughts.

"No, he's not." He sighed. "I'll have a chat with my family about it tomorrow, but for now"—he pulled up in front of yet another gate— "this one's up hill." He nodded to the gate area.

"I can reach the pedal, really." She smiled and scooted over after he jumped out.

The site was untouched, still they ran through the footage before leaving.

When he pulled into the parking lot at the hotel, he handed her a set of keys.

"What are these for?" she asked.

"Your new home. My mother expects you to move in tomorrow, so after work, if you need any help, let me know."

"I only have a bag or two. Most of our stuff is still in Brent's truck."

"Still." He waited, wanting to kiss her goodnight, but not wanting her to get out of the truck.

"Trey, there's no way I could ever repay you for all that you've done for me in the last week."

"Has it only been a week?" he joked, then his smile fell away. "No need to repay kindness. Anyone in their right mind would have done the same. Besides, you're an asset to us."

Her smile told him that he'd hit the right mark.

"Goodnight." She reached for the door handle, then stopped. "Okay, don't take this the wrong way. This has nothing to do with the fact that you're my boss." She leaned over and quickly kissed him.

When she tried to pull back, he held her still, taking the kiss a little deeper. When he finally dropped his hands, he nodded. "Damn straight that had nothing to do with who works for whom." He sighed. "There's work, then there's play."

"Agreed." She nodded. "Goodnight."

"Night." He watched her disappear into her hotel room and couldn't help a quick fist bump into the air.

Chapter Nine

*T*he following workday was the slowest day in Dylan's entire life. She'd told her brother when she returned to the room last night that she'd rented a house. She hadn't told him the details or that the rent would be coming out of their checks, equally. Still, for the first time in years, she was looking forward to going home after work.

She spent the first part of her Friday making arrangements in the payroll software for the rent to come out of their paychecks and go into Gail's account each month. They got paid bi-weekly, and Gail had agreed to take payment in two parts. She was tempted to have it all come out of her account, since she knew her brother was not going to like it, but instead, followed what had been agreed on.

When she finished, she was surprised that it had taken her less than half an hour to set everything up. The rest of the time, she emptied out the new emails, filed all the paperwork that Trent had given her that morning, answered several phone calls, and even reorganized some of the files that had been put in the wrong location.

Still, there was an hour left before lunchtime. Staring at the computer, she was at a loss for work to fill her time.

Just then, a message popped up in the chat program on her computer. It was from Trey. There was a link to an online school.

"Check it out and see what classes you'd be interested in. Once you know, go ahead and sign up. Use the corporate login info to sign up. It's in the contacts file."

She spent the rest of her day trying to narrow down which classes would work for her. She wanted to enroll in several biology classes but couldn't explain how it related to her current position. Instead, she signed up for several others that clearly did. In the end, she emailed her proposed schedule to Trey and received an almost immediate response.

The email was short and before she could open it, he stepped outside his office.

"No nerd classes?" he asked her playfully as he made his way to her desk.

"I thought about it, but in the end, these are the best for what I'm currently doing for McGowan Enterprises." She glanced at the list once more and felt a little surer of herself.

He leaned next to her and glanced over the list. "Intro to Environmental Science," he read out loud.

She was looking forward to that class the most. "I figured it might help." She glanced up at him. "For the future."

He nodded. "How would you feel if we threw in General Chemistry somewhere?" he asked. "You could drop the English." He glanced over at her. "I haven't noticed you struggling with it yet." He smiled. "Or drop Efficiency in Organization." He leaned up. "Is that a real class?"

She giggled, a sound she hadn't made in a long time. "I thought the exact same thing."

"Okay, so we're agreed. Drop that one and add in the chemistry." He stood up. "That's a pretty big workload. Are you sure you'll have enough time to keep up with all of it?"

"What else is there for me to do?" She shrugged as she moved the classes around on the school's website program. "There." She nodded, feeling even better about her schedule than before. She didn't hesitate and hit enter while he stood over her, watching.

"Done." She took a deep breath. "God, it's going to feel good to use my brain again for work and not my body." She froze the second her words were out, then turned to him, feeling her face heat. "Not what I meant." She held up her hands.

It was too late, he was laughing. "Oh, my god."

131

He held his sides as he continued to laugh. "I know what you meant, but..." He took a deep breath. "The look on your face just now was... priceless."

She relaxed. "I'm thankful I work for someone who doesn't judge me by my mouth." Once again, she felt her face heat. "Not what I meant again." She groaned as she closed her eyes momentarily.

Trey chuckled all the way back to his office. She tried to avoid him for the rest of the day, but when it was only the two of them in the office, it was a little hard to do.

Trent had come and gone a couple of times during the day. He'd been dressed in jeans, a heavy jacket, and steel-toed boots. He'd informed her that he was making the normal rounds to all the sites and would make sure everything was locked up tight. Since Trey had been on a phone call at the time, she'd relayed the message to him once he was free.

She'd heard him complain from down the hallway after she'd hung up the speakerphone. She thought she'd heard him say something about wanting to get out of the damn suit and get outdoors again, but she couldn't be sure.

Still, she was thankful he was there to help her through a few things. She still didn't know the accounting software completely. Payroll was coming up, and she had more than a dozen questions.

Trey had given her Rea's number, but since the

woman was officially retired, Dylan didn't want to bother her with too many questions. So she had spent the rest of her day going over every note and instruction Rea had jotted down. By five o'clock, Dylan was feeling a lot more comfortable in every system. She had even taken the time to reorganize a few files on the shared drive.

When Trey walked out of his office, coat in hand, ready to leave for the day, she had a list of items she wanted to discuss with him.

"You're a mess," she greeted him as she locked up her computer. "Your files are, I mean. You save files to the main folder instead of in their designated project folders." She pulled on her jacket and switched off the light on her desk.

"What?" He turned to her with a frown. "Rea always used to—"

"I'm not Rea, and there's no excuse for laziness." She held her chin up slightly. She was holding her breath, in hopes he'd see things her way. "I spent almost an hour moving files to where they belonged. If that's going to be a major part of my day, you can't expect me to get anything else done. Besides, it takes you less than a minute to pick the correct folder. Moving files takes longer, especially some of those CAD drawings where the file size is massive."

He was silent, then he smiled. "Okay, I'll make a point to be more organized." He held the door open for her. "Anything else?"

"Yes. I'll want a more detailed calendar of when and where the three of you will be. I can't just guess when you'll be coming and going. The three of you should have your calendar programs all synced up. It just takes a moment for you to schedule your days."

He nodded. "Agreed. I'll talk to my brothers tonight over dinner."

She paused. He'd offered to help her move into the house tonight. She didn't have anything for him to do, but she was conflicted as to what to say to him next. Did she mention the move?

He walked with her towards the car.

"So, we'll be over at the hotel in about half an hour. That should give you plenty of time to change. Mom's made her lasagna." His smile grew. "We're in for a treat." He was rubbing his hands together. "I'm heading home to change, then I'll see you over there."

He turned to go.

"Trey," she called after him, unsure of what she wanted to say. When he glanced over his shoulder at her, she sighed. "Thanks."

He smiled. "Sure."

As she passed the grocery store, she decided to stop in and grab a pie for dessert. It was the least she could do for a family that had gone out of their way to help her and her brother.

She had just walked into the bakery when another woman bumped into her from behind.

"Oh, I'm sorry," The brunette's face turned a slight shade of pink. She'd been looking down at her phone instead of where she was walking.

"It's okay." Dylan nodded.

"You're Dylan?" the woman asked.

"Yes." She nodded, wondering if they had met somewhere before.

"I'm Addy McGowan." The woman held out her hand. "Trent's wife." The woman sighed. "It still gets me." She chuckled. "Anyway, I'm here to get a dessert for tonight."

Dylan inwardly groaned. "I'm here to do the same." She smiled.

"Oh." Addy chuckled. "Okay, I'm on strict orders from my new mother-in-law to get the dessert. You don't want to ruin the tender budding relationship I have with my new family, do you?"

Dylan laughed, knowing instantly she was going to like the woman. "How about I grab ice cream and you get the pie?"

Addy smiled. "Smart woman."

They walked together through the store, talking about the town and the brothers. Dylan wanted to ask about what Abby had gone through recently but decided against interrogating her during their first meeting. Instead, she asked about her wedding and how long she'd known Trent. Since first grade, it turned out.

The wedding had been last fall, on the hillside up in the state park. It had been smaller than Tyler and Kristen's wedding, since Addy hadn't been into spending a lot of money on a wedding when they were in the process of building their own home.

"So, we bought new eco-friendly kitchen appliances and reclaimed hardwood flooring for our house and spent a week installing everything instead of going on a honeymoon." She laughed and leaned in. "Trust me, we hardly got any work done."

Dylan smiled. They were standing in the checkout lane, and Dylan saw the woman's entire demeanor change. Following her eyes, she saw Darla stroll in the front door.

"That woman," Addy said under her breath, "is someday going to get just what she deserves." Addy sighed and turned away before Darla could see that she was watching her.

It was too late for Dylan to turn away. Their eyes met, and Darla's narrowed as she saw how close she and Addy were standing. Then her eyebrows rose slightly, and her smile turned into a sneer.

"She's coming this way," Dylan cautioned.

Addy groaned and turned to face the threat head on. Dylan instantly admired the woman.

"Darla, I would have thought you'd learned by now not to show your face around here," Addy said quickly.

"Aren't you just full of spunk today?" Darla said sarcastically. Then she turned to Dylan and in a loud clear voice said, "So, you're the latest McGowan whore?"

Dylan felt like she'd been slapped. She'd never learned how to deal with bullies in school very well. She'd been a shy nerd who'd hidden behind long hair, baggy clothes, and thick glasses.

"Considering you're the... old whore in town, I'd say the brothers have made major improvements. Besides, everyone in town knows, you never had any of the brothers." Addy leaned forward. "Not really."

Darla glared at Addy. "I can't believe we were once best friends."

Addy laughed loudly. "Neither can I." Addy nudged Dylan forward to pay for her ice cream. "Let's go, the family is probably waiting for us."

Darla disappeared, and Dylan and Addy paid for their desserts.

"Was it true?" she asked Addy as they walked out of the store.

"What?" Addy waited.

"That you and Darla were best friends?" It was impossible for her to imagine. The pretty brunette standing before her was without a doubt, one of the kindest people she'd met. Darla, was, well,

137

completely the opposite.

"It was a long time ago. I was young and stupid."
She rolled her eyes. "You probably wouldn't
understand it, but I was the biggest nerd in town.
Thick glasses, stupid bangs." She rolled her eyes.
"Everything short of a pen protector in my shirt
pocket."

Dylan stopped. "I knew we were kindred spirits.
By the time I was eleven, I could name every
element on the periodic table and list all the U.S.
presidents in order."

"Sister." Addy shook her head. "Where have you
been all my life?"

Dylan chuckled, then frowned when she saw her
brother's truck drive into the parking lot. Instead of
pulling into a spot, the truck headed directly for
them. She pulled Addy's arm and nudged her away
from the front of the truck.

"My brother," she said quickly before Brent
rolled down his window.

"Where the hell have you been? There's all these
people in our hotel room," he called out to her.
"Better get your butt back there and kick them all
out."

"They're our bosses." She held in a choice word
she wanted to use and added, "They're helping us
move into the house tonight, remember?"

Her brother's eyes ran over Addy with a frown.
"Right, well, they can help you move. I'm heading

to the bar."

"Don't you want to help?" she asked. "It's your stuff?"

"No. I took all of the stuff out of my truck. It's on the bed. You can just put my stuff wherever you want. Not like I care." He peeled out of the parking lot.

"Nice brother," Addy said softly.

"He's an ass." She sighed. "He didn't used to be this way."

"We'd better get going." Addy frowned at her watch.

Dylan glanced at hers and gasped. "How did we spend forty minutes in there picking out a pie and a gallon of ice cream?"

Addy laughed as she made her way across the parking lot. "See you there."

***

Dylan hadn't been lying when she'd said they didn't have a lot to move. Most of it was clothes, and it was no surprise to him that all her stuff was neatly stacked.

Her brother's stuff, however, was thrown all over the small living space. Dylan had informed them that her brother was busy and couldn't help, so she'd shoved all his clothes in huge black trash bags and tossed them in the trunk of her car.

When they drove up to the house, his mother was waiting for them on the back porch, a large pan of his favorite dish in her hands.

"Welcome home," his mother called out to Dylan.

In less than fifteen minutes, everything she and her brother owned was inside the house. He wondered why she hadn't tossed all her brother's items into the apartment above the garage but kept quiet on the matter for now.

They all sat around the dining room table, eating a home-cooked meal. Kristen and the baby had shown up shortly after they'd arrived, and the women spent a few minutes cooing over his new nephew.

He had to admit that he spent a few minutes himself enjoying the little guy, even though all the kid did was sleep and suck on his pacifier.

"The kid looks like me," he said out loud, knowing that in seconds, the three brothers would be arguing over who Timothy Jack McGowan looked more like.

"Why do you want to start a fight like that?" Kristen hissed at him. His smile was his only reply.

"You're incorrigible." Addy slapped him playfully on his shoulder.

"I'm just pointing out the truth," Trey added as his two brothers continued arguing over the kid.

"I think he looks just like Kristen." Everyone in the room turned to Dylan, who just shrugged. "The nose and eyes are Kristen's." She walked across the room and leaned over the child sleeping in the small pull-out crib. "The lips are definitely McGowan, but everything else comes from Kristen and her mother." She nodded to Trisha who was helping his mother dish up dessert for everyone.

"She's a keeper." Trisha smiled at Trey as she continued to scoop ice cream onto plates.

Everyone in the room turned towards him, eyebrows raised as they assessed his reaction.

"That's why I hired her." He smiled easily. "I can tell quality when I see it." He walked over and picked up a slice of pie.

Almost an hour later, the house was finally quiet. His family had cleaned up and left, except him. He was finishing up the last of the dishes when he glanced out the window and noticed that her brother's truck had pulled up and parked directly behind his truck.

The differences in the vehicles was instantly obvious. His was a work truck, worn, dirty, and built to last. Brent's truck was shiny with extra parts that would fall off bumping down some of the access roads Trey normally took. The fact that there wasn't a speck of dirt on Brent's truck, told Trey the man had probably washed it before driving home. Knowing that the man would rather spend his time washing his truck then helping his sister move his stuff pissed Trey off immediately.

"Your brother's home," he said casually, drying his hands and setting the towel on the countertop. "I'd better get going."

"Thanks again." She followed him to the back door. "For everything."

"You'll have to stop thanking me sooner or later," he said just as the back door was thrown open. He caught it easily before it hit the back wall.

"McGowan." Brent smiled and walked past him, looking around the house. "Nice digs."

"Brent." Dylan sighed. "There's some lasagna left in the fridge. I'll heat it up for you…"

"Don't bother. I'm just here to change. I've got a date." Brent smiled as he walked into the living room.

"Want me to stick around?" he asked softly.

Dylan's eyes were on her brother but jumped to him. "No, you've really done enough. Thank—" He gave her a look and stopped her. "Night," she said instead.

"If you need anything…" He nodded. "See you on Monday."

She shut the door behind him and he walked back to his truck. He could hear her brother asking her where she'd put all his shit.

Chapter Ten

The days turned into weeks quickly enough, and before she realized it, two months had passed. Her brother had started his job that first Monday, and she'd been surprised at how easily he'd caught on. He seemed to be really enjoying what he did and the guys he worked with. She started to fall into a pattern. During the days, she focused on work, and at night, she studied and attended her online classes.

At first, she had been limited to working at the office, but then Trey had lent her an old laptop of his so she could attend her classes in the comfort of her own place.

It still shook her every time she walked into the house. Having so much space was like breathing for the first time in years. She'd picked her favorite spot, in the small library, and worked there each night.

Her brother had fallen into his own pattern of hitting the bar with his coworkers directly after

143

work and wasn't usually home until late. Most days, he didn't drive himself but rode with someone else, since he didn't want his truck to get messed up on the back roads.

She was thankful she was using her mind again, but a little sad when Tyler took over for Trey in the office. Sure, Trey continued to stop in every day. She'd been totally turned on when he replaced his business suit with worn jeans, steel-toed boots, and a flannel shirt with a white T-shirt underneath.

It was impossible, but the man looked better each time she saw him. Like some sort of lumberjack supermodel. She noticed that he'd stopped shaving and found his new beard totally mouthwatering. She spent every free moment daydreaming about him pulling off his shirt and swinging an axe. Then she would berate herself for being attracted to his type. But the harder she thought about it, the more she realized it wasn't a type she was attracted to, just him.

Her brother grew more distant to her, but she was thankful that at least they had their own space. It hadn't surprised her that he'd moved his stuff out to the room above the garage. He complained about her complaining too much when he left his things everywhere in the house and didn't pick up after himself. Less than a week after moving in, he'd moved into the garage apartment, which gave her the entire house to herself. The first week it was wonderful, but then the house started to feel too quiet. Some afternoons, she'd go down to the diner and sit in the corner booth, working on the laptop.

Sometimes she would text Addy and have her meet her down there so they could study together, since she was taking online classes as well. Addy was lucky enough to be able to take all the classes Dylan wished she could. The two of them would work until one or more of the McGowan brothers would show up.

On this particular weekend night, both Trent and Trey interrupted their studies. Trey fell into the booth next to her and then nudged her shoulder.

"That looks fun," he said in a sarcastic tone.

"It is." She smiled at him. "I never knew that environmental studies could be so enlightening." She saved her current work and started to shut down the computer, since she knew she wouldn't get any more work done until she got home. She and Addy usually waited until Trent showed up before ordering dinner. She guessed that Trey had tagged along for the evening.

"Trent tells me you two have been working hard the past few weeks." Trey turned towards her.

Trent and Addy were quietly chatting about what they wanted to eat while hiding behind their own menus.

"Yes, she's a great study partner. She's quiet, doesn't talk too much, and if I have questions, she usually knows the answers." She smiled over at Addy.

"I took all those same classes my first year in college," Addy informed Trey.

"That's right, you have a few years under your belt." Trey shifted slightly towards her. She felt the heat from his leg when it brushed her own.

Tonight's flannel shirt was blue and green, which matched his eyes almost perfectly. She found it hard to look away from him when their eyes met.

"Yup, until I became tired of hearing how I wasn't doing well enough for my parents." Addy sighed.

Addy had filled her in about how her mother used to be very condescending and manipulative towards her and her father. But, in the past year, her mother had changed so much, Addy had a hard time recognizing her. It made Dylan wonder if, had her mother still been alive, there would have been a chance for them to grow closer.

"Right," Trey added. "Talk about doing a complete turnaround. I heard your mother was just voted president of the Silver Sneakers Club."

Addy chuckled. "Yeah, stupid name, but the group meets several times every week and does everything from playing cards to line dancing in the park during the summer." She rolled her eyes.

"Line dancing." Trey chuckled. "I'm looking forward to seeing that."

"Why?" Trent broke in. "You have some sort of old lady fetish I don't know about?" he teased.

Trey kicked his brother under the table, earning him a very loud groan followed by a mumbled, "Pussy," from his brother.

They ordered food and continued chatting as townspeople came and went. At one point, an older couple walked into the diner and everyone seemed to stop talking.

"That's the Mayor of Haven," Trent told her quickly. "Martha and her husband, Steve. They're sort of the most popular couple in town." He smiled. "Nice people."

Just then, the man and woman spotted them and headed over their way.

"Hi, everyone," the woman said, giving a genuine smile. "Trent, I have a few last-minute changes on the new plans for the park," the woman said before spotting Dylan. "Hi, I'm Martha Brown."

"Dylan McCaw." She shook the woman's offered hand.

"Right, McGowan's newest employee." She nodded. "I've been meaning to stop in and introduce myself and have a chat sometime."

She was unsure why the woman would want to talk to her. Maybe she'd heard about her brother? Worry flooded her mind and she bit her bottom lip.

Underneath the table, Trey took her hand gently in his. "Martha is Haven's busybody and the town's know-it-all. She likes being well informed on everything Haven." He gave Dylan a reassuring smile.

"Speaking of which, Trey." Martha's eyes narrowed playfully at him. "Didn't I see you run the stop light on Main and First this morning?"

Trey chuckled. "No, ma'am, I didn't drive today, Trent did. I have an inner ear infection and can't drive for at least a week while I'm on the meds the doc gave me."

Dylan turned towards him. "Are you okay?"

He smiled at her. "Yeah, just can't drive until the end of the week. It's one of the reasons my brother brought me along tonight."

Just then, their food was delivered, and the older couple stepped aside, but not before Martha added, "Trent, I'll expect you to start making a full stop at the stop signs in town."

Trent chuckled and nodded. "Yes, ma'am."

Martha nodded her approval before walking off to find a table with her husband.

"See, she's harmless," Trey mumbled to her between bites. "I will, however, be stuck back in the office until the end of the week." Trey snagged one of her French fries. She snapped his fingers away, since he had a plateful himself. "I like the crispy ones and I see you avoiding them." He chuckled and tossed a few of the larger ones on her plate. He was right about her avoiding the crispy ones, so she allowed it.

"I hope the rest of your workweek won't suffer," she said.

"No, Tyler is filling in for me. We're swapping places."

For a split second, she thought about spending her week with Trey instead of Tyler and excitement rushed through her quickly. She tucked her hands close together and tried to control her breathing.

"Are you okay?" Trey asked suddenly.

"Yes." She reached for her water. "Just a little tired." She rubbed her eyes and realized she still hadn't made an eye appointment.

"Are you still wearing those contacts?" Trey

asked, frowning at her.

"I was just yelling at myself for not making the appointment." She sighed. "I'll call first thing tomorrow."

"Do you own a pair of glasses?" he asked. She nodded quickly. "Wear them tomorrow." When she opened her mouth to argue, his eyes narrowed, and she could tell he was challenging her to argue with him.

"Okay." She wanted to warn him, but instead, bit her tongue. He'd find out sooner or later just how nerdy she looked in them.

"You're going to love babysitting this guy," Trent jumped in jokingly.

"I don't need babysitting," Trey said in a low tone.

"You couldn't even walk in here by yourself." Trent chuckled.

Trey made a warning sound in his throat, but his brother ignored it and continued.

"Inner ear infection." He laughed. "Makes my brother walk like a drunk teenager."

"Is it that bad?" Dylan asked.

"No." Trey rolled his eyes.

"He's lying," Trent continued.

Addy jumped to Trey's rescue. "Honey, I'm finished here and have about another hours' worth of work. Maybe we should go."

Trent jumped up immediately. "Sure thing."

"I'm not done, I'll get a ride home with..." Trey glanced around the diner.

"I can drive you home," Dylan jumped in.

"Good, because you'll have to pick him up in the morning," Trent added. "Tyler and I have to be at the new site first thing tomorrow."

Trey groaned. "I'd forgotten. I really wanted to—"

"Too bad, baby brother," Trent interrupted. "You snooze..." Addy pushed him towards the front of the diner.

"I'll see you later," Addy said over her shoulder. "Night."

Dylan waved and tried not to chuckle.

"Brothers." Trey slumped in his seat and shoved another fry into his mouth.

"Tell me about it." She rolled her eyes.

Trey straightened a little. "What's yours done now?"

"Guess who I caught walking out of the garage apartment this morning?" She leaned back in the booth, much like Trey had just done. "I actually think she waited until she saw me leave the house, so she could time it just right."

His eyes narrowed. "Darla." It came out as a statement and not a question.

"How did you..." She sighed. "I suppose it's all over town by now." She groaned a little and glanced around the diner.

"Yup, the rumor was going around." He took her hand in his. "Sorry, it must suck. What did she say to you?"

"Oh, not much." She remembered trying to mask her shock at seeing the woman slink her way down the outside stairs over the garage. "She acted like

150

she was caught red-handed, faked being embarrassed." She rolled her eyes. "I could tell she wasn't."

"No, she wanted you to know about it. I'm sure of it. That's her M.O." He reached over and finished the last of his fries, then waved the waitress over. "Want to share a slice of cake?"

She looked at her half full plate and sighed. "Sure, I can take this home for later."

He ordered a large slice of chocolate cake with two scoops of ice cream on the side. She wondered how he stayed thin, eating the way he did. He'd ordered the same thing she had, a large burger and fries, but his plate was completely empty while hers still had half the burger and fries on it.

"Do you get ear infections often?" She decided to change the subject from her brother's sex life.

"I had them a lot as a kid. We all did. Especially when it would get cold and we didn't want to come inside."

"Were you stuck outside recently?" She shifted slightly when he rested his arm behind her shoulders on the back of the bench.

"I've been working on the weekends, clearing a spot on my land for my new house."

Her eyebrows shot up. "I thought you had a house?"

He chuckled. "I have a trailer. I'm planning on building a log cabin."

She frowned, remembering the first time she'd seen his current place. She'd assumed it was a home, not a trailer. It was nice, nicer than the last

151

few homes she'd lived in, except for the one she was currently in.

"Trent has a tractor and all weekend I was clearing a section where I'm thinking of building." He finished and sighed. "It's nestled in the woods, just behind where the trailer is."

"It snowed all weekend."

"Yeah, and I'm paying for not being smart enough to wait for warmer weather."

Just then, the cake arrived, and her eyes grew huge. "Wow," she said as he handed her a fork. "You expect us to eat that? That's a quarter of the cake and a gallon of ice cream."

He laughed. "I usually eat it all by myself."

She shook her head and dug in.

***

Trey sat silent as Dylan drove him home. The winding roads that headed towards McGowan land were usually a comfort to him, but with the inner ear infection, he found the twists and turns a little nauseating. He tried shutting his eyes, which only made it worse, so he tried focusing on Dylan's driving.

He realized she had only dropped him off at his house once before. He couldn't believe he hadn't had her up to the house before. Then again, he couldn't believe that it had been almost three months since he'd first seen her in the bar. It was easier to notice the time when he saw his nephew. The kid was scooting and rolling around like he couldn't wait to start running. His brother was already asking Kristen when she wanted to try for another one. Trey held in a chuckle. Growing up, he'd never pegged his brother as someone who would be an amazing father.

"You're quiet." Dylan broke into his thoughts.

He took a deep breath to settle his stomach before speaking. "Just thinking about Timmy." He sighed.

"He's grown so much." By the tone of her voice, he could tell she was smiling. "Are you doing okay?" she asked when he didn't respond.

"Yeah, just trying not to act like the pussy my brother thinks I am."

"Are you going to be sick?"

"No," he said mostly to reassure himself.

"I can slow down," she offered.

He opened his eyes again and noticed they were less than a mile from the turnoff to his place.

"I can make it." He took several deep breaths.

"Here." She held out her hand. "Give me your hand." She shifted and drove with her left hand.

He set his hand in hers, and she dropped it on her lap and started tapping lightly on the inside of his wrist, keeping her eyes on the road. Then she pinched lightly on his wrist. Instantly, his stomach settled.

"How did you...?" He stopped and shook his head slightly.

"Better?" she asked when he didn't continue.

"Yes." He took another deep breath. "Much. How did you do that?"

"Acupressure." She smiled over at him and gripped the wheel with both hands again as she

153

pulled into his long driveway. "I read a book about it once and it always works for me."

"Needles?" He visibly shivered, causing her to chuckle.

"No, that's acupuncture." She chuckled. "Don't you have a tattoo?" She nodded to the massive owl on his forearm. He glanced down at the owl and a mixture of sorrow and pride filled him. The creature reminded him of his father. He'd gotten it the month after his dad had passed. Rea had taken him to an artist on the reservation, a man Trey had known since birth. His name was Peta, or as everyone else called him, Blackfoot. He had been old when Trey was a child and was ancient now. But his hands had been steady, and his art spoke for itself. The owl was a perfect representation of his father's spirit animal.

Blackfoot had been a little confused when he asked for an owl, seeing as Trey was a coyote himself. Tyler was a wolf, Trent a bear. But after explaining that it was in memory of his father, the old man had quickly and quietly gotten to work.

He ran his fingers over the skin and smiled at the memory of his father.

"That's different," he said, looking down at his arm. "Do you have any tricks to help with an inner ear infection?" he asked after a moment as he rolled his shoulders.

"A few," she said, pulling up behind his truck.

"Would you... like to come in?" He tried hard not to sound too eager. "You know, to help me out?" He winced at the desperation in his words, but at this point, he'd try anything to help him with the dizziness.

She was silent for a while. "Sure." She shut off the car.

He wanted to jump out and run over to open her door, but just climbing out of the car made him break a sweat.

By the time he was upright, she was by his side, holding his arm.

"You okay?" she asked again.

"Remind me to come in out of the cold next time." He groaned as they walked together towards his front door.

"You should be in bed all week," she suggested as he tried to unlock his front door. On the third try, she took his keys from him and did it herself.

He could hear Dopey scratching and barking inside the door. "That's Dopey," he said, stopping her. "You like dogs, right?"

"Love them." She smiled as he swung the door open. "You brought him into the office once before, remember?"

"Right." Dopey jumped on him, almost knocking him over. "Down," he ordered. The dog obeyed and turned to give his attention to Dylan.

"You really are like a drunk teenager." She giggled as she bent down to give the mutt a scratch.

Instead of answering, he groaned as he walked past her, kicked off his shoes, and dropped his coat inside the door. "Come on in." He made his way towards the sofa in his living room. He wobbled across the room, knowing the room wasn't really swaying.

"Sit," she said, removing her jacket and picking up his and hanging them both on the hooks. Then she moved over to him and nudged him onto the sofa. She sat behind him, and her fingers went to the base of his skull. He felt his entire body settle in place. The room stopped spinning and his eyes burned, so he shut them on a groan.

"Better?" she asked.

Instead of answering, he groaned as she continued to move her fingers around, down his neck, up to his skull, even around to his jaw and in front of his ear.

"How does that feel?" she asked softly, when a groan escaped him.

"Like heaven." He tried not to whine when he got sick but feeling like a drunk teenager was not his idea of fun. Especially when life wouldn't slow down for him to feel better.

He hadn't realized he'd said those last thoughts out loud until he heard her giggle behind him.

"Sorry, guess I *am* acting like a teenager. You wouldn't want to make the evening complete by making out on the sofa with me, would you?" Her giggling and massaging stopped, and he held his breath when he realized just what he'd said. His eyes flew open. "Sorry." He shook his head to try to clear it from the fog that her fingers had caused. "I guess I'm a little…"

Her fingers tightened on him and then she nudged his chin back until he was looking straight up at her as her lips were covering his. Her fingers traveled down his jawline, slowly.

He hadn't felt her move, but suddenly she straddled his hips. His fingers dug into her hips, feeling the jean material under his fingertips as she slowly settled over him.

Her mouth was moving over his and it was taking all his willpower to keep himself in check. He desired a taste of her, just a small sample. When their tongues touched, he heard her moan and felt her melt against him.

"I didn't plan this," he said, pulling her closer.

"No, of course not." She sighed as her fingers closed in his hair. "I've thought about doing that since…"

"The moment we saw one another?" he finished for her. She rested her forehead on his and nodded slightly.

"Are you feeling better?" she asked softly. He realized his ear infection and headache were the last things on his mind, especially when her hips were pressed against his.

"Much." He leaned in and ran his lips over hers again. "Especially when I have someone to help take my mind off the pain," he said between kisses. He felt her body melt against his again and desperately wanted to take her, here and now.

.

Chapter Eleven

*D*ylan's mouth slanted over Trey's as she pressed her hips against his hardness. Just feeling him caused her body to burn hot.

His fingers moved upward until he touched her skin underneath her shirt. She wished he'd yank the damn thing off, but instead, his fingers slowly circled her, making her want more. She twisted slightly and had her hands under his shirt. Her nails dug into his skin and a low growling sound came from his throat, sending shivers racing through her system.

"Trey," she started to say, just as her phone started ringing. Rolling her eyes, she thought of ignoring it.

"Do you need…?" He nodded to her phone, which she'd tossed on the coffee table behind her.

She reached for it. "It is my work phone." She smiled and answered the call.

She could barely hear the voice on the other end

and had to press the phone against her ear to hear the voice.

"I'm sorry, can you—" A loud bang over the line made her scream and drop the phone. Her head exploded with pain as her ear rang from the shock of the loud noise.

She was sitting on the sofa holding her head when arms wrapped around her. She looked up into Trey's worried eyes and realized he was talking to her. His voice was muffled, and she frowned and tried to concentrate on what he was saying.

"Are you okay?" he repeated. She nodded in response.

"What... was that?" She shook her head clear.

"You tell me?" He leaned down and picked up her phone.

"No." She worried as he put the phone to his ear.

"The line's dead." He set the phone down and turned to her. "What happened?"

"Someone was talking." She rubbed her ear. "I couldn't hear them, so I pressed the phone up to my ear, then..." She took a deep breath. "It sounded like a gunshot."

When the words were out of her mouth, her heart stopped. "Oh god!" She reached for her phone. "Brent." She punched the speed dial number for the house.

"I'm sure he's okay." Trey reached for her hand, which she noticed was shaking.

Her brother picked up on the third ring.

"What?" he barked out.

"Are you..." She took a deep breath and

swallowed her fears. Even though he'd made her life hell in the past few years, he was still the only family she had. "Are you still up?"

"I wasn't, until the damn phone started ringing." She could hear the annoyance in his voice.

"I'm on my way home." She stood up and realized she was still shaking, so she tucked her free hand into her pocket. Her eyes met Trey's and she could see the worry there.

"Whatever," her brother said before hanging up.

"I take it he's okay?" Trey stood up and she had to reach for him as he almost tipped over. "Damn ears." He shook his head and almost fell over backwards.

She chuckled, the phone call all but forgotten. "Let me help you to bed." She gripped his arm.

When his eyebrows shot up, she sighed. "As much as I'd like to spend the night with a man who can't even stand up on his own... not tonight." She nudged him towards the hallway.

"We won't be doing much standing." He wiggled his eyebrows as he bumped into the wall and cursed under his breath.

"What did the doctor say?" She frowned as worry flooded her once more.

"He gave me pills, told me to rest." He shrugged as they walked into the last room, which she assumed was his bedroom.

"But you're coming into work tomorrow anyway?" She shook her head. "What will you do if I don't pick you up in the morning?"

"I'll call one of the workers to come get me." He

161

sat on the edge of the bed. She smiled as the dog jumped up and circled first, then lay down next to Trey.

"You won't try to drive yourself?" she asked.

"I'm not that stupid." He leaned back on the bed. "I'm having vertigo strong enough to make me think I'm going to fall off the mattress. Getting behind the wheel would be suicidal." He glanced up at her and smiled. "And I haven't gotten everything I want in life, yet."

She laughed. "Go to bed. I'll be here at a quarter to six."

"Are you sure I can't persuade you to climb in with me?"

"Good night, Trey." She turned to go.

"Dylan." She stopped just inside the doorway and glanced back at him. "I'm sure it was just a prank call."

She nodded slowly. "Night."

The entire drive back home she ran over what she'd thought she'd heard the voice say.

"You're next." They had been the only words before the bang.

What did that mean? Was it a direct threat?

When she pulled into her spot beside her brother's truck, she glanced around nervously before getting out and racing to the back door, keys in hand.

Leaning against the inside of the door, she flipped the lock and gave a deep sigh of relief. Flipping on every light as she walked through the house, she figured that a hot shower would calm her nerves. But when she stood naked in front of the glass, she realized that's exactly how most horror movies started.

Shivering, she glanced over at the bathtub and that scene from *A Nightmare on Elm Street* flashed quickly in her mind. She raced across her room, and jumped quickly onto her bed, covering herself in all the blankets. She reached for the remote and found a cartoon channel and watched SpongeBob until she fell asleep.

She woke to more cartoons when her alarm went off. Walking around the house, she shut off all the lights, feeling completely ridiculous about freaking out. She'd never been one to fear the dark, even after her parents' death.

Her brother must have already come and gone that morning, since there was a new mess in the kitchen. She took a few minutes to clean up the mess, then she made her lunch and nibbled on dry toast.

Glancing out the window and seeing the snow slowly falling, she pulled on her thickest coat and slipped on her boots.

Once again, she glanced around and made sure she was alone before heading to her car. She had promised herself she'd never be caught in a situation like before with Darla.

The trip to Trey's place was slowgoing, thanks to the new layer of snow on the roads. When she pulled in behind his truck, he came out, Dopey on his heels. Trey let the dog into the back seat and then climbed into the front.

"I figured I was disabled enough to have a helper today." He motioned for Dopey to sit. The dog quickly obeyed, causing her to smile.

"How did you sleep?" she asked, as she pulled out of the driveway.

"Better than the night before." He shifted and looked at her. "Sexy." He tapped her glasses, then frowned. "Looks like you had problems sleeping." He gently ran a finger over the dark circles under her eyes that she'd tried to hide with makeup and her thick glasses.

Shrugging, she tried to think of an excuse. "I was worried about the phone call. I know I shouldn't be, but…"

He ran his hand down to her shoulder and gently rubbed the tension away. She relaxed slightly.

"You're a fast learner," she said when she noticed he was mimicking what she'd done to him last night. She pulled into the parking lot and tensed when she saw his uncle's truck in the parking lot.

"Just what I want to deal with this morning." He groaned as he got out of the car. He opened the back door and Dopey followed him to the front door. She tried to catch up with him, but he was already engaging his uncle in front of the glass doors.

"Well, he's not here today, you'll have to deal with me, instead." Trey unlocked the front doors and motioned for his uncle to go through them. Dopey didn't wait for an invitation but darted between Trey's legs towards warmth.

She followed them inside and began her morning ritual as Trey guided his uncle towards the back room.

It surprised her slightly to see that the older man was somewhat contained. The last time she'd seen him, he was being carted away in the back of a police cruiser. She remembered what Trey had told her that first day and wondered why he hadn't asked her to call Mike or Tony this time. Still, she kept her phone close as she listened down the hallway.

She was surprised when the two men walked out of the office half an hour later and shook hands before his uncle walked outside.

Trey stood in the entry, looking out the front door, his hip leaning against her desk as Dopey settled at his feet.

"Well?" she finally asked. "Are you going to tell me what happened?"

She noticed the frown on Trey as he bent down to pet his dog.

"My uncle had some news he wanted to tell the family." He stood up and leaned further onto her desk. "Some... medical news."

This time, it was her turn to frown. "Is he sick?"

Trey nodded. "It's not a huge surprise, since he's spent years abusing his body." He shook his head. "Still, can you make arrangements for lunch to be delivered here from Frankie's for my entire family? I'll start calling them and tell them to come in at..." He glanced down at his watch and groaned. "Noon. I've got a few things to deal with this morning."

"Sure." She stopped him from walking away by placing a hand over his. "I've seen what your uncle is capable of and, for what it's worth, I'm sorry."

Trey nodded before walking back down the hallway with Dopey following close behind.

***

Trey tried to focus on his work, but the word "terminal" kept circling his mind. When Dylan buzzed that his mother was waiting in the conference room, he logged out of the system and made his way down the hallway.

The next hour was going to be interesting. By the time he walked into the meeting room, his brothers were already there, and so was the food, which meant he was the last to grab a sandwich.

Thankfully, Dylan had given instructions to mark the sandwiches. Frankie's knew who liked what and Trey's long-standing order of turkey with American cheese was waiting for him, as was a Dr. Pepper.

Dopey sat at his feet and begged as he dug in. He dropped a few chunks of meat to his best friend.

"Well?" Tyler asked, sitting down and digging into his food. "Want to enlighten us on why you called a family meeting in the middle of a Monday?"

"Carl paid me a visit this morning," he answered, dropping another chunk of turkey to the begging dog. He noticed that his brothers were doing the same. Dopey was almost getting more food than they were.

"Is he rotting in a cell at the moment?" Trent asked.

"No." He waited until he had everyone's

attention. "He's been told by his doctors he has less than a month to live."

The room was silent.

"We all knew it was coming sooner or later. After his last scare," Tyler said, setting down his sandwich and pushing it away slightly.

"Cancer, it's everywhere," Trey added with a sigh.

"Looks like we'll have to update our family medical history," Trent added.

"Be quiet," their mother snapped, causing the three boys to glance her way. Trey hadn't expected to see the sadness in her eyes.

"Mom," all three of them said at the same time.

"I didn't mean to upset you," Trent added. "I was trying to lighten…" He shook his head. "I'm sorry," he mumbled.

"Regardless of how many problems he's caused, he is still your father's brother. Which makes him family, even if we don't like it." Gail stood up and started pacing. "Did he want anything?" She turned slowly towards him.

"He… asked if I'd take care of the arrangements, after he was gone."

"You?" Tyler frowned. "Why you?"

"Because you weren't around this morning when he came in," Trey snapped. He instantly felt bad when his mother glared in his direction. He knew he was moody. His ears were ringing, and his head was pounding from having to remain upright instead of lying down and letting his body recover. "Sorry," he mumbled just as Dylan walked in. Just seeing her in the stylish pencil skirt and flowing white top had all his blood rushing away from his head.

"Mr. McGowan." She chuckled lightly when the three brothers all glanced in her direction. "Tyler," she corrected. "You have a phone call."

His brother groaned and then followed Dylan out of the room.

"What are we going to do?" Trent asked once the door was closed again.

"About?" He turned to his brother.

"Carl..." He motioned as if Trey should have known what he was talking about. He should have, but his mind was too busy with images of Dylan's hips swaying as she walked out of the room.

Trey shrugged. "Nothing until the time comes, then..."

"Your father would have wanted us to handle it like family, no matter what." Gail stood up. "We have an obligation to the man, even if it is after death." She started walking out of the room but stopped to glance back at him. "For god's sake, ask the woman out. I didn't raise a fool." She narrowed her eyes at him, then turned and walked out.

Trent's chuckle made him want to punch his brother, but since he was hungry and only had a few more minutes before his next call, he mumbled, "Shut up" and shoved the rest of his sandwich in his mouth.

The rest of the day he was either stuck on the phone or reading and responding to emails, and he didn't have a chance to talk to Dylan. But she was obligated to drive him home, and he figured he

168

could properly ask her out then.

At least he thought so until her brother showed up a few minutes before closing time.

"I hope it's okay, but Brent needed to ride along tonight," Dylan said as she peeked her head in his office door.

"Sure," he replied before really thinking about it. When she shut the door, he groaned. That's just what he wanted, to spend the drive home with Brent.

Shutting down his computer, he took his time standing up and was surprised that he only felt a slight tilt in the room. Not bad, he thought as he walked down the hallway, Dopey following closely behind him.

In his mind, he swept into the front area as light from the large window behind Dylan's desk played over her face and hair. He imagined himself walking up to her, swooping her into his arms, and kissing her, there, at the receptionist desk, until both of their knees went weak.

"Trey!" Dylan's cry caused his eyes to open. Instead of standing on the other side of the reception desk, he was staring up at the ceiling of the hallway. Dopey was shoving his nose in his face, trying to lick every part of his face.

"Call 911," Dylan called out.

"No!" He groaned. "I'm fine." He tried to sit up, but Dylan's hands on his shoulders stopped him. "Damn it, tell me I didn't just faint." He nudged the dog aside.

He was sure she was going to laugh, but her eyes

were filled with concern. "You did." She nodded slightly. "After you turned sheet white, and your eyes rolled to the back of your head. Luckily, I was here…"

His groan stopped her next words.

"If you tell me you caught me…" He sighed. "Just don't."

She did smile this time. "Okay, I won't say it out loud. But"—she leaned closer—"it is the first time a man has literally fallen at my feet."

He groaned, then realized her brother was standing behind her, looking down at him. His inner masculinity cringed and he rose faster than he should have. He had a death grip on Dylan's arm in an effort to remain upright.

"Head colds." He tried to roll his eyes and look nonchalant about it, but he probably looked like he was going to faint again instead.

Brent shrugged and start walking towards the door. Turning to Dylan, he noticed the worry in her eyes.

"I'm okay," he assured her. "I just got up a little too quickly."

"I really think you should be in bed." She reached over and grabbed her purse as they walked past her desk.

"Yeah, but work…"

"Trey, how do you expect to get better when you won't give your body time to heal?"

"That's what meds are for." He was half-joking.

She made a tsking sound as she locked the front door behind them. Her brother was leaning against the car, looking annoyed at having to wait in the cold.

The fact that he was still holding onto Dylan didn't go unnoticed by the man. Okay, so Trey didn't need the support anymore. He liked holding onto her and kept doing so.

He thought about how he was going to ask her out the entire car trip up to his house. He almost stopped her from walking him to his door, but instead, he allowed her to take his hand and guide him. Dopey sprinted off to do his doggie business as soon as he opened the car door.

"You should really think about taking tomorrow off," she said as she unlocked his front door for him.

"I have a few calls…" he started.

"Which I can forward to your phone here." She stepped inside with him and waited until he removed his shoes and jacket. Then she held the door open as Dopey shook himself off and rushed in to lie on the floor by the heater.

"In my new place, I'll have a fireplace." He thought that his dog would love lying by the fire. He didn't know why he'd said it, other than wanting her to be in on his plans.

"I still don't know why you need a different place," she said, glancing around his space.

"I'm leasing this place. My brother leased it and instead of returning it once he was done, I moved it here and took over." He told her. "I've got another year before I turn it back in. Which means that this spring and summer, I'll be busy." He smiled at the thought of starting on his home. "Want to see my plans?" He nodded to the kitchen table, where the blueprints were laid out. Everything was already approved through the city and county. They were just waiting for a break in the weather to finish clearing the land and start work.

She glanced towards the front door and he could tell she was worried about her brother waiting. Just then, the car horn honked.

"Go. You could come over tomorrow after work, maybe bring some takeout?"

"So you'll take my advice and work from home tomorrow?"

He smiled slightly. "If you say you'll stop by after work."

She chuckled. "It's a deal." She held out her hand towards his.

Instead of shaking it, he gripped it lightly and tugged her until she was pressed up against him. "Make no mistake, this won't be a working dinner."

"No." She shook her head. "I didn't think it..." She didn't finish since his mouth was covering hers in a light kiss.

"Go." He nudged her back. "Before your brother comes pounding on my door."

"Rest." She touched his forehead and frowned. "You're burning up." Worry flooded her eyes again.

"I'm fine," he assured her.

"Lemon and honey tea." She narrowed her eyes towards him. "A warm shower and rest," she said in a stern voice, causing him to smile.

"Yes, doctor." He saluted her. "See you tomorrow."

"I'll make sure to forward your calls."

"Thanks." He waited for her to leave before falling back onto the sofa. Collapsing onto it, was more like it.

He must have fallen asleep because he felt his feet being lifted and a warm blanket being wrapped around him. He was pretty sure it was a dream, but then his mother's soft voice drifted into his sleep.

"Sit up and drink this," she urged.

He followed her instructions and felt hot liquid slide down his throat.

"Mmm, homemade chicken soup." His eyes opened, and his mother's face came into view.

"Dylan called." His mother's eyes scanned him. "She was worried." Her cool hand rested on his forehead. "About one-oh-one, I'd wager." She frowned. "Do you think you can get more of that down?" She nodded to the soup.

"For you." He smiled and took another sip. "Isn't she great?" he said between sips.

"Dylan?" His mother settled next to him. He nodded and took another drink. "I like the girl."

"So do I." He frowned. "She's had a hard time. Her brother is an ass." He took another sip and as the hot liquid hit his stomach, he sighed at the warmth it caused. "She needs to experience what it's like to be in a good family."

His mother was silent and if he'd been paying attention, he would have seen the proud look in her eyes.

173

Jill Sanders

Chapter Twelve

/t was strange working in the office by herself. Dylan's day seemed to go more slowly without all the interruptions and trips down the hallway to any of the three offices.

At one point, she could hear the second hand on the clock across the room clicking. The soft sound almost drove her mad. She tried to focus on her work, but it was boring and she decided to study for her test the following day.

She was thankful that her online classes allowed her to set her own pace. She had already finished three classes and had her last test for her fourth class the following evening.

She hadn't told any of the McGowans that she'd finished some of her classes yet and wondered if they'd be willing to allow her to enroll in more so soon.

She already had four more classes she was interested in. She figured if they wouldn't help out, she could set some of her paycheck aside and apply for financial aid, now that she had a full-time job.

As she'd figured, Brent complained about the portion of his check that was taken out for rent each month. But, after their second month there, his complaints stopped. She knew how much each of his checks were and wondered how he spent the rest of the money he made each month. But it wasn't any of her business anymore, so she kept quiet.

She figured part of his silence about the rent money was all the time he was spending with Darla. The woman creeped her out. Every time she ran into her, Darla would have this look in her eyes. She barely wore anything to cover her ample cleavage and most of the time was dressed as if she was still at work at the Wet Spot.

Dylan hadn't been in the strip club yet, but she was sure that the way Darla was dressed was even a little over the top for the establishment. Her brother seemed to enjoy it, however, and was always pointing out how hot the woman was. It always made her cringe.

When the phone rang, she jumped out of her daydream and answered it on the second ring.

"McGowan…" she started, only to be interrupted by Trey.

"Is it five o'clock yet?" he joked.

She glanced up at the clock and sighed. "Nope, only eleven." She felt her shoulders sink.

"How about lunch then? I've put in an order at the Moose. Think you can pick it up and bring it to me? I ordered your favorite as well…" She could tell he was waiting and holding his breath.

"Sounds wonderful. I'll lock up and be there in about half an hour."

"Good, it's all paid for and under your name. See you soon."

She hung up, logged out of her computer, and was pulling out her purse when the front door opened.

Seeing Trey's uncle stroll in and glance around, she would have never imagined he was "terminal" in any way, other than he was an overweight, older man, who had obviously spent too many years drinking and smoking.

"The McGowans aren't in right now. Can I help you?" she asked, setting her purse back down.

She could tell he had already hit the bottle or something else. He was swaying slightly and had a distant look in his eyes.

"No." He continued to walk around as if he owned the place. "Just looking around." He turned to her and gave her a smile that made her skin crawl.

"I'm sorry, I'm going to have to ask you to leave. I'm running an errand and need to lock up." She reached for her purse and turned back towards him.

"Oh, right." His eyes narrowed and he almost fell over the chair in the waiting area.

He followed her to the door and she nervously locked up, making sure to flip both locks before walking to her car.

"You're Dylan McCaw, right?" The use of her full name, caused her to stiffen.

"Yes, I'm the office manager." She nodded.

177

His smile increased. "Fancy name for a secretary. In my day, we didn't attach fancy titles to make women feel more important than they were." The man's eyes ran up and down her and she shivered visibly.

Without saying another word, she climbed into the car and drove away. When she glanced into the rearview mirror, he was still there, standing on the sidewalk, smiling.

Her hands continued to shake as she pulled into the Dancing Moose. She took a moment in the parked car to get her emotions under control. Remembering that the old man wasn't long for the world didn't help any.

By the time she walked into the Moose to get their lunch order, she thought she was back under control. But then she saw Darla standing in the takeout line.

Deciding she could fake being occupied with her phone, she pulled it out and stood in line. Her ruse only worked for about two minutes, when the line moved forward.

Darla turned and chuckled at her. "Well, well, aren't you a busy one?"

Dylan glanced up and pretended she didn't know what the woman was talking about. "I'm sorry?"

Darla's outfit today was a tight black leather skirt, knee-high cream-colored pleather boots, and a grey sweater that showed enough cleavage to make even Dylan feel awkward. It was all covered by a long cream-colored coat that was left open so that her outfit and chest could be admired by all.

Dylan had never worn anything close to that skimpy when she'd worked at the bars, let alone out in public.

The woman's hair was always in the same style, as if she'd just crawled out of someone's bed. Her makeup was the only thing about the woman that was minimalized when she wasn't working.

She knew that Darla was running her eyes up and down Dylan, much like she'd scanned her.

"Getting cozy with the McGowans." She made a tsking noise.

"I work for..." She started but stopped when Darla sneered at her.

Darla leaned a little closer, and Dylan almost choked on the heavy scent of her perfume. "We all know there's more going on between you and the youngest McGowan." She tilted her head. "I myself never fancied him." Her smile grew. "Always had my eyes on his big brothers." Her chin rose slightly. "Maybe I overlooked the best in the batch."

Dylan's eyes narrowed as she thought about Trey with Darla. She held in a shiver and almost laughed because she knew Trey wasn't the kind of guy to fall for... well, what stood in front of her. "I think you should stick to my brother. He's more your speed."

Heat flooded Darla's eyes as they narrowed. Just before she could reply, the line moved forward, and it was Darla's turn at the counter.

Dylan couldn't help it, she smiled at Darla's back, knowing that at least she'd won this little battle.

Once Darla had paid for and picked up her order,

she turned around, leaned closer to her, and said quietly, "I'd watch your back if I were you." She straightened and started walking out.

"I always do," she called out. Darla didn't even glance back at her.

Fifteen minutes later, she parked behind Trey's truck and carried the hot food up to the door.

He answered on the second knock. Dopey had been scratching and barking at the door before she'd even knocked.

When Trey opened the door, the black dog jetted between her legs and rushed into the yard.

"He's been begging me to go out every five minutes." Trey rolled his eyes.

She took in everything about him. His coloring was better than it had been the day before, and she could tell that he'd gotten a good night's sleep.

He was wearing an old pair of jeans, a tight fitting black T-shirt, and no shoes or socks, which instantly registered as one of the sexiest things she'd seen in years. Hell, her mouth watered just watching him carry the food to the kitchen table.

"So, I was thinking, instead of ordering takeout, how about I cook for you tonight?" he asked, turning back towards her.

"Huh?" She shook her head clear of the thoughts that had been playing in her mind. Thoughts about peeling off that shirt of his and running her fingers and her mouth all over that sexy body.

"Dinner... tonight... I'll cook," he said slowly, smiling at her.

"Oh, sure." She nodded and moved to shut the

door just as Dopey raced in and did a few circles before begging for food from Trey.

"Is there anything in particular you like?" he asked, waiting for her to sit down at the table.

Once again, her mind went directly to sex and she felt her face flush. "No, anything." She smiled and tried to cover up her embarrassment.

Trey sat across from her, a smile on his lips as he pulled out the food and set everything out.

"So," he said after the food was set in front of her, "how's your day going?"

"Boring. It's so quiet without anyone there." She opened a container with a large burger in it.

It was strange, but all the worry and stress she'd felt earlier in the day disappeared as she talked to Trey. She told him about her run-in with Darla but kept the visit from his uncle to herself. She figured since the man was sick, and Trey had mentioned that they were trying to get along with him, that he didn't need to know about it. Besides, she was sure she had exaggerated the entire ordeal.

"So, I heard that you're only one test away from finishing your last class," he mentioned just as she finished the last of her fries.

Her eyebrows shot up in question. "How did you..."

He smiled. "Addy," he answered.

She nodded and took a deep breath. Of course, his sister-in-law had been right with her during most of her studies.

"I take my last final tomorrow afternoon." She pushed the empty container away from her.

181

"Did you pick out your next classes?" he asked, doing the same with his container.

"I have a few in mind, yes." She bit her bottom lip.

"Sign up like last time." He stood up slowly and carried their containers to the trash. "It's nice setting your own pace." He turned and leaned against the counter. "You and Addy have that in common."

She stood and waited, her eyebrows raised slightly.

"For some unknown reason, you like school." He shivered and laughed. "Not me. I couldn't wait to graduate."

"Oh, what were you going to do after school?" She moved closer. "Work for your father?"

He shook his head and she stopped directly in front of him.

"Bartend," he answered with a grin. "It's where I met Rainah, my ex. The tattoo artist."

She nodded, remembering their conversation.

"You bartended?" For some reason, she was having a hard time seeing him stuck behind a sticky counter, popping the tops on beers.

"Sure, I was good at it too." He reached for her. "Course, I got tired of the crowds and the noise." He shook his head as he brushed his hand over her hair slowly. "I guess I've changed a lot since back then."

She felt her heart kick in her chest as his eyes moved to her lips.

"I know your lunch break is almost over, but I really want to kiss you right now."

She melted against his chest, a smile on her lips

as she leaned into him.

"What's stopping you?" she asked under her breath.

She tried to get the kiss out of her mind as she drove back into town, but the feeling of his mouth on hers was seared into her brain.

She parked, pulled out her purse, and walked to the doors. She frowned as they slid open before she'd had a chance to unlock them.

Figuring that either Tyler or Trent had stopped in, she walked in, tossed her purse on her desk, and made her way towards the back offices. Noticing the door to the supply closet was open, she moved towards it. She heard a noise behind her and turned, only to be shoved backwards. Her feet flew out from underneath her. She reached out for something, anything, to catch her fall. Pain exploded at the base of her skull as her head hit the wood shelf in the closet. Blackness overtook her before she even settled on the cold tile floor.

***

Trey paced as he held his cell phone close to his ear. "What do you mean she's not there?" He almost screamed it.

"Easy brother," Trent replied. "I'm looking around. Her purse is on the desk, but I don't see her... Hang on..." He heard his brother drop the phone. "Damn it." The phone went dead.

"Shit, shit, shit." He punched his brother's number again.

"Sorry, hey," Trent answered. "I... I've got to take Dylan to the clinic. She's bumped her head

183

pretty bad."

His entire body tensed. "What happened?"

"Jesus." Trent sighed. "There's a lot of blood. I'll call you when I know more."

"I'll meet you at the clinic." He hung up before his brother could argue.

Grabbing his keys, he jumped in the truck and, before starting the engine, took a few deep breaths and assessed his situation. "Damn," he groaned. There was no way he should be driving. He picked up his phone and dialed his mother.

Twenty minutes later, he rushed into the clinic, totally overcome with panic. Both of his brothers were in the waiting area.

"She's okay." Trent met him. "A few stitches, here." His brother pointed to the back of his head. "She doesn't know how long she was unconscious, but Tony's in with her now, taking her statement."

"Tony..." Suddenly his worry turned to anger. "Someone attacked her?"

"We don't know yet. She thinks she slipped. The tile was wet. She hit her head on the bottom shelf in the closet, knocked it clear off the wall." Trent added, "The shelf, not her head." He shook his head. "But she mentioned something on the trip here about the door being unlocked and hearing a sound. She doesn't remember anything else."

Trey walked towards the receptionist.

"She's in room five," Trent called after him.

He swung past the woman behind the desk and made his way down the hallway.

The clinic wasn't large, but big enough for the

town's basic medical needs. Surgeries and X-rays were in a separate building across the parking lot.

When he got to the door, he could hear Dylan talking to Tony, answering his questions.

"I thought I heard something, but... I'm not sure. It could have been..." She stopped talking when she noticed him in the doorway. "Trey?"

"How are you feeling?" he asked, moving towards her.

"Like I hit my head on a thick wood shelf," she tried to joke. She was pale and lying on the gurney. Thick sheets covered her, but he could see the dried blood on her clothes.

He moved over and noticed the white bandage on the back of her head. "Heard you got a few stitches?"

"Three." She nodded, and he could see the pain in her eyes.

"Did they give you something for the pain?" he asked.

"Yes, I took something a few minutes ago."

"Ms. McCaw, if you think of anything else, give me a call," Tony broke in.

"Have you checked out the office to see if anything's out of place?" Trey turned to Tony.

"Dale and Mike are over there now. I hope you feel better." Tony tipped his hat before walking out, leaving them alone.

When Dylan patted the side of the bed next to her, he sat down, and she took his hands into hers.

"I'm okay." She met his eyes. "You look scared to death." She smiled. "It's a bump on the head."

185

"It could have been worse. I should have been there." His mind had run through a million different scenarios while he waited for his mother and on the trip into town.

"I'm okay," she repeated. "I didn't mean to scare everyone."

He sighed. "What happened?"

He listened to her story of how she arrived back to the office and found the front door open. After that, she didn't remember everything. She thought she'd heard a noise, but she couldn't remember if it was from an office or the supply room. She had woken in a pool of blood when she'd heard Trent's voice.

"It's my fault. I must have forgotten to lock up. I know I forgot to set the alarm. Your uncle... he made me nervous."

"Carl? He was there?" he asked. Upon seeing her look, he jumped in. "Hey." He squeezed her hand. "It's not your fault. We shouldn't have to always punch in the alarm code."

"Are they going to keep me here overnight?" she asked him.

"I don't think so." He glanced towards the door, wanting to talk to the doctor himself. "I'll go check."

Less than five minutes later, he walked back into her room. "You're all set to go home. They want someone to keep an eye on you tonight. Addy has agreed to stay with you, if it's okay with you."

"Sure." She sat up, then groaned when she noticed her shirt, which was covered in dried blood.

"I'll buy you a new one," he promised, helping her up.

After checking her out of the clinic, he helped her into Addy's Jeep and climbed into the back seat.

"You're coming too?" she asked.

"I'm sticking by your side. There is plenty of room at your place. Besides, I promised to cook dinner for you." He smiled.

"Oh, are you going to make your spaghetti?" Addy asked, sounding excited.

"Third wheel," he tossed to Addy, who only smiled back at him. "I'll make the garlic bread." She wiggled her eyebrows. "And I can have Trent pick up a pie or cake on his way over."

Trey groaned as his date night turned into yet another family dinner.

Dylan glanced back at him with a smile. "We can postpone our dinner until next week, when we're both feeling better."

"Promise?" he asked, feeling a little better that she understood. Her smile was her answer.

As far as dinners went, he couldn't complain much. He hadn't enjoyed time with Trent and Abby, outside of the presence of the rest of his family, since they'd gotten married.

Seeing the pair together was simply amazing. He'd grown up with Addy and had had some classes with her. She'd been the silent nerdy type, much like he imagined Dylan had been. The pair of them got along wonderfully. They chatted over the spaghetti dinner about classes, and which ones Dylan was going to take next.

187

He had to admit, he was feeling a little undereducated after listening to the pair of them talk. Maybe he should take a few classes himself. Running his father's business wasn't what he'd imagined doing growing up, but with the direction they were taking McGowan Enterprises, it wouldn't hurt him to sign up for a few online classes.

They sat around the living room and ate chocolate cake with raspberry sorbet, one of his brother's favorites.

Trent and Addy were snuggled together on the sofa, while Dylan was leaning back in the recliner, close to the fireplace. Trent had brought Dopey over to stay the night, and his own dog, Happy, was curled up to its sibling next to the fire.

"So," Addy finally said once Trey had cleared all the dessert dishes, "who do you think it was?"

The room was silent.

"It could have been Darla. After all, it's all around town what you said to her at the Moose," Trent pointed out.

"She doesn't have a key to the office. How did she get in?" Addy asked.

"Carl," Dylan said softly.

"What?" Everyone turned towards her.

Her eyes scanned his. "He stopped by before I locked up for lunch."

"What did he want?" Trent asked.

Dylan shook her head slightly. "Nothing, he... just made a comment about my job title. I ushered him out, locked up and..."

"You're sure you locked up?" Trent asked.

"Yes, I locked both locks. I did forget to set the alarm, but I remember locking up."

"Did you test the door after?" his brother asked.

Dylan frowned. "No, why?"

Trent sighed. "The only thing our dear uncle taught us was how to open a locked door."

"How?" Dylan frowned.

"You don't," Trey answered, his eyes turning to hers. "You waltz in before they lock up, when the door is unlocked, and slide a piece of duct tape over the holes. That way when someone locks it, the bolts won't engage."

"It's an old trick. One I thought our locks were impervious to." Trent stood up and pulled out his cell phone and stepped into the kitchen.

"I…" She looked at him. "I should have checked."

He shook his head and moved over to her. "You didn't know. He showed us a few other tricks—how to break into cars, figure out the code to our father's safe, those kinds of things." He sighed. "Great influence," he added sarcastically.

"Tyler's heading back down there to check. He was sure he tested the door once he locked up, and he set the alarm, but he'll look for tape marks on the doorjamb."

They all sat around in silence until Trent's phone rang a few minutes later.

"Okay, thanks." He hung up.

"Well?" Trey asked.

"No sign of tape, but he's down there putting in a new camera. The front door one didn't catch

189

anything, there was a gap."

"Gap?" Trey asked. "What gap? I installed those cameras myself."

"The wind must have turned it so that it was pointed at the parking lot, instead of the door."

"Bull..." He glanced towards the ladies. "Sorry,"

"I think I'm going to head up and take a bath." Dylan rose from the chair.

"Are you feeling okay?" he asked, worried.

"Yes, but I think it will help relax me some." She glanced around. "Thank you, everyone, for everything."

Trent nodded. "I'd better get going myself. I've got an early morning." He leaned in and kissed Addy. "See you in the morning."

"Night." Addy held onto Trent a little. "Call me," she told him.

"I will." Trent smiled wickedly at his wife.

"Eww." He rolled his eyes. "Phone sex hints."

Addy chuckled. "You're just jealous." She pushed him and walked with Trent towards the back door.

He turned to Dylan. "Are you sure you're okay?"

She smiled. "If you're waiting for me to ask you to come take a bath with me..." She paused and moved closer to him. "You're out of luck tonight, buddy," she added as she strolled by him.

"Shot down, he crashes and burns," Addy joked as she walked back into the room. "You can help me do the dishes." She turned to him as he watched Dylan disappear up the stairs.

This was not how he'd planned the night ending,

but still, he enjoyed his sister-in-law's company as they cleaned up.

He wasn't looking forward to sleeping on the sofa, but Addy was taking the guest room. Still, it was a comfort knowing he was there if she needed him. Plus, he wanted to keep a close eye on her. He was pretty sure someone had moved the front door camera and had attacked her. Which pissed him off.

Thoughts of installing more cameras crossed his mind as he lay there in the dark, listening to Dopey snore at his feet.

He heard a floor board creak and jumped up, only to see Dylan standing at the base of the stairs.

"Sorry, I needed some water to take these." She held up the bottle of pills she'd gotten from the clinic. "I didn't mean to wake you."

"You didn't." He moved into the kitchen with her, grabbed a glass, and filled it for her. "Feeling any better?"

"Much." She swallowed the pills. "I'm sorry for scaring everyone."

"You didn't." He nodded out the window towards the garage. "I haven't seen your brother yet."

"He... I talked to him earlier. I told him not to worry."

"Doesn't mean he shouldn't have checked in on you."

He noticed her frown and placed his hands on her shoulders lightly. "I'm sorry, I didn't mean to..."

She shook her head. "No, you're right." She sighed. "Things are... strained between us. They

191

have been since… for a while." She glanced out the window and he wondered if he could ruin the night any further.

Chapter Thirteen

Talking to Trey came naturally. They sat up until almost midnight, talking about family troubles. From her perspective, the McGowans were perfect. Even as Trey filled her in on past problems, she couldn't imagine the family being anything but poster children for *Leave it to Beaver*.

She climbed the stairs almost two hours after she'd gone down for a glass of water. Somehow, she was more relaxed than when she'd descended the stairs. She fell asleep instantly instead of replaying what had happened to her over and over again, which she'd been doing ever since she'd woken up on the floor of the supply closet.

When she woke the next morning, her head felt like it was about to explode.

She groaned as she climbed out of bed. Showering helped, but when she tried to wash her hair, her fingers brushed the bandages.

Dressing in comfortable slacks and a thick

sweater, she applied her makeup and tried to do something with her hair that would hide the bandages.

She walked downstairs to the smell of pancakes. Addy was standing at the stove, and Trent and Trey were setting the table.

"I think I could get use to this," she said, sitting in the chair Trey pulled out for her.

"Too bad, I miss my husband too much," Addy joked, setting a plate of pancakes in front of her.

Much like the night before, the four of them sat down to the meal and talked. It was nice, pretending to be part of a family, even though she knew it wouldn't last long.

When her brother walked into the house, Darla hanging off his arm, all the happiness was sucked out of the house and out of her.

"Brent." She stood up. "We've talked about this…" She took her brother's arm, but he jerked free and walked past her.

"I figured since you had company over, I could have my own." His eyes narrowed at her.

They had both agreed to keep his company contained to the garage.

"Don't worry, we've got to get going." Trent stood up and took Addy's arm.

She glanced down at her watch and hissed. "We're late."

Trey frowned down at his own watch, then picked up his dish and carried it to the dishwasher, like Trent and Addy had done.

"Don't worry, I'll clean this all up, later." She

glanced towards Darla, who had made herself comfortable at the kitchen table. Even though all the food was gone, she appeared to be waiting to be served.

"Brent." She gripped her brother's arm. "Aren't you going to be late for work, too?"

Brent shrugged. "If the bosses can be late..."

Her eyes narrowed, and she lowered her voice. "Go, now. Get her out of here."

Her brother's eyes narrowed. "We'll leave after we have some food."

"Ready?" Addy said, cheerfully.

Grabbing her purse and jacket, she followed the rest of them out of the house.

"Wow, talk about leaving a sinking ship," Addy said after getting in her Jeep.

Trey and Trent had jumped in Trent's truck and were following them to the office before Trent had to go to his meeting.

"I can't believe Brent is seeing her." She closed her eyes and rested her head back, then hissed when she bumped her stiches.

"Men. Some of them think with their lower brains." Addy rolled her eyes.

Dylan chuckled. "Thank god none of the McGowans are dumb enough to fall for that."

"Oh, there was a time when Tyler and Darla were an item. Long ago," she added.

"Tyler?" Dylan cringed.

"Back in school, back when Darla and I were friends."

"I just can't see either of those two scenarios."

She smiled over at Addy. "You're too smart and Tyler is so in love with Kristen."

Addy chuckled. "I hear they couldn't stand each other when they met."

"Really?" She leaned in and listened to Addy tell the story as they drove towards her work.

When they arrived, the three McGowan men were standing at the front doors.

"What's all this?" she asked, stopping by Trey.

"New security system. I installed it last night." Tyler pointed up to the new camera next to the old one. "There's a new key pad too." He moved inside. "It alerts anytime the door is opened and locks via a phone app." He pulled out his cell phone. "Everyone will have to download it."

For the next half hour, she learned the new system. It was really cool being able to see on her phone if the system was on and which doors were open. She also liked setting the alarm remotely.

By the time she sat behind her desk, she was feeling more relaxed about being alone in the space again, but all three of the brothers had changed their schedules around so that they were sitting behind their desks for the rest of the day. Tyler and Trent had canceled their important meeting, just for her.

After the workday, she drove herself home in the borrowed company car. She'd been thinking about buying a used car herself. Maybe a Jeep like Addy's. She seemed to like hers and talked about how nice it was to be able to get around after a snowstorm.

She had, with Trey's help, signed up for her new

classes and was as prepared as she could be for her final that evening.

She took a hot shower to clear her mind from work before logging into the laptop to take her test. When her brother walked into the house with Darla hanging on his arm, she groaned and wondered what it would be like to be an only child.

Deciding not to fight with him, she gathered her things, went upstairs, and locked herself in her room. She wasn't surprised when, half an hour later, loud music was playing downstairs.

She tried to block out the noise as she focused on the test, but part of her knew her score would be lower due to the incident.

Slamming her laptop shut, she marched downstairs to find Darla bouncing up and down on her brother's lap, her shirt around her waist and her ample chest smacking her brother in the face.

"Oh my god!" she cried out, covering her eyes. "What the hell?" She stomped her foot. "You have your own place to do that in."

She wasn't surprised to hear Darla giggle. Actually, she wouldn't have put it past the woman to have planned it this way.

"Hell, haven't you heard of knocking?" Brent joked dryly.

"Get the hell out!" She pointed towards the door, keeping her eyes shut. "And don't come back!"

She heard them moving around and wagered it was safe to look again. Darla had just thrown her jacket over her chest and left it open enough that Dylan could still see her belly button.

"Out!" She stomped her foot again, wondering if she'd ever get the image out of her mind.

"I pay rent here too, you know," Brent started.

"You pay half of what I pay, which gives you full access to the garage apartment, not the main house," she replied. It was an argument they'd had in the past a few times. She'd set it up that way on purpose after catching Darla coming down the stairs that first time. There was no way she wanted that woman to have access to the rest of the place, so she could do what she'd just seen her doing.

"Listen," Brent started, but Darla was pulling him towards the door.

"Come on, sugar, let's go finish our party." Darla gave her a strange look, then winked at her.

Dylan felt a shiver of repulsiveness race through her and felt the chicken salad she'd had for dinner threatening to surface.

When they left, she locked the door and rested her head on the cold glass.

Okay, maybe instead of a car, she'd buy a place for herself. Someplace in the woods, where her brother and Darla couldn't bother her.

Just then her phone chimed in her back pocket.

Seeing Trey's number, she swiped the message open.

-So, did you pass?

-Ugh! Just caught Darla bouncing on my brother. I don't know, they had the music up loud and I couldn't concentrate.

-okay, first off... gross! Second... GROSS!

She chuckled as the image of Darla and Brent

198

faded and Trey's face came into focus.

She moved over to light a fire, but then stopped herself.

-What are you doing? she texted him

-Now?

-Yes.

-Well, I was about to pour myself a glass of wine and take a bubble bath. Why?

She giggled and replied.

-I thought you were a beer and shower kind of guy?

-haha, everyone knows sparkling wine and bath bombs are my kind of thing.

She was really laughing now.

-Can I join?

-Thought you'd never ask. I'll leave the door unlocked.

Her laughter died as she typed the next message.

-Seriously, I thought I'd bring over a carton of ice cream and we can chat.

-I like chocolate chip.

-Be there in ½ hour

-See you then, drive safe.

***

Okay, why was Trey nervous? It wasn't as if it was the first time he'd be with a woman. It was, however, the first time he'd had one over here. Hell, the first time he'd had one anywhere since returning home. He glanced around and made sure the place was moderately clean.

When Dopey let out a bark, he took several deep

199

breaths and moved to open the door.

She held up a bag. "Chocolate chip."

He took the bag from her and swooped in before she had a chance to say anything else. His lips took hers as her body formed against his own. The kiss changed, and suddenly, he was pushing her backwards, pinning her to the door, which slammed behind her. The bag of ice cream dropped to the floor as he used his hands on her, over her.

"I need…" she said against his mouth.

"Yes," he agreed and started walking her towards the bedroom. They made it to the sofa instead. She giggled as she tugged his shirt over his head.

Her eyes ran over him quickly as she bit her bottom lip. She pressed against him and he felt his entire body respond to the way her hips felt in his hands.

She pushed him on the shoulders playfully. Normally, he would have gained control, but he was still a little off kilter and felt himself falling. Reaching for her, he took her down with him and landed on the soft cushions with her on top of him.

The move didn't slow her down. Her hands moved over his chest, gripped his shoulders, as she continued to trail kisses over him.

He was quickly losing control and desperately wanted to enjoy every moment. Using his hips, he flipped them over until she was tucked underneath him.

Her short hair was fanned out on the cushion.

"I didn't come over for this," she said, looking up at him. Her dark eyes ran over his chest. "But, mmm." Her fingers traced his pecs and he couldn't stop his muscles from responding to her touch.

"Then why?" He smiled. "For that bubble bath?"

She smiled, then giggled. "Your dog isn't going to eat the ice cream, is he?" She glanced over towards the door, where, sure enough, Dopey was sniffing the bag.

He sighed, then rolled up and set the bag in the freezer. He walked back over to her, and just seeing the way she looked at him made him want to jump her on the sofa.

"How about we slow down?" He reached for her hands, then pulled her up next to him.

"Do we have to?" She wrapped her arms around him. "Do you know how long it's been since…?" She closed her eyes and rested her forehead on his chest. "Too long," she answered.

"Ditto," he replied, "which is why I want to take things slow and enjoy myself."

She looked up at him and after a moment, nodded. "Okay." She took a deep breath. "Lead the way."

He chuckled as he started to move.

"Dancing?" Her eyebrows rose.

"Why not?" He took hold of her hips and spun her towards the bedroom. "As long as we dance that way." He nodded towards the bedroom.

She laughed again. "Or the sofa. How about the kitchen counter…"

He covered her lips with his and she moaned with pleasure.

"Bed first. Kitchen and sofa later."

"Promise?" she said as they stepped into his room. He was thankful he'd taken the time to clean up and put new sheets on the bed.

"You cleaned," she said as they walked in.

"Stop looking around and start enjoying." He nudged her closer and took her mouth again, tilting her head and drawing her back into the moment, losing himself a little as he did so.

Her knees hit the edge of the bed, but he stopped her from pulling him downward.

His fingers had hooked into her yoga pants and he nudged them lower as her fingers traced the skin just below his jean line, causing him to hold his breath.

"Ticklish?" she asked between kisses.

"No, and if you tell my brothers otherwise, I'll deny it," he said, bending down in front of her as he pushed the material down to her knees.

He heard her gasp as he did so, his eyes taking in every curve of hers.

"Beautiful," he whispered, his voice cracking. Her fingers dug into his hair when he moved forward to nibble on her flesh. "Mine," he whispered next to her skin. She smelled of lilacs and tasted like nectar.

Her hands gripped him as he dipped his tongue into her skin and lapped at her until he felt her knees go weak. Only then did he nudge her to sit on the edge of the bed. He pulled her leggings the rest of the way down her legs. Using his palms, he spread her thighs wide and dipped a finger into her as his eyes locked with hers.

She moaned and threw her head back against the mattress.

"No," he said, "look at me. I want to see your eyes change."

Her eyes returned to his and her tongue darted out to wet her bottom lip.

"My god," he groaned, his eyes returning to what he was doing to her. "You're perfect." He moved inside her, and she spread her legs further, giving him full access.

With his free hand, he nudged her towards the edge of the mattress. "Wrap your legs around me." He knelt and replaced his fingers with his mouth. She gasped and gripped his hair and shoulders, her nails sinking into his skin. Her inner thigh muscles gripped his head as he took her. Her feet rested on his lower back as she leaned back. Soft moans encouraged him onward. He felt the moment she convulsed and tasted the sweetness of her release on his tongue.

"My god," he groaned, pulling the condom from his back pocket, then reaching for his jeans.

She was there, helping him slide them off his hips. "My turn." She smiled up at him, then her eyes ran over him as she nudged the denim downwards.

"Wow." She smiled, her eyes remaining on his cock. "Wow." She licked her lips before dipping her head and taking him fully into her mouth and throat.

"My god," he groaned as his fingers tangled in her hair. Just seeing those pink lips of hers wrapped around his cock had him almost bursting.

He'd never had anyone take him as deep before,

and he almost came when she licked his balls while he was fully in her mouth. He jerked her back and tossed her onto the bed. He slipped on the condom faster than he knew was possible and jerked her legs wide.

She was smiling up at him when he settled between her legs. "Hold onto me, it's going to get crazy."

She laughed as she pulled him in. "Good, I love crazy."

Chapter Fourteen

She woke to being licked on the face. Not by Trey, unless he had stinky doggie breath.

"Dopey!" She laughed and tried to push the dog away from her face.

"He likes you." Trey chuckled and rolled her over until she lay across his bare chest. "So do I." He leaned up and kissed her.

Just then, her stomach growled. "There was promise of ice cream." She leaned up and looked down at him.

He chuckled. "As I remember, there was also promise of kitchen sex."

She laughed. "After the ice cream."

"Deal." He rolled them both until they stood. When he started walking out of the bedroom, completely naked, she escaped his hold and backtracked to gather her shirt and yoga pants.

"Shy?" he asked.

"I've lived with a brother. I know that they forget

205

to knock. I don't mind showing my business to you." She leaned up and kissed him. "I would, however, mind if Trent or Tyler saw it all."

He chuckled. "That's why we have our own places. They wouldn't dare…" He stopped himself when he remembered that, even though his brothers were married, and he always knocked, his brothers hadn't adopted the same rule with him.

"See." She nodded and held up his jeans for him. "Told ya."

He groaned. "Okay, going to have to have the brother talk with them soon."

He slid the jeans on and, for good measure, slipped a few more condoms into the pocket before following her out into the kitchen.

She already had the ice cream out and was searching his cupboards for bowls.

"They're in the dishwasher." He walked over and took two bowls out.

"You only have two of them?"

"Sure. One's usually clean." He shrugged. "I was going to buy more… when my house was done." She shook her head and laughed.

She sat on the kitchen counter eating ice cream while he leaned on the counter next to her, watching her eat ice cream and occasionally taking a bite of his own.

"I thought you liked chocolate chip?" she said when he'd all but let his melt in the bowl.

"I do." He frowned down at the melted mess. Then he smiled up at her. "I like watching you eat ice cream better than eating it myself."

"Oh?" She took the spoon and put it into her mouth slowly and licked it. He slid between her legs, his eyes glued to her mouth.

"You're killing me." He groaned as his fingers dug into her thighs.

She set her spoon down, pushed her bowl away, and wrapped her arms and legs around him to pull him closer. "There was also mention of countertop sex…" She bit his bottom lip and sucked on it.

He hoisted her up, yanked her yoga pants down past her ankles, and then pulled out a condom.

She quickly undid his jeans and took the condom from him. She slid it on him slowly, enjoying the feel of him in her hand.

"God," he groaned before stepping back between her spread legs.

His hands gripped her butt cheeks, hoisting her up, until she felt herself give as he slid into her fully.

Rolling her head back, she closed her eyes and held on as she felt something new inside her begin to build.

Two hours later, she drove herself home, her body still pulsing from Trey's touch. Even though he'd begged her to stay the night, she knew she couldn't, shouldn't. Not this soon.

At home, she tossed and turned in the large empty bed, wishing she had stayed. What would it be like, waking up next to a man in the morning?

Not that she hadn't had plenty of sex before Trey. But none of it had… mattered, really.

When her alarm went off, she felt oddly energized, knowing she'd see Trey soon.

It wasn't Friday yet, but she swung by Belle's Bakery for donuts and coffee. She chatted with the owner for a while as she waited for a fresh batch of donuts and her coffee order, then headed into the office.

"What this?" Trey smiled as he walked in the front door, followed closely by Tyler.

"I needed a pick-me-up this morning and couldn't resist the donuts," she answered.

Trey shocked her by walking around her desk and planting a kiss on her, right in front of his brother.

"Don't worry, if he didn't know when he picked me up this morning, seeing the donuts would have guaranteed it," he whispered.

"Didn't need the donuts. The stupid look on Trey's face said it all." Tyler took two donuts and his coffee with him to his office as he chuckled.

"See, told you," Trey said, taking a donut and leaning against her desk. "So, did you get your test score back?"

She'd completely forgotten about her test. "I can log in now." She turned and logged into her computer. Trey hung around, sipping his coffee and nibbling on his second donut.

"Ninety-eight." She groaned.

"That's great," he said excitedly. "Isn't it?"

"Yes." She turned towards him. "It would have been a hundred if—"

He leaned in and kissed her. "Shut up and have a donut. You passed, you should be proud." He smiled down at her.

She took a deep breath, then nodded. "Agreed, and I am." She relaxed slightly. Still, the ninety-eight gnawed at her. She had an extensive line of one hundreds in her past. The only lower grade she'd received had been in the month after her parents' death.

"Good." He grabbed another donut and his coffee cup. "Now, get to work." He winked at her and disappeared down the hallway.

The day seemed to fly by. Maybe it was all the sugar pulsing through her blood, but lunchtime arrived faster than normal. The three of them drove over to the Moose and sat in the back booth, where Kristen and baby Timothy Jack joined them.

Dylan had to agree that the kid was the spitting image of his dad. A true McGowan through and through, right down to the little dimple to the side of his mouth.

"I think he's going to have his uncle's blue eyes," Trey said in a baby voice as he looked down at the sleeping child.

"Nope, they're already turning darker," Tyler said, raising his chin slightly.

"Boys." Kristen sighed. "They'll find any reason to fight."

It was strange, but Dylan felt like she fit right in with the family. They were so welcoming, so open to her. She'd never experienced anything quite like it before, even with her own family.

As they drove back to the office, Trey glanced at her. "So, I figured I'd come over tonight. I have a few things I want to ask you."

209

Her eyebrows shot up, but since his brother was driving, she nodded and tried to hide the smile.

If the morning went by quickly, the afternoon seemed to drag on. The full stomach didn't help, or the lack of sleep. She found her head dropping several times and had to go back to the break room and make a pot of coffee.

"Is that coffee?" Tyler poked his head into the room.

"Yes." She held out a mug.

"God." He sighed. "Timmy kept us up last night." He took the mug from her and held it out as she poured a cup for him and then one for herself.

"Babies do that." She smiled.

"Yeah." He rolled his shoulders, a move she'd seen Trey do before.

"Heard you aced your test." He leaned against the countertop.

"Aced?" She shook her head. "Ninety-eight."

He smiled. "That's a better score than any of us ever got on a test." He held up his mug for her to clink hers with. She did so and sipped.

"Congrats. So, um…" His eyes moved around the room. "Things won't get weird between you and Trey, working together?"

She almost coughed up the sip of coffee she'd just swallowed.

"No," she said quickly, almost too quickly.

"Good," he said slowly. "I don't think we can stand to lose you around here. Trey?" He shrugged. "He's just dead weight."

"I heard that," Trey yelled from the hallway.

"Which is why I said it," Tyler called back. He leaned closer to her. "I knew he was eavesdropping." He winked at her. "But, seriously, in the past three months, you've proven yourself invaluable." He toasted her with his coffee cup again before leaving the room.

Trey walked in, a frown on his face as he grabbed an empty mug and poured a cup for himself.

"Damn brothers always sticking their noses in my business."

She rested her hand on his arm. "I bet that feels wonderful." She leaned up and placed a quick kiss on his cheek as she heard the phone ring up front.

Trey followed her out front, and she answered the call. It took a moment for it to register, but after the second loud noise, she quickly hung up the phone.

"What?" He frowned.

"Prank call." She tried to remain calm, but Trey moved around the desk quickly and took her shoulders.

She'd gotten them a few times now, the loud banging noises with whispers in the background.

"Same as before?" he asked, taking her hands in his.

"Yes. On my cell and here." She glanced down at the phone. "Like you said, I'm sure it's just kids." She shrugged.

He picked up the phone, punched a few numbers, and then listened.

"Unregistered number." He set the receiver back down. "I'm sure it's just kids. What do they say?"

211

She shrugged, not sure how he'd respond. "You're next."

He tensed, and his eyes changed. She'd seen him angry before, but this was different.

"What kind of sounds?" he asked.

"Loud banging."

"Like a gun?"

"No, more like a lid of a trash can being dropped." She'd worked it out for herself. After the first call, she'd ruled out a gunshot. Whoever was calling, there was no doubt they wanted to scare her. At this point, all they were doing was wasting her time.

"It's okay, really." She smiled and placed her hand on his arm. "They're just prank calls."

"After someone pushed you into a closet and caused you to get stitches," he added.

Her eyes narrowed. "The calls started before that," she mentioned, then wished she hadn't.

"Dylan." He turned her until she faced him. "There's been some crazy stuff going on in the past year or so. Mark my words, if you're getting calls, it won't end there. We have to deal with this, now."

She sighed and asked, "What do you suggest?"

"I'll give Tony a call, see if he can stop by and take a statement. He might be able to do something we can't to track the call."

She nodded. "I'll call Tony. You've got a meeting with a supplier starting..."—she glanced down at her watch—"five minutes ago." She motioned for him to go.

"Tyler's probably already on it." He glanced

down the hallway. "Call, I'll be quick." He leaned in and kissed her, then rushed down to join the call.

By the end of the day, she had instructions on how to handle the calls and had filed a police report.

When she drove home, she was exhausted and wanted a hot shower and her bed. But then she remembered Trey was coming over. Her bed would have to wait.

She showered, pulled on some comfortable clothes, and lit a fire. Even though the sun had been out all day, they were a few months away from warmer nights.

There was a knock on the back door, and she smiled as she opened it.

***

Trey could tell immediately that Dylan was tired. Feeling bad, he stepped in.

"You're tired." He frowned.

She chuckled. "For good reason. Someone kept me up most of last night." She leaned up on her toes and kissed him.

"For good reason." He smiled. "This can wait."

"Trey, you're here, what's up?" He followed her into the living room.

"I brought Chinese." He held up the bag with the takeout.

"Good. Sit, eat, talk." She motioned to the sofa.

He tried to keep the conversation light as they ate. Still, he felt a little nervous about what he had to ask her. It wasn't every day you made a decision this big that would change the course of your life.

When her box of rice noodles and beef and

213

broccoli was half empty, she motioned with her chop sticks. "So, what's up?"

He set his own food down and jumped in with both feet. "I want you to help me pick a couple classes to sign up for. I'm not good at that sort of thing... school." He rolled his eyes. "And, with my workload, I'll need something light to begin with." He took a deep breath.

"Trey." She stopped him from rambling. "Of course, I can. Let me go up and grab my laptop." She smiled at him reassuringly before disappearing upstairs.

He was nibbling on his food when the back door flew open. Her brother stormed in the back door, muddy boots still on, and walked past him like he wasn't there. Glancing back, he frowned at the still open back door.

"Any problem with shutting a door?" he asked as the man began rummaging around the kitchen.

Brent glanced over his shoulder quickly. "I'll be out of here as soon as I find something to eat."

"By then, it will be freezing in here." Trey got up and shut the door himself, just as Dylan came down the stairs, laptop in hand.

"Brent!" She set her laptop down on the table and glared at her brother. "I just mopped the floor yesterday."

Her brother shrugged. "You can do it again today."

When Dylan started to pull the mop out, he stepped in.

"I think since you're the one who made the

mess"—Trey held out the mop—"Dylan can finish helping me while you clean up after yourself."

Brent turned on him, his eyes narrowed. "You McGowans can boss me around while I'm on the clock, but in my house—"

"It's not your house," Dylan broke in in a low voice, handing the mop to her brother. "It's mine, and you've just made a mess in it."

Brent shrugged and started hastily mopping up the mess.

"What was it you came in here for?" Dylan asked.

"Food." He shoved the mop back at her.

"What happened to your own kitchen?" she asked, crossing her arms over her chest.

"Nothing," he replied, eyeing the Chinese on the coffee table.

Dylan stepped between it and her brother. "As you can see, we're having a meeting. You'll just have to run and get something yourself."

Brent gave Dylan a strange look as she pushed him towards the back door. "And next time, have the decency to take off your muddy boots, or I'll make you mop the entire floor." She shoved her speechless brother out of the back door, then shut it and leaned against it.

"That felt good," she said with a smile as she sat back down.

"Sticking up for yourself feels good." He gathered her close and kissed the top of her head. When he felt her shoulders slump and her body shake with her tears, he held on tighter.

"Are you okay?" he asked when her tears lightened up.

"I cried all over your shoulder." She sniffled but remained still.

"It's okay." He smiled and kissed the top of her head again. "I can deal with a little salt water."

She chuckled and leaned back. If he'd thought Dylan McCaw was beautiful before, seeing her dark eyes pink from tears solidified it. He was a goner.

Tugging her towards the sofa, he sat down and pulled her into his lap. "You're tired and pissed." He gently brushed the tears away with his fingers. "Why haven't you stood up to him before?"

She sighed and rested her head on his shoulder. "I have, it's just never gone in my favor before." She looked up at him. "But you were here and, I don't know, I felt empowered."

He sighed. "You may not see it, but as far as the two of you go, you're in charge."

She tilted her head as her eyes narrowed. "What do you mean?"

"I mean, even though he doesn't show it in the normal brotherly way, he respects you. He may even look up to you."

She laughed. "Right," she said sarcastically.

"Take it from someone who has two older brothers. What we just witnessed was his way of giving you respect. Think about it—he mopped the floor and left your kitchen without taking anything." He shrugged. "That's as close to respect as you can get."

She was silent for a while, then climbed from his

lap to take up her laptop. "Thanks." She smiled and wiped her face. "Now it's my turn to help you." She sat at the table and motioned for him to sit beside her.

Less than an hour later, he was signed up for two classes, with a promise from her that she'd help him if he needed.

Dylan's eyes were drooping, so he kissed her goodnight and drove home. He was thankful that the inner ear infection had pretty much run its course. He still had some occasional ringing, but his balance had returned.

When he parked in his usual spot, a faint glow in the distance caught his eye. Stepping out of the truck, he pulled out his phone and called Tyler.

His brother answered on the first ring. "Hey." Trey could hear the baby crying in the background.

"Looks like we have a squatter on the far west side of the hill. I see a fire going midway up the hill."

"Damn it. Call Trent. We'll get the ATVs and go check it out."

"I'll meet you at the barn." He hung up and called his brother.

Trent answered on the third ring. "What's so damn important?"

Trey chuckled. "Sounds like I'm interrupting something."

"What do you want?" His brother punctuated each word.

"Squatters on the property. Meet us at the barn, we're going out." He chuckled when his brother

217

flung some choice words in his direction before hanging up.

"Yup," he said as he climbed back in his truck, "definitely interrupted something."

It took them almost forty minutes to find the campfire. By then, whoever had started it was long gone. The fire had been left to burn out, so Trent dumped some water on it to put it the rest of the way out.

"Looks like there's tire tracks over here," Tyler said from behind them. "They lead back up the hill."

"Think we scared them off?" he asked.

"For now." Tyler glanced at his watch. "We'll take the long way back and check out the gate at the service road, just to make sure."

Another hour later, Trey walked into his house, muddy and cold. Someone had broken the lock on the service gate, which they'd had to replace with another. They talked about installing a wild game camera but figured whoever it was had been spooked off by the sound of the ATVs. Still, if Trey knew his brothers, the cameras would be going up that weekend anyway.

He showered and climbed into bed with Dopey just after one in the morning and fell fast asleep.

The fire alarm didn't wake him. It was Dopey scratching at his face, hard, that jolted him from his sleep. He sucked in a deep breath of dark smoke and coughed. Realizing what was happening, he yanked the sheet from the bed and covered his head with it, scooping up his dog with his other hand.

The hallway was already blocked and full of

smoke. He could see the flames consuming the pictures he'd hung up in the hallway.

Turning back into his room, he rushed into the bathroom and glanced around. Only then did he realize he'd left his cell phone on the nightstand. He turned back but decided he couldn't chance returning to the pitch-dark room. The smoke was too thick. Yanking open the small window, he tossed Dopey out first then shimmied his way out. He cursed when rocks dug into his bare feet.

"Trey!" He heard several people shouting his name.

"Over here," he called out as Dopey circled him, barking frantically.

"My god!" Tyler rushed over and wrapped his arms around him. "I thought…" His brother held on as Trent rushed over.

"You're naked." Trent laughed and hugged him.

Trey glanced down and cursed under his breath as Tyler removed his jacket and handed it to him.

"Son of a bitch!" He glanced at the place, fully engulfed now. "What the hell happened?" He ran his free hand through his hair, the one that wasn't holding the jacket over his crotch.

They walked to the front of the place, going slowly since he was barefooted. His feet were torn up from all the rocks and branches.

They reached the front as his mother's car jerked to a stop. She rushed out and raced towards him. Tears were streaming down her face as she embraced him.

"Don't ever scare me like that again." She kissed

his check before slapping it lightly

His brother handed him a blanket from the back seat of his truck, which he wrapped around himself quickly.

"Yes, ma'am." He pulled his mother into a hug and held on.

Chapter Fifteen

"What happened?" Dylan rushed into the office first thing the next morning and hugged Trey. The entire family was gathered in the reception area, along with a few others, including several police officers.

Trey had called her from his mother's place earlier that morning and told her that his place had burned down and that he and Dopey were both okay. He told her to head into the office at the normal time. She had tried to argue, but he told her they were all meeting there.

"I'm okay," he assured her, running his hand over her hair. "Dopey woke me and we crawled out the bathroom window."

"That small thing?" She pulled back and looked at him. "How did you fit?"

"He shimmied out of it, butt naked," Trent said, laughing as he slapped Trey's shoulder.

She turned to him. "All your stuff?"

"Up in smoke." He sighed.

"Don't worry, a lot of his stuff is still in my garage," Gail added. "Good thing he was too lazy to haul it away."

"I was waiting until my house was built," Trey said, wrapping an arm around his mother and kissing the top of her head.

"We won't know much until after the inspector gets done going through the rubble." Tony stepped forward. "Until then, we'll need to make sure everyone stays clear of the property."

"I don't need anything from there. Sucks that I lost my cell phone and truck keys, but I'm having someone come out and make a replacement. My new phone will be delivered later today. Thank god we sprung for the insurance on those."

"Food's here." Addy walked in with Kristen and the baby. Tyler was following with a stack of boxes from the donut shop. "Coffee's here too," she added, holding up two holders full of cups.

Everyone flooded into the conference room and sat around talking about last night's ordeal. Speculations swirled around the room, but Dylan remained silent as she kept her eyes on Trey.

She'd been so scared when he'd called. Seeing him tired and trying to act cool only made her more so.

"I was thinking"—she leaned closer to him— "about your living arrangements."

He leaned closer and smiled. When he wiggled his eyebrows, she chuckled.

"I have a spare bedroom."

This time, it was him that laughed. "Sold." He wrapped an arm around her. "As long as Dopey can come too."

She glanced down at the dog sleeping at his feet and nodded. "He can sleep with me."

She didn't know what had caused her to offer her place, other than the fact that she felt better with him around. She'd been telling the truth when she said she felt more empowered with him there. She knew she had to learn to deal with Brent on her own and seeing Trey stand up to her brother had given her the courage to do so.

She'd done a lot of thinking last night about what Trey had said about Brent's attitude towards her. She had thought that maybe he was right. Maybe her brother had his own way of showing her that he cared.

But then she'd rushed out of the house that morning to find his truck parked behind her car. When she'd banged on his door and asked him to move it, he'd tossed her the keys and told her she could move the damn truck if she wanted it moved. Which, of course, had removed all doubt from her mind about how her brother acted.

For the rest of the day, people came and went, checking in on Trey and Dopey. Several delivered gifts to Dopey after hearing how he had woken Trey and warned him. He now had a new dog bed, toys, bags of dog food, and lots of treats. So many things had been delivered, Trey finally stepped in and told everyone to deliver the donations to the local shelter instead.

Over the next few days, she couldn't believe how smoothly things went. That first evening after the fire, Trey and Dopey had moved into the house with her.

Of course, she hadn't forced Trey to stay in the guest room. She was a little shocked at how right it felt to sleep next to him each night. Her brother had remained silent on the move, but she could tell he had plenty to say about it, just not in front of her, apparently.

Still, it was nice to have Trey there, planning dinners, helping her out with the chores, and keeping her sexed every night. The last part was a major perk. She was going to be fully satisfied, exhausted, and happy.

It was interesting to see Brent and Trey skate around one another at the house. After the first few days, Brent steered clear completely. Only once did he try to bring Darla back into the house. Trey easily shut him down without saying a word. How he did it left her speechless and impressed.

They had been snuggling on the sofa, watching a movie, when her brother slammed the back door open, took two steps into the house, and turned and saw that Darla had followed him inside. Her brother's eyes met Trey's and her brother froze on the spot.

Trey snapped his finger, which sent Dopey jumping off the end of the sofa and into a barking fit. Her brother made a quick retreat, pushing Darla out of the door as she complained.

When she asked Trey about it, he shrugged.

"Dopey doesn't like your brother or Darla."

She got the feeling there was more behind it, some training he'd done, but she decided not to push it. Maybe she didn't want to know what went on between the two men. Ignorance was bliss, after all.

Most evenings they spent huddled over their laptops for their classes. She helped Trey by reading his English paper, and he helped her by making dinners and cleaning up after them. It was odd how good of a cook he was. She doubted her brother knew how to make a peanut butter and jelly sandwich, let alone chicken Florentine.

The inspector had found the cause of the fire and a full investigation had been launched. Apparently, a wire on the front porch had been snipped and fuel had been poured on it.

If it hadn't been for the minute traces of fuel, they would have assumed it was an accident. Now, however, they were looking for whoever purposely burned down Trey's trailer and tried to kill him. More important to her and the McGowans was why. Why try to kill Trey? Were the other family members in danger as well?

The police had interviewed her brother and Trey's family; she had even gone in and answered questions herself. In fact, most of the McGowan employees had volunteered or been requested to come in. She'd had to make arrangements for each of them to take time off to go in during the workweek.

At this point, they were no closer to figuring out who had started the fire. They spent a great deal of time trying to figure out why he was the target. They had their own suspects, but the police claimed each of them had alibis for the night the fire was started. Still, Uncle Carl and Dennis Rodgers remained on top of their lists.

Carl lived alone in an old trailer at the top of a dirt road. He'd moved several times in the past year. Apparently, he'd been kicked out of his home after the bank had taken it back.

Dennis had taken up residence in an apartment in one of the old buildings downtown since his divorce. The man lived alone and, to Trey's knowledge, worked a part-time job driving a truck. He'd lost everything when he'd been locked away shortly after Kristen's kidnapping. The proof of his embezzlement had gone up in smoke when the NewField building had burned down, but that hadn't removed all his legal woes.

Life continued to fly by her. She had gone into the ophthalmologist and gotten new contacts as well as a new pair of glasses that Trey had helped her pick out. He told her he found her irresistible when she wore them, so she started wearing them more often to work, since the contacts irritated her eyes.

She was shocked when she noticed a flower growing in the flower bed between the garage and the back door. It took her a moment to realize what it was.

"What's wrong?" Trey asked, his hands loaded down with bags of groceries.

"That." She pointed, frowning down at the green sprout sticking out of the dirt.

He glanced over the top of the bags and chuckled. "Don't they have daffodils where you come from?" He started to move past her, but she stopped him.

"When did it become spring?" She glanced around and suddenly realized spring wasn't just in her flower bed, but everywhere in her yard. "It's only March." She frowned.

"April," he corrected. "Tax day, remember?"

She frowned. Of course she knew it was April. After all, she'd spent the last few week faxing paperwork to the CPA that handled McGowan Enterprise's taxes, not to mention pouring over hers and Trey's taxes in the evening between classes and tests.

"I remember, it's just… time is flying by so quickly." She opened the back door for him.

He leaned in and set the bags down, then gripped her hips and pulled her close.

"Time flies when you're having fun." He kissed her, and she melted against him. "And when you're with me." He turned and picked up the bags and walked into the kitchen to set them down. "Don't worry, we still have a few more snowstorms in our future before summer gets in full swing." He started to put the groceries away, moving around the space comfortably and looking good doing it as well.

"How about chicken enchiladas for dinner?" Trey wiggled his eyebrows. She felt her stomach growl.

"I have a test," she answered. Her frown caused him to smile.

"I don't. You go up, get ready, test hard, and I'll get cooking." He walked over and kissed her again. She wondered what she'd done before he'd come along and if he would always make her melt with just one kiss. When he broke the kiss, he nudged her towards the stairs.

"Good luck."

She climbed up the stairs, tossed her work clothes into the hamper, and glanced around their room. Trey wasn't as tidy as she was, but he was a good deal cleaner than her brother had ever been. His shoes sat at the base of the bed, and a jacket and some jeans were tossed over the chair on his side of the bed. Then again, there was a pair of her panties and a bra over the back of her chair. He had peeled them off her the night before. Her body heated at the memory of what he'd done to her.

Changing into a pair of shorts, she frowned at her pale legs and replaced the shorts with leggings, promising herself she'd spend some time in the sun that weekend to work on her tan. Grabbing her laptop, she moved to the window seat in the hallway and logged in.

She heard her brother's truck pull in the driveway halfway through her test. She had just answered the last question when she heard shouting. Glancing out the window, she saw her brother pull back his fist and punch Trey directly in the face.

She must have screamed, because her brother looked up, giving Trey a chance to grip her brother's fist so it wouldn't fly towards his face again.

By the time she ran out into the yard, barefoot,

Trey was shoving her brother towards the garage stairs.

"Go sleep it off," he said, turning to catch her.

"Are you okay?" she asked, flying into his arms, her eyes scanning his face. There was a red mark under his left eye that would probably become a black eye by the morning.

"I'm fine." Trey sighed. "I've been sucker-punched loads of times before. I have two brothers, remember?" He was trying to joke with her, but she wasn't laughing.

Her eyes burned into her brother, who was standing at the top of the stairs, glaring down at them.

"What's your problem?" she called up to him.

"Fuck off," he said softly. Then he turned and slammed the door behind him.

"Darla broke it off with him," Trey said, gently pulling her back into the house. "You're barefoot." He nudged her to sit down on the bench by the back door, then gently wiped the mud from the bottom of her feet with a towel from the dryer.

"How do you know that?" she asked, looking down at his blonde curls. She enjoyed pushing her fingers into the softness and loved the way each curl wrapped around her fingers, as if hugging them.

"The entire town knows it. I heard it at the grocery store." He shrugged.

"Why did he punch you?" she asked.

"I was there." He helped her up. "Dinner's almost ready."

"Trey." She stopped him from walking away.

229

"I'm sorry."

"For?" He blinked down at her. "You need to stop apologizing for Brent."

"He's my..." She wrapped her arms around herself and sighed.

"What?" He waited. "Responsibility?"

Closing her eyes, she shook her head. "Brother," she finally answered.

"I don't apologize for Tyler or Trent's fuck-ups." He leaned closer and kissed her. "Besides, he punches like a girl."

She chuckled and followed him into the kitchen.

***

Trey lay in bed at night with Dylan wrapped around him, her breath gently floating over his chest, causing the little hairs there to sway with each of her exhales. He hated lying to her about Brent.

Well, he hadn't fully lied. It was true that it had gone around town that Darla had broken things off with him a few days back. But the reason he'd approached Brent was the four missed days of work and Brent's refusal to answer his calls to find out why he was missing work.

He and his brothers had agreed to talk to him personally, before doing something as harsh as firing him. Of course, Brent had made himself scarce the past few days. When he'd heard the truck pull up, he knew it might be his only chance to confront him.

He'd approached it like any boss would. He'd mentioned the missed days and asked if there was anything going on that he could help with.

Brent's response had been to yell at him and throw a sucker punch to his jaw. Trey had thrown his own punches, but without his fists.

"You're fired, unless I see your ass at work bright and early tomorrow morning. Your pay will be docked for the time you missed," he had added.

"Bullshit," Brent had challenged. "I've got sick leave." He had almost toppled over as Dylan had rushed from the house.

He had kept her mind off what would no doubt be a black eye come morning by talking and finishing dinner. He asked about her test, talked about his family, anything to keep her apologies for her brother at a minimum.

After dinner, he'd taken her upstairs and occupied her in the most pleasurable way possible. Touching her, kissing her, was like magic. Each time he slid another piece of clothing off, it was like unwrapping the best gift ever.

When his cell phone buzzed, he had just drifted off to sleep. He reached over for it without waking Dylan, but Dopey was now stirring, which meant he was probably going to have to let the dog out or allow him to jump up on the bed.

"Yes?" he asked after seeing Tyler's number.

"We've got more problems." Tyler sounded pissed.

"Where?" He gently nudged Dylan aside, thankful she was a heavy sleeper.

"The new site." His brother covered the phone and spoke to someone else. "Better hurry." His brother hung up.

231

When he jumped out of the bed, Dopey climbed up and laid down in his spot.

"Keep it warm for me." He tucked the blankets around Dylan. "Watch out for her."

He pulled on his jeans and was just putting on his boots when Dylan sat up.

"What?" She blinked a few times, looking around.

"Sorry." He rushed to her side. "Problems at the site. I'll be back soon."

"I can…" She started to get out of the bed, but he stopped her.

"No, go back to sleep." He nudged her, and she fell back into bed. "I'll be back soon."

It took almost half an hour to get to the site. When he arrived, his brother's truck was parked on the hill, behind Mike's police cruiser.

"What's up?" he asked, pulling the jacket around him more tightly.

"Looks like someone's blown up our trailer."

"What?" He glanced around and noticed all the shards of wood where their new construction trailer had been parked less than a week earlier. "Damn it," He ran his hands through his hair. "We just bought that trailer."

"Looks like we'll be buying another one," Tyler added dryly.

"Did the video show anything?" He turned to the area he'd helped his brother place the cameras.

"That's what I needed you for. You have the passcode for this one, not me."

He groaned. "I forgot." He pulled out his phone

and logged into the app. It took longer than usual since their wireless hub had been blown up, and he had to use his data plan.

They all stood around in the truck's headlights and watched his phone screen. A black blob raced across the screen, then stopped just in front of the trailer. He flicked the screen and zoomed in for a better look.

"Son of a…" he heard Mike catch himself.

"Carl." Tyler sighed and started pacing.

"The son of a…" He glanced up and took a deep breath. "SOB doesn't look much like he has only a few weeks left to live." He watched his uncle crawl under the trailer and set the charges, something he had been trained to do years before Trey or his brothers had been born. He used his thumb to fast-forward to the moment the trailer blew, making sure the old man had cleared the area before everything went up. The screen timer showed that the trailer blew about five minutes after his uncle left the site.

"We'll bring him in." Mike turned to go.

Tyler surprised him by saying. "We don't want to press charges."

"The hell we don't." He shoved his phone into his back pocket.

Tyler walked over and leaned close to him. "Think about it. How bad would it look for us to put a dying man in prison? We've got insurance and can have a new trailer out here by the end of the week."

"Tyler, he—"

"Thanks, Mike. We'll deal with this family matter ourselves." Tyler reached over and shook the

233

man's hand.

"Suit yourself. If you need anything..."

"Thanks."

They both watched Mike jump into his patrol SUV and maneuver his way around Trey's truck.

"Okay." He turned to Tyler. "What gives?"

Tyler glanced at his watch. "It's late, let's talk over breakfast. How about we meet at the Moose at ten?"

"Ten?" His eyes narrowed. He knew as well as Tyler did that ten was late enough that most people will have come and gone in the diner, giving them the entire place to themselves.

"Sure, whatever." He turned to go.

"Trey," Tyler called out. He turned and looked over his shoulder at his brother. "Keep this under wraps for now."

"Whatever." He shook his head and drove back home.

When he crawled back in bed with Dylan, he had to nudge Dopey until the dog made room for him.

"Everything okay?" Dylan asked, sleepily.

"Yeah, go back to sleep." He kissed the top of her head and lay there listening to her soft breath as she slept. His mind refused to shut down. He was beyond pissed. He almost vibrated with it.

When the sun hit him in the morning, he figured he'd gotten less than a few hours of sleep. He rolled out of bed, showered, and dressed before Dylan had a chance to open her eyes.

"I have to go in early. I'll see you at the office later." He kissed her and thought about crawling back in bed with her. Instead, he pushed away and, after letting Dopey do his business, climbed into his truck to drive up to his uncle's place to get some answers.

When he stopped at the end of his uncle's driveway, he was slightly surprised to see the patrol car blocking the dirt road.

"Mike." Trey nodded to the man leaning on the hood of the SUV.

"Trey." He glanced at his watch and chuckled. "You're late. I had a twenty on you arriving before six."

Trey sighed. "Tyler put you up to this?" Mike nodded and met him at the side of the car. "You're not going to let me pass, are you?"

"Nope." Mike smiled. "Tyler says he's the head of the family and as such..." Mike stopped when Trey let out a string of bad words. "Don't let your mother hear you talking like that." Mike chuckled.

"Yeah." He stormed back to his truck.

"See you later," Mike called after him playfully.

He drove angry and when he pulled into the gravel driveway at his brother's new house, he let the tires lock for a split second. Before he could get out, his brother was on the front porch, fully dressed, smiling at him.

"Mike call?" he called out as he stormed towards the front. When Kristen and little Timmy came out the front door, his anger dissipated completely.

"Damn it, don't hide behind your woman's skirt and a new baby." He nodded to where Kristen stood.

Tyler glanced over his shoulder and laughed.

235

"She's not wearing a skirt, and I'd never hide behind anything." Tyler stepped off the porch. "What did Mike do? Clock you?" His brother frowned and nodded towards Trey's shiner.

He'd forgotten about it and realized that last night at the site where their trailer had been it had been too dark for Tyler to see the damage Brent had caused.

"Don't change the subject." He stepped up to his brother. The two of them stood eye to eye. For many years he'd had to look up to both Tyler and Trent. Now they were finally equally matched in weight and height.

"Don't make me knock you on your ass in front of my wife," Tyler warned.

"I'm old enough to handle things myself," Trey added.

"Sure you are," Tyler agreed, "but family matters—"

"Are just as much my business as they are yours." His eyes narrowed.

"As head of the—"

"Fuck that," he said softly so Kristen didn't hear. "That's bullshit and you know it. Mom's head of the family."

"I'm glad we agree on this point." His mother's voice came from directly behind him.

Trey had a moment to wince before his ear was pinched and tugged until he was looking down into his mother's angry brown eyes.

"I taught you both better than to cuss and cockfight like this, and in front of the baby, too."

His mother dropped her death grip on his ear and rushed up the porch to take the baby from Kristen's arms. She turned back around to the two of them. "I think we can all go inside and have a decent family discussion now." She turned and walked into the house as Trent's truck pulled into the driveway.

He didn't know what upset him most. The fact that his family knew him so well or the fact that they had changed the meeting time and place without telling him.

He sat in a chair at the kitchen table stewing, until his mother settled the baby in his arms. Suddenly, all the anger drained from his body.

"Now," Tyler said a few minutes later, "since we're all here, I guess we won't have to meet at the Moose later today." He turned to his mother. "I've filled everyone in on what happened last night, and we need to hear a few options on our next course of action. Then we'll vote."

Kristen walked up and took the baby from his arms. "He needs to be changed." She smiled down at him. He was about to argue that the kid was fine, but then the smell hit him, and he gladly handed the baby up to her.

"He should be rotting in a cell until he croaks," Trent said softly. "What if he'd done that when someone was there? If he had set a timer…"

"But he didn't," their mother said.

"He could have." Trent narrowed his eyes. "It's obvious after last night that he's the one that set the trailer on fire and almost burned Trey alive. What if he gets it in his demented mind that one of our

237

homes should be his next target?"

They all heard a gasp and turned to see Kristen hugging the baby to her chest.

"Sorry." Trent sighed. "I should have…"

"No." Their mother stood. "You're right. I've been trying to justify his actions as just anger aimed at the school, but in truth, the school is all of us. It's our baby." She turned and smiled at Kristen, then back at the three boys sitting around the table. "As a mother I don't know what I would do if any harm were to come to you three. And now all of you have your own families, and I think that you understand how it feels to be afraid for their safety. Carl is your father's brother. They had a falling out years ago, and the man is obviously sick." She sat back down. "I suggest we make a move to have him institutionalized."

"Vote?" Tyler said after everyone was silent for a while.

In sync, four fists rose into the air. At the count of three, four thumbs were raised.

"Then it's settled." Tyler stood. "I'll see if Mike can help us make arrangements to take him into custody as soon as possible."

Trey stood up, but before he could go, Tyler laid a hand on his shoulder. "I'm sorry about earlier."

"Don't worry about it." Trey looked past his brother to where Kristen stood, rocking the baby.

"You're still my family," his brother said softly, "always." He held out a hand and Trey hesitated for less than a second before taking his brother's hand in his own.

"I've got to get to work. If you need my help cleaning up out on the site today, let me know."

"Thanks." Tyler smiled and then turned back to his family.

Trey drove into town, unsure of his next move. He glanced at the clock and sighed. It was an hour before Dylan was due in the office. He turned right at the end of the driveway and headed to his land.

Seeing the black spot where his trailer used to sit was depressing. His brother's tractor was still sitting there from the cleanup, so he decided to kill an hour clearing a place for the house he had always dreamed of.

When the engine roared to life, something settled deep inside him and he lost himself to the hum of the beast as it tore out tree stumps and roots.

The trailer had sat closer to the main road, but he wanted his log cabin home to be nestled down by the brook that ran through their land, down in the trees, in the thick of everything. He'd have a large garage up where the trailer used to sit, maybe even a barn for the horses he planned on having. His mother's horse was pregnant and due to drop her colt any day. He planned on convincing her to let him take the animal for his own. He also wanted a chicken coop, maybe even some pigs as well.

When his phone vibrated in his pocket, he ignored it. Hell, he could take a day off once in a while. After all, he was the boss.

When his phone buzzed for the third time in half an hour, he shut the engine off and answered his brother's call.

239

"What?" he barked out.

"Need some help?" He heard a horn honk behind him and glanced over. Tyler and Trent stood leaning against his truck. Both men were dressed to work in the dirt and mud and smiling over at him.

"Jump in, but if you think I'm getting out of Bessy…"

Tyler laughed. "She's all yours." His brother slapped Trent on the shoulder. "Sorry, he's got your woman for the day."

Trey could hear Trent reply, "Damn it" but then he flipped the key and the engine drowned out the rest of his brother's words.

They worked until lunch, when Dylan delivered meals from the Dancing Moose. He hadn't called her, hadn't told her where he was or what he was up to. His brothers must have done it at some point. He felt bad but remained silent about it, since he was still stewing and didn't want her to get any of the anger. She didn't deserve it. He didn't deserve her. That fact was becoming more apparent the longer they were together. She aced every exam, every class she was in without even really trying. He'd worked harder than she had and had barely gotten a pass in the two classes he'd taken. Hell, she'd had to help him through most of it, talking to him softly. He felt like a damn kid infatuated with his teacher.

Sitting across from her on the picnic table he'd built, he felt guilty for not including her in his plans. After all, when he imagined the log cabin home by the brook, he imagined her in it with him.

Chapter Sixteen

$\mathcal{D}$ylan knew something had changed with Trey. She'd heard about the trailer being blown up. After all, she was the one who had to fill in and file the insurance reports. She didn't have all the information yet, but Tony had stopped by and given her a copy of the police report and told her that Carl hadn't been found yet. He assured her they had an APB out on him, and that someone would be watching the office building until he was in custody.

She'd found out that the family wasn't pressing charges from Tony, and that they had plans to have him committed instead.

As she drove away from Trey's property and headed back to the office, she realized Trey had barely said two words to her over lunch. She'd seen his pissed-off look before, but this was something entirely new, and she feared it could be the beginning of the end for them.

After all, why did he, recently, have a new desire

241

to clear his land? Sure, he'd worked on it occasionally in the past, but in the past few days he'd spent most of his free time working on it. Since he'd moved in with her, he'd mentioned starting on the construction of his new house at least a few times. She'd seen the plans to the log cabin kit home he'd ordered. It was a lot like his brother's place. But ever since the fiasco with Brent last night, Trey'd had a fire under him to get working on it now. Was that his way of telling her that he wanted out?

She worried about it the rest of the day. When evening came, she wasn't surprised at all to get a text from him saying that he was going to continue working and would be home late.

When she asked if she could bring him dinner, he replied that his mother had already dropped something off for them. She had a week before her new classes would open to her online, so she spent her evening cleaning the house and then made herself a grilled cheese sandwich and snuggled with Dopey on the window seat in the library to read a book.

She must have fallen asleep, and when she heard a door open and close, she jolted. Frowning, she nudged the sleeping dog off her lap and glanced down the hallway.

When she realized it had been the front door opening, she frowned. Trey never used the front door. It took a few seconds for the dark figure moving towards the stairs to register in her mind.

Her entire body tensed and tingled with fear. She

sat there, almost in shock, as the figure ascended the stairs.

When she heard the top stair creak under a man's weight, she wrapped the throw blanket around Dopey, who whined, picked him up, and rushed out the front door.

She hadn't expected to come face-to-face with another dark figure, who had been standing on the front porch, watching the road as he smoked.

She must have gasped, because the man turned around, his dark mask raised and a cigarette hanging out of his mouth. She saw his face completely and for a moment thought to berate him, but then he moved towards her, darkness in his eyes and she knew she had to do something.

Tossing the blanket off Dopey, she held him out like a weapon. The dog weighed close to twenty pounds, and to her relief, showed his teeth and started growling at the man.

He backed up a step, his hands out as he started muttering. She didn't need any further encouragement to escape and sprinted down the stairs, holding Dopey under her arms as he continued to bark and growl.

At the end of the block, she slowed down and set the heavy dog on the ground next to her. Glancing around, she realized she'd forgotten her phone inside. Encouraging Dopey to follow her, she knocked on the first door with a porch light on. When an older woman answered, she rushed to tell her story.

"Don't worry, honey, come on in. We'll give

Mike a call."

Less than five minutes later, the patrol car pulled up out front. The woman had lent her a leash for Dopey, and the two of them walked out to meet Mike.

"I sent the guys over to the house to check it. We'll wait here until we get the all-clear call." He sighed and waved to Mrs. Anderson, the woman who lived there. "Thanks!"

She turned and smiled at the older woman who'd helped her. She had given her some cookies and Dopey a treat while they waited.

She walked back to the patrol car with Mike and it was no more than a few minutes before his radio came to life.

"All clear," someone said.

Mike turned to her. "Hop in, I'll drive you back. You must be freezing." He nodded to her bare feet.

She nodded and told Dopey to get in, then followed him and sat in the back of the car. When they arrived, she was surprised to see Trey's truck parked beside two other patrol cars.

When she stepped out, he rushed over and gathered her in his arms.

"Are you okay?" he asked, burying his face in her hair. She felt him shaking and before she could respond, he was gathering her up in his arms. Dopey's leash tugged on her hand as the dog raced around Trey's legs.

"I'm fine," she said several times. "Really," she added when Trey set her down inside on the sofa.

"What happened?" he asked, as Mike stepped

inside.

Her eyes traveled between them. "I only saw one of them." She took a deep breath. "It was Jake. He was on the front porch, acting like he was watching out."

"Jake?" Trey frowned.

"I don't know his last name. He's hung around Brent before. He's dropped him off from work a few times before."

"Jake Williams?" Trey turned to Mike, who nodded quickly.

Just then, her brother walked in, followed by Tony.

"Looks like he was fast asleep in the apartment over the garage. He claims to have not heard anything," Tony added.

"What's going on?" Brent looked around.

"Someone broke into the house and had your sister running barefooted for her life down the street." Trey's eyes narrowed as he approached her brother.

"What?" Brent looked over at her, and a hint of worry flashed quickly behind his eyes. "Who was it?"

"Jake," she answered.

She was shocked when her brother began to laugh.

"He told me he'd get me. I just figured he knew I lived over the garage." Her brother relaxed and held up his hands. "It's all a mistake, I'll call him..." He pulled out his phone.

"Breaking and entering is not a mistake," Mike

said, stepping forward.

Brent held up a hand to the officer. "Yo," Brent said into the phone. "The cops are here, saying you broke in?" He listened for a while, then laughed. "That's what I thought. I live over the garage, stupid." He laughed again after listening. "Yeah, come on over." He hung up and turned to them. "They were coming to get me for Seth's stag party."

"Seth Williams?" Mike asked.

"Yeah, he's getting married this weekend, and Jake's throwing him a huge stag party. They didn't tell us when or where it would be, only to be ready sometime this week. They were *kidnapping* guests on the invite list," he said, using air quotes when he said *kidnapping*. "They had joked about doing that, but I didn't think they really would. I'm heading up to get ready." He didn't even turn his eyes towards her to see if she was okay. Instead, he turned to Mike. "I wouldn't be surprised if you have a few more calls about it tonight." He laughed as he left.

Just then, all three of the officers' radios squawked to life and a woman's voice came over the line. *"We have a 207a at 202 Stine Road."*

Mike sighed loudly. "Damn it, those brothers are worse than you lot." He waved Tony and the other officer out of the house.

Trey turned his eyes towards her. "I may have to kill your brother," he said softly as he once more gathered her into his arms as the front door shut.

"You won't get a chance," she replied. "I'm first." She leaned back. "I'm thinking of asking him to find his own place. I don't know how much longer I can deal with this sort of thing."

"Has something like this happened before?" he asked, and she could see worry in his eyes.

"No, just the whole Darla thing. I'd hoped that since that fiasco had run its course I'd have some peace."

"My god." He leaned his forehead on hers. "I'm still shaking. When I drove up and saw the flashing lights…" He reached up and cupped her face. "I should have been here." He kissed her gently. Suddenly, without warning, tears streamed down her face.

"I'm sorry." She wiped at them.

Trey shook his head. "*I'm* sorry." He kissed her softly again. Something deep down inside her popped. If this was close to the end, she at least wanted this moment, this last moment, to be with him, to take what she wanted. She'd make it last a lifetime if she had to, but for now, she just needed him.

Her fingers dug into his hair, holding him to her lips. She pushed his shoulders until he leaned back against the sofa, then she straddled his hips and took the kiss deeper.

She heard him groan as his fingers fumbled to nudge her shirt up.

"Now," she cried out as she tugged his shirt over his head. She sunk her teeth into his shoulder and lapped at the little red mark she'd left as she reached for his jeans. She wanted to mark him like he'd marked her. He'd ruined her for every other man. She would never feel the way she did about him,

247

never again.

"Dylan." It was a warning, but she didn't care. She needed him, now, raw, hard, and more desperately than she'd needed anything in her life. When she gripped him, he jerked in her hand and suddenly she was falling as they rolled to the floor.

Clothes were tossed aside. She scraped her nails and teeth across every inch of his exposed skin as he lapped her up. The roughness of his unshaved face scraped her tender skin, sending shivers racing through her entire body.

Moans and demands echoed in her head as he filled her, giving her exactly what she'd never expected she'd ever get in life.

Even through the roughness, his gentleness broke through the stronghold she'd placed around her heart, and as they reached the peak together, she told him how she felt.

***

Hearing Dylan say she loved him before he'd gotten the chance to say it himself made him smile.

"You beat me to it," he said once his breathing had settled.

They were in a heap on the carpet in front of the dying fire. He was pretty sure he had a few bite marks and rug burns in places he hadn't thought possible. Yet it felt wonderful. He wanted to do it all again in about half an hour, after he'd had a chance to recover fully.

She nudged him until he rolled slightly so he

could look down at her.

"I've never said it before." Her eyes narrowed. "You aren't one of those guys that goes around telling every woman he's with that he loves her, are you?"

He chuckled. "No." He kissed her quickly. "And, technically, I still haven't told someone yet." He settled beside her, resting his head in his hand as he looked down at her, his free hand running slowly over her naked body. His eyes roamed over her skin as the firelight danced over her skin and tattoos. "Hmmm," he sighed. His fingers traced one of the tattoos on her shoulder. This one was a small delicate flower with a lady bug crawling out of the soft petals. His eyes returned to her darker ones. "I never thought I'd find someone like you, someone smart, sexy, strong." He started feeling like a fool.

She smiled. "Go on," she encouraged him.

He chuckled slightly and tried to think of better words and finally came up with something he knew she'd appreciate.

"You're like a cross between Wonder Woman and Black Widow, with the mind of Marie Curie and…" He couldn't think of another example. Then he smiled. "Seven of Nine."

She chuckled. "*Star Trek* fan. Now I know I'm in love with you."

His smile dropped. "I'm crazy for you. From the moment I saw you, I lost my heart to you. It's yours." He leaned in and kissed her. "I love you."

She rolled over quickly and straddled him, their lips joined as she started moving over him. He no longer needed time to recover, not when she could build his needs up again so easily.

This time, instead of speed, they let the passion between them fuel their movements. Slowly they moved together, discovering new pleasures, new desires that had changed with the admission of their feelings. He'd never experienced anything equal to its power.

They fell asleep in each other's arms and slept until the chill woke him. Then he carried her up the stairs, and cradled her in his arms as they slept.

The ringing of her cell phone woke them a few hours later.

"Damn it." She frowned down at the number. "Hello?" she answered. He listened as she talked briefly to someone. "I'll be there..." She glanced over at him. "No, wait." She bit her lip. "No, I won't." She smiled at him. "I think he can deal this time on his own." She listened then smiled. "Thanks." She hung up.

"Well?" He shifted to get a better look at her.

"Seems like the stag party was an enormous success. Brent's down in the holding cell on battery charges. Apparently, they decided the best way to end the party was to have their own version of *Fight Club*."

He groaned and sighed loudly. "And?"

Half a dozen guys are in the drunk tank. The other half are being booked."

"Your brother?" he asked, already knowing the answer.

"Can find his own way out of the mess." She

snuggled back into his arms. "I'm done bailing him out."

He smiled and brushed a hand down her hair.

"Why should I be there for him, when he hasn't been there for me?" she asked.

"Because you're a better person than he is," he answered.

"I know. Carol says he'll be released in the morning with the rest of the drunk ones. He'll have to go to court, but..." She sighed. "There's no reason for me to go down there and sit in an uncomfortable chair the rest of the night waiting for him. He can find his own ride home in the morning."

He chuckled. "I think you've had two major insights tonight."

"Oh?" She glanced up at him. "What was the first one?"

He chuckled and kissed her. "You finally figured out that you love me."

She smiled. "I've know it for weeks, I just didn't think you felt the same way." Her smile fell away. "Actually, after yesterday, I was thinking you wanted to break things off with me."

"Why?" He shifted so he could see her better.

"You acted so... remote yesterday."

He nodded. "I'm sorry, I had... things on my mind."

"About your uncle?"

"No, I was trying to figure out how to convince you to move in with me once the house is done." A look of surprise crossed her eyes.

"You want… me to move into your new house?"

"Yes," he said, his hand still running through her hair.

"As in…" She sat up slightly and his eyes went to where the sheet fell away, exposing her skin. She tucked her knees to her chest, wrapping her arms around them. "A permanent thing?"

He took her hands. "As permanent as it gets." He frowned. "God, that sounds awful."

She laughed. "You can make it sound better tonight, when you take me out for dinner." She leaned in and kissed him. "I can give you my answer then." She lay back down, turning her back to him.

"Hey." He frowned.

"Go back to sleep." She chuckled.

He pulled her close, her body pressed against his. "I don't think I can, now." He wiggled her body against him and she moaned with pleasure.

"No, I suppose not." She shifted.

He moved her slightly, using his hand against her inner thigh to spread her as he slid slowly into her heat.

"Mmmm," she groaned as his lips found a tender spot just under her ear. His free hand wrapped around her, holding her where he wanted her, needed her.

"Tell me again," he whispered against her ear as his movements built.

"I love you." It was a sigh in the night, sending him over the edge.

Chapter Seventeen

*N*othing went right for Dylan the following morning. First, her trusty blow dryer, which she'd had since sixth grade, died on her, which left her heading out to work with damp, curly, out-of-control hair. Then she hadn't been able to find the boots she'd wanted to wear, so she'd pulled on a pair of flat closed-toe shoes that didn't have a chance of keeping her feet warm all day.

Trey had an early morning meeting on a site and had disappeared almost an hour before she went, so she'd eaten breakfast alone.

When she pulled into the parking lot at the old brick building downtown, her brother was standing there, looking haggard and pissed.

"What the hell?" Brent said as soon as she climbed out of the car. Her brother loomed over her, and she straightened her shoulders so she stood at her full five-foot-seven height. Anything to make herself feel less small around him.

"Oh, good, you did find your own ride." She smiled and reached for her purse.

Her brother's hand circled her arm as he pulled her back.

"Dylan, why the hell did you leave me there?"

Her eyes narrowed. "I don't know, Brent. Why the hell did you allow two of your idiot friends to break in and scare me to death? Why didn't you give a damn about me when someone broke into the office and knocked me unconscious? You didn't even stop by the clinic to see if I was okay!" She hadn't realized she'd been screaming in his face until her last words echoed off the bricks. Lowering her voice, she took a step back and crossed her arms over her chest. "You've been less like a brother to me every year since the accident. I'm tired of playing parent to you. I need to focus on my own life. I don't have the strength anymore to raise you." She rubbed her fingers over her forehead. "I can't keep caring about someone who doesn't care about me." She turned to go, but once again, Brent's hand on her shoulder stopped her. She turned, prepared to yell some more, but what she saw in her brother's eyes shocked her. Tears filled the brown eyes that matched hers perfectly.

"I'm sorry," he said softly. "I... didn't know..." He shook his head. "I fucked up." He sighed. "No one asked me if I was prepared to take on such big responsibilities at such a young age." He closed his eyes. "I've been pissed at our folks." His eyes opened, and she could see something behind them that she had either been too blind to see or hadn't

254

noticed before. Pain. "They should have made better choices. They should have planned for something like this. Instead, they continued living like…"

"Children?" She sighed.

"I was thrust into adulthood when I was only twenty-one. I didn't know what to do to make house payments. Hell, they didn't either. They were months behind on the house payment when they died." He ran his hands through his hair.

"What?" She blinked. It was the first she'd been told about it.

"One of the cars had already been repossessed before we took the trip." He leaned against her car. "My truck was next. Thankfully, they had enough life insurance policies to pay it off."

"Brent." She reached up and touched his shoulder.

"I wanted you to go to college." He closed his eyes. "Hell, everyone knew I wasn't smart, but you." He smiled down at her. "Wile E. Coyote." The use of his old nickname made her smile. "Super genius," he finished. "I had always expected that you'd go to Harvard or Yale. Then… they left us with a mess and nothing mattered anymore." His shoulders slumped. "I fucked everything up. Just like they did."

"Hey." She stepped closer. "You've gotten us this far." She wrapped her arms around him and held him close for the first time in years. "You can go the rest of the way. I'll help you."

He shook his head. "No, I don't want to drag you

down with me. You've got a fresh start here." He glanced around. "You'll be better off if I leave."

She remained silent, her heart sinking slightly. "What about your job?"

He glanced around. "I have a chance to transfer to a job site in North Dakota for the McGowans. I think I'll take it. Jake is heading there after Seth's wedding. I've told him I'll drive. I've already packed."

It was a blow but seeing the excitement in her brother's eyes as he talked about going to North Dakota eased the pain a little.

"When do you leave?" she asked.

"Monday. I've already told Tyler I'll take the job." He looked back down at her. "I just didn't have enough courage to tell you, until now." He ran his hand over her shoulder. "I'm sorry,"

She nodded, then realized she'd been crying and wiped the tears away. "You'll be back?"

He nodded. "It's just a temporary transfer. I need to…" He looked around. "Take a break."

"Did she break your heart?" she asked suddenly.

"Who?" He laughed. "Darla?" She nodded. "No, I broke it off with her. I found her poking holes in my condoms."

"What?" Instantly she was pissed.

"Yeah, seems like she's desperate to have kids." He shrugged.

"I'm sorry." She hugged him. "If you need anything…"

"No. I'm sorry about leaving you high and dry with the rent, but Tyler assured me that they would work something out."

"Don't worry, Trey's been covering it."

He nodded. "You serious about this guy?" he asked.

"Yes," she answered quickly. "Very,"

Brent nodded. "Good, he's… Hell, a lot better than I am to you."

She smiled. "You're my brother."

"That's no excuse." He glanced around as a truck drove up. "I've got to get to work. I'll see you tonight."

"Brent," she called after him. "I love you."

Her brother smiled. "Right back at ya, kiddo."

It was a statement he'd made all his life and love flooded her heart. As bad as her morning had been, her day was looking up and she knew that evening, it was only going to get better.

Just remembering the tenderness that Trey had shown her the night before kept a warm glow spreading throughout her the rest of her workday.

Trent and Tyler came and went. Trey had called and canceled their standard lunch date so he could play catch-up for missing the day before.

Since she was on top of all her work and her next classes weren't open up to her yet, she decided to finish cleaning up some of Rea's old files on the computer.

She'd started organizing the old files and emails the week after getting hired and every time she had downtime, she would work on them.

There were a few new emails she questioned, several from a lawyer named Steven Rice. She

257

forwarded them on to Tyler, knowing he would take care of them, then got back to work archiving the rest.

Today, she figured she could get through all of Rea's old emails. She was going through the oldest emails when she had to stop and read a few several times.

It was a grouping of emails between Carl and Rea. Carl used to work for McGowan Enterprises, and there had been hundreds of such emails, which she had either filed or deleted due to lack of official business in them, and nothing stood out about these emails at first. After glancing through the rest, she'd gathered that Rea wasn't too fond of Carl. But then she got to this email.

I know we agreed never to talk about that night, but I found a letter from a clinic in Helena. Gavin went there and was tested. They say that he's sterile. I don't know if I should give it to him or not. What am I going to do? -R

The reply was short.

Throw it away.

There was another one from Rea, marked two days later.

The clinic keeps calling. I'm scared. -R

Again, Carl had only a few words in reply.

I'll handle it.

The last one from Rea was short.

Gavin knows that Brian isn't his.

She got to the end of the emails and sat there rereading them until her phone rang, jolting her out of the trance.

"Hey." Hearing Trey's voice made her wonder if they knew.

"Hey," she said, unsure what to do with the emails and the knowledge.

"What's wrong?" he asked.

"I... found something out." She closed the emails down. "I..." She opened them again and hit print. "We can talk later." She tucked the prints into her purse.

"Is it bad?" he asked.

"Um, I don't know." She remembered that Rea's ex-husband had killed himself years ago and wondered if the dates were close to when the emails had been written. "It has the potential to be."

"I'm heading to the office. I'm done for the—" His phone buzzed, interrupting his words. "Got another call. I'll call you right back."

"Okay." She hung up and did a quick search on the local newspaper's website to see if she could find Gavin Laster's obituary announcement.

The emails were dated days before the man was found hanging from the bridge on Interstate 41.

Dylan's heart skipped. When her phone rang, she knew she had to tell the McGowans.

"Hey, there's an emergency up at the Meier Ranch site. I'll be about an hour."

"Should I call your brothers?" she asked, tucking the emails back in her purse.

"No, I've got this. I'll see you when I get there. It should be shortly after five." He took a deep breath. "I can't wait to hear your answer tonight."

She smiled and nodded. "I'll see you then."

When they hung up, she turned back to the computer. She decided to not move the string of emails, but just to continue through the remaining ones.

There were several she'd printed out from Carl to Trey's father, Thurston. In the beginning, the brothers had gotten along, even joked with one another. Sometime shortly after the emails between Rea and Carl, things had changed. A pattern of Carl going downhill had emerged. She immediately wondered if it was due to Gavin Laster's death.

Over the next hour she built a chart of events. She searched the newspaper archives for any information on Carl and Rea, and even on Trey's father.

She was surprised when an article with a massive image popped up on her screen. The image was of a six-year-old Thurston Noah McGowan the third, who was standing in front of the baseball fields holding a large trophy. His long blonde hair was curling down in front of his blue eyes as he smiled widely, showing a large gap where his front teeth should have been.

She couldn't help but smile at the kid he'd been. Then, without warning, a daydream filled her mind of how their son would look just like that. Her entire body tensed as the imagination took flight. A son who looked like Trey, and also a look-alike daughter.

When the phone rang, she shook the daydream off and answered the call as she glanced at the clock, Trey should be there any time now.

"The McGowans have been warned." The voice was low, and she had to pinch her other ear closed to hear. "His blood is on their hands." The line went dead.

Her heart jumped a beat and she fumbled as she punched the button to call Trey's line. When he didn't answer, she called Tyler, who picked up on the second ring.

"I can't get a hold of Trey. Someone called. They said his blood is on your hands." She knew she sounded hysterical, but she couldn't control herself.

"What?" Tyler asked.

She repeated herself and she could hear as Tyler turned to someone. "Call Trey." He came back to her. "I'm with Trent. Where was he last?"

"Um, he was heading to the Meier Ranch. He received a call saying there was an emergency up there."

"We're turning around and heading there now." She heard tires squeal. At the same moment, Dylan felt the earth rattle. Everything in the office shook and pictures fell off the walls. She held onto her desk as the entire building jumped.

"Jesus!" Tyler screamed in her ear. "Oh Jesus, no!"

***

As Trey drove up to the Meier Ranch, he thought about the perfect night he had planned.

Dinner was being delivered to his property sharply at six o'clock by Basia, a local chef who owned a catering business in town. She made some of the most sought-after meals in town and had catered both Tyler and Trent's weddings.

He'd ordered her specialty meal with pierogi, a dumpling stuffed with meat, cheese, and potatoes, along with a salad, hors d'oeuvres, and the champagne that she had suggested. The evening would be perfect.

He'd asked his brothers to set up the scene after they got off work. They were hanging lights and putting their mother's good tablecloth on the picnic table, along with setting up candles and the portable fire pit so they could enjoy the evening without getting too cold.

If all went well, everything would be perfect and in place by the time they arrived at six-thirty. The only thing left for him to do was come up with the right words. This had been his problem all day long.

Words weren't his strong suit. Hell, he'd flunked eight grade English class. Okay, it was mainly Susie Grimes's fault. She'd sat in front of him all year long with her pretty blonde hair and her freshly grown boobs. He'd blamed the new hormones pulsing through his fifteen-year-old body for his grades that year.

Now the only eyes he thought of were a pair of honey brown ones that looked up at him with love and lust mixed together.

Dylan was his ideal woman, the one he'd never imagined he'd find. Even though they'd been rough, his words to her last night had been from the heart.

He'd never imagined he'd find someone like her. He'd been jealous watching his brothers find and fall in love with their new wives. There had been bumps in the road, but it had always been clear that the two older McGowans would get their happy ever after. Not that he thought he wasn't worthy of getting his, but he'd always imagined something getting in the way of it.

Trey parked his truck alongside the oil pump. The Meier's site had been setup last year. There were six pumps on their ranch and, so far, it had given the couple enough profit that they'd retired and purchased a house in Florida.

Why was it that everyone always retired to Florida? he wondered as he got out of his truck. The sound of the pump was deafening. Something was off. Normally, they made a low humming noise or a squeaking noise from the rusted metal. This one, however, was making a terrible grinding noise and wasn't turning at all.

He must have taken no more than two steps towards the machine when he heard a clicking noise. As if in slow motion, he watched a spark fly from the pump's drive area. He took a step backwards and watched in horror as the small explosion grew. When the blast hit him, he knew he was screwed.

He'd hardly had time to jump behind the wheel well of the truck before the second, bigger blast shook the ground. The wheel well shielded him from most of the flames shooting his way. Still, he felt his clothing and skin heat as the fire circled him.

He was fully surrounded within a matter of seconds as the pump shook once more. He knew he only had minutes before the fire would reach the valve that led to the main pipeline. If he couldn't get to the switch to shut the valve off, the entire damn field could blow. He crawled, army style, under his truck and glanced around as the green grass surrounding him charred with flames.

The switch was across the road and surrounded by some of the bigger flames. It was too far away for him to get to in time. His only hope was to find shelter from the blast that he knew was coming.

Glancing around, he noticed the long ditch that the Meier's had used to bring fresh river water to their crops and animals in the far field. From this angle, he couldn't see if it was full of water, but with the snow thawing the last few days, he prayed it was.

He was halfway across the space when he heard a change in the sound coming from the pump. Instead of the high-pitched hiss, there was now a low rumbling sound coming from somewhere underground. He was too late.

He dove for the ditch, praying that he'd survive to see Dylan one more time.

Chapter Eighteen

*D*ylan sat in the front seat of her brother's truck, biting her nails, as he drove up the hill.

At this point, the entire hillside a few miles from Haven was engulfed in fire. The newly green trees were all burning, sending smoke up to fill the darkened night sky. It had been less than fifteen minutes since the earth had shaken with an explosion could have been felt across all of Montana.

She tapped the fingers of her free hand on the phone in her lap. She kept looking down at the screen, waiting for Tyler to call her back.

Looking at the growing glow they were driving towards, all she could think of was that Trey was in there somewhere.

When her phone did ring, she fumbled and almost dropped it.

"Hello?"

"Hey, we're blocked. We can't get up the hill the

rest of the way. The fire is too bad up this way. We'll have to go around or wait for the fire crew. Mike's warned us not to go in, but…"

"He's your brother," she answered. "Be safe. We're heading up there now."

"No. Do me a favor and head on down to my mom's place. Everyone's gathering there. When we find Trey, he'll kick our ass if we let you anywhere near this mess."

She looked over at her brother. He'd shown up a few minutes after the explosion to check on her, a new step she had been thankful he'd taken, since she didn't think she could have driven herself anywhere. She'd convinced him to drive her towards the fire instead of away.

"Tyler, I can't… I need to…"

"Dylan." Tyler's voice lowered. "Please, don't make me beg. Go make sure my family's okay and take care of my mom. She's probably a mess."

She sighed. "Okay, only if you promise to call the moment you know anything."

"I promise," he said before hanging up.

"Head to the McGowan's place instead." She glanced out the window at the glow just over the horizon.

"You sure?" her brother asked.

"Yes, it's too dangerous. I'm supposed to wait there with Trey's family."

The truck turned and suddenly she was heading away from Trey. Her heart sank as they turned a corner and the full effects of the fire could be seen. At this point, it was more than just one hill on fire.

From this view, it appeared the entire horizon was glowing red.

When she arrived at the McGowan's place, Gail was on the front porch, as if she'd been waiting for her. Her phone was in her hands and Dylan knew that Tyler had called to let his mother know she was on her way over.

Before she could get out of the truck, she was being drawn into the older woman's arms in a hug that forced all the wetness out of Dylan's eyes. Crying on the woman's shoulder drained her of any energy she had left.

"Come on inside, both of you. Everyone's arriving. I'm sure we'll have plenty of food while we wait." She nodded to a few more cars that were pulling in behind them.

Sure enough, within the hour, the kitchen table and countertops were completely full of wonderful-smelling dishes. Dylan couldn't stomach eating anything. Even when Addy delivered a plate to her, she set it down and pushed the food around without eating anything.

Every time the phone rang, she jumped. The TV in the main room was on the local news with the volume set to low. They had coverage of the fire and were able to get more updates from the TV than they were from phone calls.

Each time Tyler or Trent checked in, they didn't say much other than they hadn't found Trey yet and that they were safe.

Dylan noticed that they called her instead of their mother. It was after the first hour that she realized

267

that Gail wasn't in as bad a shape as Tyler had let her believe she was in. Dylan was in far worse shape than anyone in the house.

Dylan hadn't bitten her nails in years, but she found herself biting them now and pacing across the wood floor.

Addy was by her side the entire time. She had at one point fallen asleep in the chair but woke when Dylan's phone rang again. Her friend looked worried and very tired.

"They spotted his truck from the helicopter," Trent told her. "It was sitting where they believe the explosion happened."

"Oh god," she cried out, covering her mouth as she sat down. A hand went to her shoulder as she closed her eyes. The entire room was quiet as they waited to hear more.

"No, that's a good thing." He added. "They had enough space to get close. He wasn't in it or anywhere near there, which means he's on the run somewhere. The fire near that part of the hill is still out of control, so they're having to back off until they can drop another bucket of water. The emergency fire crews arrived on scene and have kicked us out, but we're going to stick around here."

"What can we do?" she asked, looking around the room.

"Stay put, pray, keep watch over my mother and family." He added, "I'll call again soon." He hung up.

Waiting was pure hell. The clock ticked slowly as everyone came and went. Blankets were draped over her as she sat in the chair. At one point, she felt her head dipping and her eyes closing. Jolting awake, she walked into the kitchen and poured herself a cup of coffee, then stepped out on the back patio, into the chilled night air, and watched the bright red glow from over the hills. Now it appeared the entire mountain was on fire, glowing like a massive volcano hovering over the town.

"How are you doing?"

Dylan turned to see Kristen's mother, Trisha, step out onto the deck, a cup of steaming coffee in her hands.

"I'm scared," she admitted to the woman. They had chatted a few times when she'd seen her at the store or the Dancing Moose.

"I know the feeling. When Kristen was taken last year… It's the worst feeling in the world, having to wait for news." She leaned against the deck and looked out over the darkness. "What a mess."

"What happened?" she finally asked.

Trisha leaned back. "I don't know. You said he was called out there on an emergency call?" Dylan nodded. "Maybe he arrived too late to stop whatever happened?"

"Pumps just don't blow up. I've been doing a lot of research since I was hired. Once the pump is in place, the chance of it sparking and blowing are very slim. The Meier property was set up a few months ago. Everything had been inspected and signed off on. There shouldn't have been any issues."

Trisha sighed. "I don't really know much about

what happens, but obviously something went wrong."

Dylan thought over everything she'd learned in the past few months since working at McGowan. She'd even gone to the length of watching safety videos. Usually, problems were related directly to employee errors. Trey couldn't have been there long enough to do anything. Nor was anyone else on the site at the time. She hadn't known that until after the fact, when every employee had been accounted for. The other troubling item was that no one admitted that they had called him about an issue at the Meier's Ranch.

She hadn't told anyone yet about her fears or her speculations. But their uncle was an expert in explosions, and she had a gut feeling that, no matter what Trey had done, the outcome would have been the same. She knew that the family probably thought the same, especially after catching him blow the trailer on video. It was a jump from blowing up a vacant trailer to blowing up your nephew, but still, if it was true that Carl was out of his mind, maybe he'd crossed that line.

Her stomach ached as her mind wondered about the possibilities. When her phone rang again, she was ready. Tyler had taken to calling on the top and the bottom of every hour.

"Any news?" she asked, still looking out over the darkness.

The long pause told her it wasn't good. She didn't hear the glass door open behind her but felt the presence of several other people on the deck with them.

"They have found a body." Tyler sighed. "They haven't given me any other information other than it appears to be a male. But the body they found was in a car, so there's a good chance it isn't Trey. They think it was someone trying to escape the flames."

Her head spun quickly, and she realized in slow motion that the phone had slipped from her fingers. By the time it hit the deck, blackness had overtaken her.

**

Trey was up shit's creek. Literally. His entire body was covered in the wet smelly stuff. All the water had evaporated shortly after the fire surrounded him, blocking him in his current location. After the massive explosion that had knocked him on his ass, he'd let the water he'd jumped into carry him down the hill as fast as it could. He figured he'd traveled almost a full mile before the rushing water had slowed to a trickle.

Then he'd gained his feet and run as fast as he could through the knee-high sludge. When the water had stopped all together, he knew it had been blocked somewhere upstream by the fire that lapped at his heels. So, he'd run even faster.

He stayed by the dry water bed, hoping somewhere it would open to a lake or a stream. He realized that somewhere he'd dropped his phone. Maybe it had flown out of his pocket when he'd been carried away by the cool water. Hell, maybe he'd left it in his truck.

It didn't matter now. He doubted it would have survived the wet trip anyway. Still, he knew his family would be worried sick and wanted to ease some of that pain. But every time he glanced around, he realized quickly that he wasn't out of the worst of it yet.

He was about to lose hope. The ditch had dried up completely and the mixture of mud and cow dung at the bottom was caking up so that it was almost impossible for him to run through. Fire lapped at either side of the banks, singeing his skin and clothes.

He had covered his face with the T-shirt he'd ripped off his back and soaked in the water before it had disappeared. Breathing was becoming almost impossible. He'd traveled almost another mile when finally the ditch opened up to a larger creek. He was thankful, as he'd been starting to get light-headed.

Diving into the cold water, he felt his skin sizzle and soothe. Relief turned to sheer panic when he glanced around and realized the fire was already surrounding the waterway.

His best bet was to move to the center of the creek and float until someone spotted him. He'd thought a few moments ago that he'd heard the whiz of a chopper overhead.

He didn't know how long he'd been gone or how long it had been since the explosion, all he knew was that he was exhausted. His legs ached and as he floated in the freezing water, he imagined just letting go and drifting away.

Part of his mind screamed that it was shock and

he should get out of the cold, but the bigger part of his mind told him he could take a few minutes more to enjoy the peacefulness of it all.

Glancing up at the night sky as he floated downstream, he watched the flying sparks mix with the stars overhead. The roaring sound of the fire mixed with the calm sound of the rushing water. His mind drifted and thoughts of floating away almost overtook him.

He had just closed his eyes when his mind snapped an image of Dylan quickly behind his eyelids. Her eyes were red, and she cried out his name over and over. The image shook him out of the trance. His body jolted, and he spit out the water that he'd sucked into his lungs.

He fought the water, forcing himself to find a stronghold and plant his feet on the rocky bottom of the growing river.

The sky had turned a lighter color and it took him a moment to realize that it wasn't because of the fire. The sun was slowly rising over the east hills. He had to blink a few times to realize that he was no longer surrounded by fire and destruction.

Instead, he stood in a green field near the edge of a slow flowing river. It was the most beautiful sight he'd ever seen. He crawled out onto the rocky bank and glanced around. His mind and body were too cold to register just where he was.

He shook his head several times but still wasn't able to focus. His body shook with the cold and every time his breath escaped, puffs of white smoke floated overhead.

273

He rung out his wet shirt and thought about putting it back on, then dismissed the idea of putting something even wetter than he was over his chilled skin.

The other side of the lake was a steep incline uphill. The side he'd crawled out of was muddy and full of tall grasses. He slowly made his way out of the muck, getting stuck several times and almost losing his work boots in the process.

By the time his feet hit dry ground, the sun was bright enough that he could figure out where he was. There was a bead of sweat rolling down his shoulders as he looked around.

"Jensen's cabin." He practically screamed it, and his voice and words echoed back to him, bouncing off the rocks around him.

His legs muscles screamed at him as he rushed across the small field towards the cabin. He knew that old man Jensen had an old CB radio in the hunting cabin. When he reached the door, he didn't hesitate to use the hidden key under the wood carving of Jensen's old dog, Buddy, to unlock it and step inside.

Taking the blanket from the back of the sofa, he wrapped it around himself and sat in front of the radio and flipped it on.

Chapter Nineteen

*D*ylan rushed from the truck and met the paramedics as they wheeled Trey out of the cabin. She reached for his hand but stopped when she noticed the white bandages wrapped around his arms.

"Hey, gorgeous." He smiled up at her. His skin was red, his blonde curls singed, but he was the best thing she'd seen in years.

"Hey." She smiled down at him as tears rolled down her face. She wiped them away quickly.

"Don't do that." He looked like he wished he could reach up and touch her, but he was strapped down to the gurney. Even though his face was red, as if sunburned, she could see how pale he was under the burns.

"God, don't cry, baby. You're breaking my heart."

"How is he?" she asked the paramedic.

"We'll know more once they give him a full

275

examination. Right now, we're treating his immediate burns and dehydration along with hypothermia."

"Hypothermia?" She glanced down at Trey.

"Only my baby brother could get hypothermia in the middle of a fire," Tyler said from beside her.

Trey chuckled then winced. "Damn it." He sighed. "Shut the hell up,"

Tyler laughed, then turned to her. "He won't be able to live this one down. Why don't you ride with him? We'll meet you at the clinic." Tyler pushed Trent towards their truck.

"How are you feeling?" she asked as they loaded him in the back of the ambulance. She climbed in behind him and settled next to him as the paramedic strapped her in.

"Well, right now, everything is still pretty frozen from my nice lazy float downstream. But when things start to wake up..." They started bumping down the dirt road towards the highway.

He was talking slower than normal and she could tell it was costing him a great deal of effort, so she decided to talk to him instead of asking him questions.

"Your mom and everyone else went directly to the clinic." She told him everything that had happened, who had shown up, what food they had brought. When she finally took a break between words, she realized Trey had fallen asleep.

"He's exhausted, ma'am. Besides, we've given him a little something for the pain." The paramedic assured her, "His vitals are very strong and steady.

The burns are only on his arms and neck area. His body temperature is back to normal, so he should make a full recovery. He's lucky. Real lucky."

"Yes." She smiled down at him. "Yes, he is."

When they reached the clinic, she stood back as they pulled him out of the back and wheeled him inside. Trey's eyes opened slightly as he was wheeled past his family. Gail began to cry as soon as she saw him.

"I'm okay, really," he reassured her.

"You don't look okay," she said softly. "You look like you've run through the gates of hell and back."

He smiled. "I feel like it, but... I'm here."

"We'll have to talk about how you are and what happened when you're feeling better," Tony said, standing next to Gail.

Dylan saw Trey's demeanor change. His eyes turned darker. She followed him into the back room. Several nurses entered, and she stood out of their way as they got to work cleaning Trey up and treating his burns.

She relaxed when she saw that his burns weren't as bad as she had feared.

Most of the red marks were on his upper body. He must have, at one point, removed his shirt, since there were red marks all over his chest, back, and arms. They covered him with salve, then wrapped what they could in clean bandages. He had a few large cuts as if he'd landed on his knees at one point, as well as a slice just below his left shoulder blade. They gave him a few stitches for the slice and covered the cuts on his knees with more bandages.

She hadn't realized he'd been watching her until her eyes returned to his.

"So, am I still sexy?" He smiled at her.

She laughed. "You surprise me." She moved to his side and took his freshly bandaged hand.

"Oh?"

"It's not as bad as we all feared. How did it happen?" she asked as the last nurse finished up.

Trey's smile fell away. "There were several small explosions, which caused the main pump and pipe to go."

"Your uncle?" she asked. Trey sighed and nodded.

"I don't know who else, at this point. Unless they find proof..." He leaned his head back and closed his eyes.

"You must be tired." She stroked his hand with her fingers.

"Don't leave me, okay?" His eyes opened slightly.

"I'm not going anywhere," she assured him as he fell back asleep.

She pulled a chair over towards the bed he was resting in. Nurses came and went, some checking his vitals, others wrapping him in fresh warm blankets. His mother and brothers entered the small room and made themselves comfortable as he slept.

When Addy and Kristen came in later, the sky outside the window had grown dark again.

"Any news?" Addy whispered.

"He's been resting." She smiled and took the coffee mug Addy handed her, then hugged her friend when she brandished a box of donuts.

"I hope there's some of that for me." Trey's voice caused everyone in the room to jump.

"We didn't mean to wake you. I was trying to be quiet," Addy said.

"You didn't. The smell of coffee and sugar woke me." He leaned up, then winced.

"Here." She set her coffee down and hit the button on the side of the bed to sit him up. Then she turned and handed him the cup to sip from.

"Nectar from the heavens." He sighed after a long sip of the hot fluid. "Did I smell donuts?"

"I don't know why we even worried about him in the first place," Tyler joked.

"Stop it," Gail said, waving at her oldest son as she moved over to Trey's side and held out the box Kristen had handed her.

"Are you sure you're cleared to eat that much sugar?" Trent asked.

"Shut up," Trey said between bites.

"So," Tyler said when Trey had finished his second donut, "are you going to tell us what happened, or do we have to see it on the news?"

Trey hit the button again and sat further up. "Someone blew the pump. Two quick pops and I had less than two minutes to find shelter before it hit the main pipe."

Everyone in the room was silent. "I think we'd better ask Tony and Mike to come in." Tyler stood up and walked out. Within five minutes, Mike and Tony followed him back into the room.

"Go on." Tyler motioned as Mike pulled out a

notepad.

Trey glanced around. "I arrived after receiving a call."

"Who from?" Mike interrupted.

"I'm not sure at this point. I thought it was someone from NewField. It sounded like a standard call from one of their dispatchers."

"About?" Mike asked.

"A pump in distress, at least that's what he said. I drove out, parked, before I took two steps, the first explosion hit. Blew me back a few steps." Trey sighed heavily and reached for Dylan's hand. "Things went to hell after that."

"Did you see anyone nearby?" Mike asked.

"No," Trey answered.

"What happened next?" Tyler asked.

"I knew the big one was coming, so I ran towards the water ditch, the one that runs down to the other side of the property. I floated, then ran, then floated until I ended up at Jensen's place."

"You mean to tell us you spent your time floating down the river like a lazy river ride?" Trent asked.

"It beat running in the burning woods." Trey smiled. "Of course, the water was freezing cold."

"I'd take hypothermia any day over burning," Tyler said softly.

"Smart," Mike added.

"Not too smart. Something blocked the flow of water, and I spent half the night outrunning the fire in mud and cow dung."

"Do they know who they found yet?" Tyler asked, turning to Mike.

"No, I'm heading over to the coroner next to see if we have an ID."

"You found someone?" Trey broke in.

"Less than a mile from the blast site. On the side road, heading up to the Meier's house."

"It was empty, right?" Dylan asked.

"The Meier's moved to Florida just before Christmas. The place was empty until they found renters," Mike answered. "No one should have been up that way."

"Do you think it's him?" Tyler asked, glancing over to his brothers.

"Do I think it was Carl who lured me out there and tried to blow me up?" Trey was silent for a while. "Hell, every part of me is screaming, yes. But I just don't know. Something about it doesn't sit right. Why tell me he's dying? Why the whole sob story?"

"To throw us off?" Tyler suggested.

"Instead of sitting around speculating, why don't we get a healthy meal into Trey and let him rest?" Gail stood up.

"We'll head down and get something for him in the cafe." Tyler took Kristen's hand.

"I'll go with them." Gail turned and gave everyone else in the room a look, and they all followed her out the door with their own excuses.

Dylan found herself alone with Trey as the door to the room shut behind the last visitor.

"How are you feeling?" she asked, suddenly nervous.

"Come here." He motioned to the spot next to

281

him on the bed.

When she walked over to the side of the bed, he reached up and gently tugged her until she crawled in bed next to him.

"Now I'm better." He sighed as he settled his arm around her carefully.

"You might hurt yourself," she warned.

"It'll be worth it."

She rested her head gently on his shoulder. "I thought I'd lost you," she said softly. She'd cried all her tears, or so she'd thought.

"Hey now." He nudged her chin up with his bandaged hand. "If you do that, then I'm going to have to explain to my family why I spent this time alone with you wiping your tears away."

She smiled. "Yes." She searched his eyes and waited until recognition of the unasked question hit the blueness of them. She was slightly surprised by the humor she saw behind them.

"I haven't officially asked, yet." He wiped a tear away with his fingers and it soaked into the cotton bandage.

"You don't have to ask." She took his face in her hands. "You never did." Leaning slightly, she touched her lips to his chapped ones. "I can't imagine my life without you, I don't want to."

This time it was her turn to wipe the wetness from his face.

"I've been looking for the words to tell you how you make me feel." He closed his eyes and took a deep breath. When they opened again, they were focused. "The truth is, there are no words. You're more to me than anyone or anything has ever been in my life. If you were by my side for two lifetimes, I doubt I'd have the right words to express just how you make me feel."

She placed a finger over his lips. "Thurston Noah McGowan the third, ask me." He smiled at his name on her lips.

"Dylan..."

"Grace." She supplied her middle name with a smile.

"Dylan Grace McCaw, will you marry me?"

"Yes," she said before gently placing her lips over his.

"Finally," someone said from the doorway, "now we can eat." Tyler barged in, followed by the rest of his family.

***

Trey was glad to be back at home. Dopey was curled up at his feet on the sofa while he watched the news about the ongoing fight against the fire, which was now almost ninety percent contained. Dylan and his mother were in the kitchen making dinner.

He'd gotten a somewhat clean bill of health, along with a bottle of pain pills and a request to return to the doctor in a week to check his progress.

His brothers had updated him on the news that it hadn't been their uncle in the charred car. The age was all wrong. The remains had been a male in his late forties to early fifties.

The town was currently trying to figure out who was missing. More than a hundred homes had been evacuated on the far side of town. Half a dozen people were camped out at his mother's place. The rest of them were crammed into the local community center, the town hall, and even the school's gym.

Television stations from all over the state and nation were now parked outside the mayor's office. For her part, Martha Brown had done more television interviews than he was sure she ever thought she would when she became mayor of the sleepy old town.

McGowan Enterprises had, of course, been associated with the fire, but it was being made clear by both the mayor and the police that the fire was not due to any employee's negligence, and that sabotage was suspected.

The news stations spun their own webs about the suspect being the forty to fifty-year-old male they had found burned in the car, which had been parked less than a mile away from the initial explosion.

When a knock sounded on the front door, he was pushed back into place by his mother who rushed to answer it.

He wasn't surprised to see Mike and Tony walk in.

"What's the news?" Dylan asked, walking in from the kitchen, wiping her hands on a dishrag.

Mike spoke first. "We've got an ID on the person who rented the car. Dennis Rodgers. We haven't positively ID the body yet, but the description fits.

We did find other explosives in the trunk of the car. For the past week, he'd been staying at a hotel in Helena, since he had been kicked out of his apartment in town. You know that Crystal had filed for divorce. She ended up getting everything—full custody of the kids, the house, you name it."

"Yeah," Trey said, "she deserved it all."

"She hasn't seen him since the explosion, but we're checking just in case."

"Do you question it's him?" Gail asked.

"Until we have a positive ID, we can't afford to assume, but..." He shook his head.

"Do you think he worked alone?" Trey asked the question he'd been wondering.

Mike ran his hand over the back of his neck. "We can't officially say anything further." His eyes moved to Tony's. Then he groaned. "Go ahead. Hell, we both know Trey had nothing to do with it. Besides, it'll be on here in a few minutes." He nodded to the television

Tony nodded. "The official ruling on the death was murder."

Trey heard both Dylan and his mother gasp.

"Can you give us any more details?" Gail stepped forward. "Have you found Carl?"

"No, we're still out looking, but with the fire and all the press, we're shorthanded at the moment."

"I understand, thank you." She walked over and hugged Tony. "Be safe out there," she said softly to the man who'd helped her get over the death of a man she described as the only love of her life. Losing his father had been hard but seeing his

285

mother lonely had been even harder. He and his brothers hadn't liked the idea of their mother dating at first, but seeing her with Tony had changed their minds.

Tony was one of the best kind of men. He and his brothers had always looked up to the man, who had lost his first wife long before Trey could remember. He'd been a widower without any kids and had put his career helping the town of Haven before anything else.

As the men left, Trey turned up the volume of the TV as Martha stepped into focus in front of town hall.

They listened to her latest update, informing the population that the police believed that the body found was the culprit behind the explosions. She didn't name names, since his family members hadn't been informed yet. But she did state that investigators had confirmed that McGowan Enterprises has been cleared of any wrongdoing. Then, to his surprise, she added a small statement about the Thurston McGowan Flathead Drilling Training Center plans.

"Nice plug." Dylan smiled down at him.

"Yeah." He hated that all the destruction Dennis had caused would probably end up being good for his family's business.

"Do you think Carl helped Dennis, then killed him?" Gail turned to him.

He shrugged, then instantly regretted the move and winced.

"Rest." His mother laid a hand gently on his arm.

286

"Dinner's almost ready. Everyone will be here before we know it."

"Everyone's coming over?" He hated that it came out as a groan, but he had planned to cuddle with Dylan and Dopey on the sofa for the night.

"Family meeting," Gail added. "Sorry. We'll be quick so you can get your rest."

He watched the newscast with little interest. The overhead shots of the fire were heartbreaking, especially the image of the shell of his burned-out truck. Still, he could see that the fire was under control now.

Close to five thousand acres and half a dozen buildings, including the Meier's home, barn, and garage, were all destroyed. The land would slowly make a comeback, and homes would be rebuilt, but the lives of those who'd survived would always be changed, including his.

He doubted he could hear a loud noise without wincing or enjoy a swim in a cool lake without remembering the time he'd spent wondering if he'd survive.

He glanced over at Dylan and smiled, knowing she was going to be by his side for the rest of his life.

By the time his brothers and their wives arrived, he was starved and tired. He couldn't determine which he wanted more, sleep or food.

Instead of having him join everyone at the table, a plate was delivered to him on the sofa. Still, he could hear the conversation in the other room perfectly. There was talk of Dennis Rodgers and

Carl and how the two of them were tied together.

"I don't know if this might explain the relationship between Dennis and Carl, but, well, I was going to show this to Trey when I had a chance…" Dylan shocked them all with the piece of paper she pulled from her purse.

Chapter Twenty

Reading the emails to Trey's family was nerve-wracking. It may not have anything to do with Dennis and Carl working together, but it might shed some light on Carl's behavior in the past.

"Brian is Carl's son?" Gail shook her head. "That doesn't..." She was quiet for a while then sighed. "I suppose part of me knew it long ago." She glanced around the table.

Trey had picked himself off the sofa and moved over to the table to sit next to her. She could tell by the way he walked that he was hurting, and she hated seeing him in pain.

"Why?" Trey asked.

Gail looked over at him. "The four of you, when you were young, used to play together in the office when we were busy or Rea had to step out for a call or meeting. One day, I came to pick you three up and picked up Brian by mistake, instead of Trey. I laughed it off since I'd been tired and overworked that week, but… Brian could have easily passed as your brother. And you took after your dad so much." She glanced at Trey with a smile

"Lucky me," Trey said softly.

"No one thought anything about Brian's blue eyes and blonde hair because Gavin Laster had both as well," Gail added.

"Do you think Carl had anything to do with Gavin's death?" Dylan asked the question that had been burning in her mind since she'd first read the emails.

The entire room grew silent.

"I'm going to call Rea. Is it okay if I have her and Tom come on over?" Gail glanced around.

"I'm wide awake now," Trey commented, taking Dylan's hand under the table.

Less than fifteen minutes later, Rea and Tom walked through the front door.

Gail made small talk for a while, asking if Brian was doing well.

Dylan had met Rea on several occasions. Since retiring, she was enjoying fixing up the house that she and Tom lived in a few blocks from Dylan's place. Rea also had come into the office on several occasions when Dylan had needed some help at the beginning.

She had instantly liked the woman. Rea had given her some American Indian bead earrings and a bracelet that Dylan wore often. She'd purchased some baked goods that Rea sold at the grocery store as well.

"Brian's doing wonderful. It really helped when

he decided to leave Haven. He's been in Helena for a few months now, going to school. He works part time at the golf course over there," Rea gushed.

"It seems like the kid has finally found his place," Tom added. He was still in his uniform and every now and then his radio would buzz. "I'm still on call, but I was on dinner break when you called," he explained, turning down the radio.

"The reason we called you over here was... these." Gail held out the emails to Rea. "We know it's a private matter, but... we're family." She touched Rea's shoulder. "We have been for as long as I can remember."

Rea smiled and nodded. "We sure are." She smiled, then her smile fell away when she scanned over the emails. Tears started rolling down the woman's dark brown cheeks. "I..." She shook her head, and Gail handed her a tissue.

"It's true?" Gail asked.

Rea nodded. "I thought... I'd hoped that it wouldn't come up."

"Does Brian know?" Gail asked.

"Yes. I told him a while back, when I..." She looked over at Tom.

"Shortly after we started dating last year," he explained. "She told me, and I suggested that she tell him."

"I should have told him years ago."

"Suddenly, so many conversations we had make sense," Addy jumped in, getting everyone's attention. "He changed, suddenly, last year. Just before he took off, he told me that he'd had a lot of

291

pent-up anger until recently. He said that just before he left town."

"I think he was relieved that Gavin wasn't his father." Rea glanced around. "It was a well-known fact that Gavin was very abusive towards us. I think when he found out he had... well, McGowan blood instead of Gavin's, he started to have a drive for something better."

"Does this mean we have to start being nice to Brian?" Trent asked, earning him a playful slug on the shoulder from Addy. "Ouch," he whined, as he faked being hurt.

"Yes," she hissed at her husband, "he's your cousin."

Dylan could tell the entire McGowan clan was thinking that one through. "Damn, now I'm going to have to give him a call and offer him a job," Tyler added.

"Don't you dare," Rea hissed. "Brian may have been upset at one point that you hadn't offered him a job, but now he would know it was a handout and he'd hate you for it. Besides, he's doing great at school, really great. He wants to finish it. Then, and only then, if he earns it, you can hire him, fair and square." Rea's eyes narrowed at the three brothers.

"Yes, ma'am," Tyler replied.

Trey had told Dylan that they had looked up to Rea as if she was their second mother, so she knew they'd take her words seriously.

Just then, Tom's radio came to life and he stepped out of the room so he wouldn't wake the sleeping baby.

"I'm sorry, I've got to go." He glanced around the room. "I'll drive Rea back home." The pair left quickly.

Dylan sat next to Trey as everyone cleaned up and left until it was just them and Gail left.

"I'm heading out too," she said, coming back into the dining area. "I don't know that we made much headway, but at least one secret is out there."

"Thank you for all your help tonight." Dylan stood up and followed Gail out after she had kissed Trey on the top of the head.

When she came back, Trey was back on the sofa with Dopey between his legs.

"Come on over here." He shuffled over so there was plenty of room for her to sit in front of him. "I want to spend the rest of the evening snuggling with my fiancée and our dog while watching something funny on the television." He turned the channel away from the news and flipped the stations as she settled next to him, toeing off her shoes and grabbing the blanket from the back of the sofa to cover them.

"Here." He settled on a classic romantic movie and set the remote down on the coffee table. "Just what we need, a happy-ever-after story."

She rested her head gently on his arm. "Am I hurting you?"

"No," he said softly. "I'm not fragile."

She glanced over her shoulder at him. "You're literally covered in bandages at the moment." She motioned to his arms and hands.

He responded by wrapping them tighter around

293

her. "It's only the top layer of my skin. I'm still strong under here." He rolled her quickly underneath him. His growing smile told her that he wasn't in any pain.

Wrapping her arms around him, she pulled him down until he was a breath above her. "Prove it to me."

"As you wish," he said softly as he humorously wiggled his eyebrows. Then he gave her a passionate kiss that put the romantic movie to shame.

***

Trey woke the next morning and felt every ache in every muscle, and every scratch on his very tender skin. Before he could sit up, Dylan was there with a glass of water and a pill. He wanted to deny that he needed them, but he could see the determined look in her eyes and knew she wasn't going to take no for an answer.

"Can I shower?" he asked her after making his way into the bathroom.

She turned and gave him a look. "The doctor said it all depends on how your skin looks." She carefully helped him off with his bandages.

He was surprised at how good his skin looked. There were red spots with small blisters in some areas, but for the most part, he doubted he'd have any major scars. He was thankful he'd had the water to protect him most of the time.

When she unwrapped his left hand, he winced.

His fingers were puffy and swollen.

Dylan let out a quiet gasp when she saw them. "You'll have to keep this hand out of the water," she said. She looked at him with sad eyes, and he gently took her hand.

"I'm here and I'm in one piece. More or less." He tried to lighten the mood by joking, but seeing the sadness in her eyes, he pulled her close. "I'm okay, really." He tested his left hand and relaxed slightly when the pain there was minimal. "See?" He moved his hand several times for her. "Minimal pain. It's just swollen."

She nodded and wiped a tear from her eyes. "When I think of how lucky we got..." She held onto him again. She was right, they *had* gotten lucky. They had another chance, another day together. There wasn't going to be a day from here on out that he didn't remember just how lucky he was.

She pulled back and scanned his face, then she chuckled and put her fingers into his hair. "We'll have to do something about this mess."

"Chop it all off." He nodded to the scissors on the countertop.

"I... I don't think I can."

"Then I will..." He reached for the scissors, but she stopped him.

"No." She took them up. "I'll do it. Maybe I can save some of it."

He shrugged. "It grows back fast."

For the next hour, he sat still as she took her time chopping off his hair. As the curls dropped to the floor, he wondered how he'd let it grow that long in the first place.

Dylan had been right—time had flown by since he'd moved in with her. Spring was in full swing and it seemed like just yesterday that he'd spotted her sexy legs on the sticky dance floor.

She handed him a mirror and he smiled at the very short haircut.

"Remind me to give you a tip, later." He smiled and pulled her close. "Come on, I think I'll call this good enough to shower." He pulled her into the shower with him, and she helped him gently clean his skin. Then he sat on the edge of the bathtub while she lathered salve all over him and rebandaged the worst areas.

When her phone chimed, he reached for it. He'd told everyone to contact him at her number until his new phone could be delivered later that day.

"Tony wants us down at the station. I'd hoped to avoid being seen in public for a few days." He glanced down at the bandages. He knew that all of Haven knew exactly what he'd gone through, and he wasn't ready for all the attention he was sure he was going to get.

"How about we stop off and get some donuts and coffee for the entire station? After all the demanding work they've had in the past few days, they deserve it," Dylan suggested.

"Sounds like a plan." His stomach growled at the mention of donuts.

She helped him get dressed, which was a little more difficult than he'd imagined. His skin was still tender and with his sore muscles, he moved more slowly and stiffly than before.

After stopping off at the donut shop and loading up with five boxes of donuts, they pulled into the parking lot of the station. The place was packed with news vans, and he immediately wished he could hide.

"Think we can sneak in the back?" Dylan asked, looking out the front windshield.

"It looks like it's too late." Several cameras had already turned their way.

"How about we run for it?" she suggested.

"You take the donuts. I'll handle this and meet you inside." He took the coffee cups and reached for the door handle.

"No, I'm not leaving you to the wolves." She glanced out and he realized the car was surrounded already.

He chuckled. "I'd hate for you to get swallowed. Go on inside. I'll answer a handful of questions then head in."

"Okay, but if you need me..." He took her hand in his and raised it to his lips to kiss it gently. Several camera flashes went off and he groaned at the lack of privacy.

He was bombarded with shouted questions the moment he stepped out of the car. Out of the corner of his eye, he watched Dylan being shuffled towards the back of the growing crowd.

"How did you get out of the blast zone?"

"Is this a family feud?"

"Did you have anything to do with the

explosion?"

He stood in front of the station doors and held up his hands.

"Thank you all for your concern. I'm very lucky to be here today. Our prayers go out to everyone who has been affected by the fire. We wanted to shout out a huge thank you to all the firefighters and emergency personnel who have worked hard to ensure the safety of everyone in town." He took a breath. More questions were shouted at him and he decided enough was enough. "Thank you," he turned and entered the building.

"Nicely handled, kid." Tony slapped him on the shoulder, and Trey winced. "Sorry."

"It's okay." He smiled, then glanced around. "Where's Dylan?"

"In the back, handing out donuts."

He followed Tony into Mike's office.

"Good, you made it through the buzzards," Mike said as Trey took a seat.

"We have a positive ID of the body found near the site." He glanced up at him. "Steven Rice."

"Not Dennis?" Trey asked.

"No, the car was under Dennis' name, but with dental records, we've positively ID'd that Rice was the one found."

"Why would Dad's lawyer be in a car rented by Dennis Rodgers with the trunk full of explosives?"

"We've been asking ourselves that question since we found out," Mike said.

Chapter Twenty-One

7he entire town of Haven was on edge the following few days.

Dennis Rodgers was brought in and questioned. Everyone wished they could be in on the questioning, but so far, the police were keeping the outcome quiet. The fact that he was released less than five hours after walking into the station told everyone that the police had no proof Dennis had killed Steven Rice or knew anything about how the man had ended up in a car leased to him.

The rumor going around was that he hadn't known of the rental car and there was no proof he was the man who'd picked up the car in the first place. His ex-wife, Chrystal, confirmed that he had been at her place picking up their kids for a planned visit when the explosion had happened.

No one doubted her word anymore, now that she was officially free from his grasp.

Dylan was thankful when the media frenzy died down in Haven. Now that the fire was completely out, the town quickly went to work cleaning up the mess. The town came together to help those who had lost their homes. Donations were collected, temporary housing was arranged, and everything seemed to get back to normal.

It was Trey's first full week back out in the field. He'd been stuck in the office for almost two full weeks.

No one had seen or heard from Carl since he'd stopped by the day that she'd been attacked. Still, she was never left alone at the office, and she was thankful for it. She doubted she could handle another bump to the head.

They'd had a few other McGowan family meetings, which were always planned around meals. They'd discussed what they should do next and how to keep everyone safe, and Dylan started to feel like part of the family. It felt wonderful.

Their weekends were spent working on the new house on Trey's property. Even her brother pitched in before he left for North Dakota. He'd postponed his trip a full week after the fire. Seth's family had lost their barn and he had helped rebuild it before they headed out to their new jobs.

It was hard seeing the garage apartment empty and not seeing his truck parked in the driveway. This was the first time she'd ever been away from him for any length of time. She knew it was a good thing for him to get out on his own, but she hadn't thought she'd miss him this much.

She'd run into Darla several times at the store. She swore the woman showed up whenever she pulled into the parking lot. The last time, she'd planned out what she would say to her. It had gone over just as she'd imagined and, since then, Darla hadn't bumped into her again.

Dylan smiled remembering the run-in. She'd gone to the store after work to get a few items for a dinner she was planning to make for Trey.

She'd turned the corner aisle towards the back of the store, near the milk and eggs. Darla had been standing in the middle of the aisle, her arms crossed over her ample chest, blocking the way.

"Darla." She'd tried to pass by her, but the woman had gripped her cart, her eyes narrowed in her direction.

"Where's your brother?" she'd hissed.

"He's moved on. Isn't it about time you did the same?" she said clearly.

"I'm pregnant," Darla had blurted out. If she hadn't heard how Darla had dealt with Addy's family, she would have believed her. Instead, she maneuvered her cart around her. "Once you have a paternity test confirm it's my brother's kid, our lawyer will be in contact. Until then"—she narrowed her eyes—"try barking up someone else's tree."

"You'll see when I have my baby, *our* baby," Darla had screamed after her. Several people rolled their eyes in Dylan's direction when they passed by. "I *am* pregnant!" She stomped her foot and shouted at the passersby.

Dylan had almost laughed as she walked out of the store.

A spring snowstorm hit shortly after that. Trey had helped her cover her flowers with trash bags before the storm hit so they wouldn't be shocked and freeze. They had sprouted up even faster after the cold weather passed.

It was strange, having seventy-degree weather the day after a snowstorm that had brought in almost a foot of the white stuff.

Now everything was melting and muddy as the men worked on laying the foundation for the new house. The cement was due to arrive in a few days, and the men were hooking up the rough-in plumbing and electricity.

The log home kit had arrived, and the massive pieces were set where Trey planned on building a three-car garage. A large crane had been set up to lift the pieces into place.

It was another warm Saturday and Dylan and Addy were glued to their computer screens as they sat in the shade of a cluster of trees. Her classes had started up again, and she was worried that this time she'd bitten off more than she should have. She had thought she had plenty of time to take six classes, but she was finding it harder to set time aside now that she was helping Trey out at the property. Not that she was doing much, just giving her opinion and helping rake dirt now and then. But she found it harder to concentrate on her classes when Trey was strutting around in front of her without a shirt on, all sweaty and looking like a true mountain man.

After the haircut she'd given him to fix the parts of his hair that had been singed by the fire, his hair had grown back quickly. It was still shorter than before, but the curls were already coming back.

Trey's skin had healed quickly with her help. He only had one little scar on his wrist, just under his owl tattoo. He mentioned often how good it felt to regain his strength.

His brothers still gave him grief about his shorter hair, but for the most part, Dylan could tell they were happy he had come out of the ordeal nearly unscathed.

They were just shutting down for the evening when a truck pulled into the driveway. A man in a suit stepped out and worry flooded Dylan instantly.

"You must be lost," Trey called out.

"I'm looking for the McGowans?" The man walked slowly towards them.

"You found them." Tyler tossed down the towel he'd been using to wipe his face. "I'm Tyler McGowan. Can I help you?"

"I'm here about Carl McGowan." The man extended his hand.

"You are?" Tyler asked.

"I'm Don Hathaway, Carl McGowan's new lawyer. He's hired me to oversee his affairs."

"What affairs?" Tyler asked.

"Well, that's what I'd like to meet with you all about, if possible." The man glanced between the three brothers. "Do you have someplace we can talk?"

"Back up at the main house." Tyler pointed to his mother's place. "I'm sure our mother would want to hear what you have to say."

"I'll follow you up there." The man walked back to his car.

"Just what we need, another lawyer," Trey said under his breath.

"Let's see what the man has to say. I'm curious what our dear uncle thinks he needs a lawyer for," Tyler added as they all piled into their trucks.

When they arrived up at Gail's place, she was waiting for them. Tyler had called her and let her know they was coming.

They all gathered around the living area and, after introductions were made, Don Hathaway pulled out a piece of paper.

"As I mentioned, I was hired to represent Carl McGowan in a suit to contest his brother's will."

It wasn't a big surprise to the family. Dylan noticed several of them sigh with frustration.

"I'm sorry to interrupt, Mr. Hathaway, but this will be the second time Carl has tried such actions," Gail said.

"I'm aware of that. I'm also aware that your late husband, Thurston, has been deceased almost two years now. The statute of limitations in the state of Montana only allows up to two years, which is why Carl is contesting his brother's will now."

"Son of a..." Tyler ran his hands through his hair.

"My husband's last will was sound. It's already been proven..." Gail started.

"I'm sorry, I haven't made myself clear. We are not contesting the will that was read shortly after your late husband's death."

"Then what are you contesting?" Gail asked.

304

"The new will that has been filed in the last few months. The one that Carl McGowan found at the hunting lease that post-dates the first will read."

"What?" several people said at once.

"The will was filed by a…" He shuffled through his paperwork.

"Steven Rice?" Tyler asked before the new lawyer could find the name.

"Yes, how did…" The man shook his head. "Anyway, the new will was presented and verified on the twenty-second of last month."

"The day before the explosion," Trey added softly. "The day before Steven Rice was found shot to death."

To his credit, Don Hathaway looked shocked. He set down the stack of papers he held. "I'm sorry, did you just say—"

"Steven Rice, the lawyer who filed my father's supposedly new will, was found murdered a day after he filed it. We have reason to believe that Carl had something to do with his murder."

Dylan hadn't heard that bit of news, but figured Tyler knew more than she did and kept her mouth shut.

"I see." The man sighed. "In light of these new circumstances, I'll postpone my own filing until I can do a little digging myself." He moved to get up.

"Mr. Hathaway, is there any chance you have a copy of the new will my husband supposedly made?" Gail asked.

"Yes." The man dug through his case. "In the will, Thurston McGowan the second left everything

305

to his youngest son, Thurston Noah McGowan the third."

The room was silent as every eye turned to Trey. Everyone remained silent as Gail showed the lawyer out.

"What the hell?" Tyler turned back to the room. "There is no way in hell Dad would leave everything to only one of us."

"Of course not," Gail said as she walked back in. "This is just another way for Carl to get at us," she said, looking down at the paperwork. "The signature looks real." She held it up for the three boys to see.

"I've seen Dad's chicken scratches enough to know that it's real, but the question is, did he know what he was signing or is it from something else?" Tyler sighed. "I'll take this home and read through it."

"Why would Carl be contesting this will? Does he really think he could win this fight when he didn't win the fight against a will that left everything to all of us?"

"You don't think..." Trey started but then stopped.

"What?" Dylan encouraged him.

"You don't think that Carl blew the pipe with me standing next to it so he could contest the new will that, upon my death, left everything Dad left us, including McGowan Enterprises uncontested?"

***

The fact that his uncle had probably tried to murder him to get his hands on his family's business and money weighed heavily on Trey, and he found it impossible to sleep that night.

There had been lots to discuss after the lawyer had left and everyone agreed that, no matter the signature, the document was an obvious fake. It went against everything his father had set in motion with his mother. His parents' relationship had been solid. So solid that they had talked about every aspect of their lives, including their deaths.

After trying to sleep for about an hour, he pushed Dopey off his feet and slowly got out of the bed, making sure not to wake Dylan.

Taking her laptop, he crept downstairs and sat at the table to do his own research. The first thing he looked up was the new lawyer. Don Hathaway had an office in Butte, which lead him to question what Carl had been doing in Butte. Could he be hiding there still?

A few hours later, he gently woke Dylan up as the sun started to rise.

"What's up?" she asked, scooting up and blinking.

"God, you look amazing in the morning." He leaned in and kissed her softly on the lips. It was true. He'd spent a few moments just watching her sleep before waking her.

She laughed. "Are you drunk already this morning?" She blinked a few times and stretched her arms over her head.

"No." He rubbed his hand over her shoulder.

307

"Instead of working on the house today, do you want to take a drive with me?"

Her eyebrows jumped slightly. "A drive?"

"I was thinking of hitting this little café I know for some of the best chocolate-chip pancakes ever. Then we could swing up to the national park, take a hike with Dopey, and maybe find someplace quiet to eat dinner on the way back."

"You had me at chocolate-chip pancakes." She chuckled.

They showered and dressed. He enjoyed seeing her in the tight worn jeans and the new hiking boots he'd bought her. She pulled on a flannel jacket, and they strapped Dopey into his car harness, tossing his water bowl on the floor.

"I still can't believe they sell these things for dogs." Dylan chuckled as the dog happily laid down with the safety harness.

He drove to the little café in Dillon, a small cozy town much like Haven. It was a good hour away but totally worth the long drive.

They sat out on the front patio, Dopey lying by his feet, and ate the sugary pancakes as they watched the sleepy town come to life.

"I can't believe I've lived in Montana this long and still haven't explored much of it," Dylan said between bites.

"I've lived here all my life and still haven't been to a few places myself," he said.

"Like?"

"Well, I haven't been to Great Falls or Flathead National Forest." He thought for a moment. "I might have been there once when I was a kid, a fishing trip, but I'm not positive." He shrugged.

"Where are we going today?"

"I thought we'd hike at Table Mountain." He waited and decided it was time to spill the beans. "The real reason I wanted a drive was that I found out that the lawyer, Don Hathaway, has an office in Butte."

She set her fork down and tilted her head. "Are you thinking of stopping in on him?"

"Not really, but I was thinking of asking around to see if anyone in town has seen or dealt with Carl."

"Trey," she said softly, "you could have trusted me with this. You didn't have to persuade me with chocolate."

"But it helped." He smiled and reached for her hand.

"Trey, what do you hope to gain from this? I'm sure the police have already thought of looking for him here, especially after your mother called and talked to Mike last night."

"Yeah." he sighed. "I just needed to try."

She was silent for a while, her eyes searching his. "We'll go to Butte first, then go on our walk."

"Thanks." He took her hand up to his lips and placed a kiss on the back of it.

They left the sleepy town and headed for Butte. The town wasn't a hopping metropolis, but compared to Haven, it was city life.

They started by stopping at the police station and showing them a picture of Carl. The local office was already looking out for Carl and had no news as to his whereabouts but told them they were free to ask around town.

They walked Dopey through the main streets and asked anyone they ran into. Everyone seemed nice enough, but no one had seen him.

They passed by the lawyer's office, but it was closed for the day.

"What about here." Dylan motioned towards the grocery store. "If he's been in town, he would have needed something from the store."

"Good idea." He took her hand and crossed the street. "You stay here with Dopey." He nodded to the sign that said no pets allowed. "I'll go in and check."

He walked into the small store and made his way towards the checkout clerk.

He was waiting in line when he glanced out the window and saw Dylan talking to a young mother who was coming into the store. She showed the woman the picture of Carl on her phone and her eyes grew big as she nodded her head.

Trey stepped out of the line and made his way outside.

"Well?" he asked. The woman had already left to go inside.

"She says she saw him at the gas station just this morning." She motioned to the end of the street. "She remembers him because he fell against his car and she helped him up. She said he looks weak, like he's sick."

Trey's stomach rolled. "Maybe there was something to him being sick after all." He took her hand and they started walking towards the gas station.

They were halfway there when a horn blasted. Glancing around, he sighed. "I should have counted on this."

His brothers pulled up in the parking lot and got out. "Like minds…" Tyler said, giving Dopey a scratch on the top of his head.

"We have a lead." Trey filled them in on what the woman had told Dylan.

"I'll head in and ask around," Tyler suggested.

The rest of them chatted as they waited outside.

When Tyler came back out, he had a frown on his face.

"The clerk says she's seen him a few times. The address on his checks is Beef Trail Road. She's given me instructions." He held up a piece of paper. "How do we deal with this?"

"We need to call the police," Dylan jumped in. "They need to handle him." When the rest of them were silent, she glared at him. "It's the smartest move. The safest," she added.

He sighed loudly. "She's right." He knew the three of them wanted to confront the old man, but if something happened… His eyes met Dylan's. He knew he couldn't live with the knowledge that someone he loved had gotten hurt because of his pride. "She's right," he said again, this time with more strength behind his words. "We'll drive back to the local PD. They're just down the street." He motioned to where the police station sat.

"Why don't you guys go ahead? Trent and I were

311

going to grab some food." Tyler motioned to the diner across the street.

"We'll meet you there after we're done," Trey said, taking Dylan's hand as they started walking again.

"They aren't ditching us, are they?" She glanced back over her shoulder.

He watched his brothers walk into the diner. "No, they aren't that sneaky. Besides, I heard Tyler's stomach growl." He smiled and walked a little faster.

Chapter Twenty-Two

She was surprised that Tyler and Trent were just finishing up their lunches when she and Trey walked up to the patio area.

"So?" Tyler glanced up at them.

"They're sending a car up to the address now. They said they'd give me a call when they know something." Trey sat down and grabbed a fry from his brother's plate.

They ordered sandwiches and the four of them sat around until Trey's phone chimed.

She listened as he talked to the police. When he hung up, she knew the trip there hadn't done any good.

"The place was emptied out. They said it looked like he'd been staying there but had moved out sometime during the night." He ran his hands through his hair in frustration, a move the three of them did often.

"What do we do now?" Trent asked.

Trey glanced over at her. "Now Dylan and I go

313

on our hike, and we all regroup when we get home tonight."

"Sounds like a plan." Tyler glanced at his watch. "I promised Kristen I'd watch Timothy so she and her mother could do some shopping."

"I've got to go with Addy to her mother's place, help her move a few heavy things," Trent told them. "We'll have to regroup after. How about the Dancing Moose around eight?"

"See you then." Trey tossed down some cash to pay for their meal.

Dylan watched the landscape pass by her outside the truck windows. Dopey was fast asleep in the back seat and Trey was quiet as he drove.

"We'll find him," she assured him.

"Yeah. It kills me knowing he might be the one who caused all this mess."

"Who else could it be?" She'd thought long and hard about it. "I mean, you said that he was skilled in explosives. He was the last person I saw before leaving the office that day. You caught him on camera blowing up the trailer. Who else would have reasons to start the fire? To kill the lawyer?"

"Lots of people," Trey answered. "We haven't heard from our usual suspects. Darla's been quiet since your brother left town. No one has seen Dennis in weeks, since after he was brought in for questioning. Still, no one can prove he was the one who rented the car they found Rice in." He turned off the main road and pulled into the parking area of the hiking trail.

"How is that possible?" she asked as they got

out. Dopey jumped out, excited to see dirt and trees surrounding them.

"The rental place says that someone picked up the car using a code that allows you into the vehicle. The man who called it in put the rental under Dennis' name but paid with a disposable credit card. For all we know, Rice could have rented the car himself."

"And shot himself in the head and threw the gun away?" she asked.

"Right." They started walking up the trail. He'd thrown the backpack with their water over his shoulder. "Still, they found Rice in the passenger seat. That means someone else drove him up there."

"Someone who wanted everyone to think it was Dennis Rodgers." She glanced over at Trey. "Is Dennis a smart man?"

He thought about it before answering her. "He wasn't smart enough to remove Kristen's shoe from the back of his truck after he kidnapped her."

She nodded. "Still, he did walk free after that."

"Yeah." Trey sounded disgusted. "Maybe he's smarter than we all were led to believe."

"He's worth looking into. I'm sure the police have done so."

"He's still a free man," Trey reminded her.

"Right. Still, maybe he killed Rice long before the explosion. Set a timer of sorts, then showed up at his ex's just as everything went down."

Trey was silent for a while. "It's worth considering." He took her hand. "Later." He nodded to the view.

They hiked up the hill, quiet as they made their way. She was huffing and puffing by the time they reached the first peak.

"I don't think I could ever get tired of these views." She sighed and smiled as she looked out over the valley. A lake sparkled down in the basin surrounded by green hills and blue skies with only a few puffy clouds overhead.

When Dylan turned around to smile at Trey, he shocked her by bending down to one knee.

"I know we've already done this, but I needed to do it properly. Someplace like here." He smiled at the view. "Dylan McCaw, I can't imagine a day without waking up beside you, watching you sleep. I love you more than I ever imagined loving someone." Her heart did a little jump and tears filled her eyes when he pulled a small box from the backpack pocket. "This time, let's make it official. Will you marry me?"

He slid open the box and she gasped at the beauty of the white gold ring. There was a beautiful blue diamond and several smaller diamonds around it. It sparkled in the sunlight. She'd never seen anything like it.

"Yes, a million times, for the rest of our lives, yes." She chuckled as he slipped the ring on her finger. "Get up here." She pulled him into her arms. The kiss was just as powerful as the first one he'd given her and that amazing kiss he'd given her after the explosion. His arms around her was the best feeling she'd ever experienced. She couldn't believe she'd been lucky enough to find someone like him and to know that for the rest of her life, she would enjoy him, like this.

"Now that we've made it official, there's just one more thing I have to ask you." He smiled down at her.

"Anything," she said, smiling back up at him.

"Can we stop for ice cream on the way back?"

She laughed. "I was hoping you'd ask me that. Let's go. I'm already hungry again." Dopey let out a playful bark and raced around them.

Going downhill was a lost faster than going up. Dopey kept tugging on her arm, so Trey took his leash and helped her when the path got too steep.

"Next time we go hiking, I get to pick the path," she joked after tripping over a stone.

When they arrived back at the truck, his cell phone chimed. "We must have been out of range." He frowned at the messages that kept coming.

"We have to go." He tossed the bag into the back and snapped Dopey into his harness.

"What's up?" she asked, strapping her seatbelt on quickly.

"Family meeting has been moved up. Here." He handed her his phone. "Read the rest of the messages out loud as I drive."

The first message was from Tyler.

-We made it back to Haven and ran into Dennis. The man was acting pissed and strange.

The next one was from Trent.

-Man, you'd better come back to town. It looks like they are going to bring in Dennis. They found more evidence in the car.

317

Tyler messaged again.

-Dennis is on the run. No one knows where he is. Word got out that the police had evidence. I'm not sure it's true, we're heading down to the station now. I'll keep you posted. p.s. I hope Dylan likes the rock you picked out.

She looked over at him. "I love it," she said. He smiled over at her and took her hand as he hit the highway.

"Your mother texted you next." She read the text out loud.

-We're all down at the station. They want us all down here for our own safety. Where are you?

"Call her," Trey broke in.

Dylan hit redial and speaker. When his mother picked up, Trey spoke up.

"Mom, we're coming back into town. We should be there in about half an hour. What's going on?"

"Okay, sweetie. Well, we'll go over everything once you get here. We're heading over to the Dancing Moose now with Tony and Tom. We'll be there until you arrive. Keep your eyes peeled and drive safe."

"Will do, tell everyone we're on our way," he added before she hung up.

"What is going on?" Dylan asked, unable to believe that things could take such a turn so quickly.

"I'm not sure. Looks like we'll find out when we get there." She let him focus on driving as she continued to scan his family's text messages. There were a few other messages, all about meeting with the police. A new message popped up and she read

318

it for Trey. This one was from Mike.

-If you see either Dennis or Carl, do not engage. Call or text us immediately.

"Reply back and tell him we'll be in town in about"—he glanced down at the clock—"twenty minutes."

She texted a quick message back. She noticed then that her fingers were shaking.

"Hey." Trey reached over and took her hand. "It's okay. I'm sure they just found more proof that Dennis had something to do with Rice's murder."

"Yeah, that's not what worries me. The fact that the police are worried for your family, that's what worries me."

The thought of something bad happening to any of the people she'd grown to love in the past few months was unbearable.

"Hey, we McGowans are made of tougher stuff than that." He smiled over at her. "We've survived fire, being blown up, and being frozen." He raised his eyebrows at her.

"Yes, but this is different."

"I know," he said softly. "We'll get through this. I promise."

***

Trey parked next to his brother's truck. Dopey was fast asleep in the back seat, and he decided to let the dog enjoy the sleep. The dog barely opened an eye as they got out.

"He should be okay." He had walked over to help

Dylan out of the truck and assured her as she glanced in the dog's direction. "I think we wore him out with that walk."

"Him and me. My legs are going to be sore tomorrow." They were halfway across the parking lot when a sound caused him to turn around.

He had less than a second to push Dylan from his side. She went face first into the asphalt parking lot, catching herself on her hands and knees. A second later, the sedan slammed into his hip, and he flew across the parking lot.

His shirt was torn away as he skidded across asphalt. The sting of his skin tearing was instant.

Before he could recover fully, he was staring down the barrel of a gun.

"You had to ruin everything by surviving the trailer fire and the blast. No one should have been able to survive the blasts." Dennis Rodgers stood over him, the weapon aimed directly at Trey's heart.

One part of his mind heard Dylan scream and the sound of several people running. He was sure that before his family reached him, he'd have a bullet through his chest.

He was sprawled out on the black asphalt, bleeding from his new scrapes and cuts.

"Dennis." He blinked a few times. What could he say? How could he stall the man? "What's this all about? At least show me the decency of telling me why I deserve to die."

The older man's eyes narrowed. "You still don't know." The man chuckled, the weapon never wavering from its mark. "I can't believe he never told you."

"Told me what? Who?" he asked, trying to see out of the corner of his eye if help was on its way.

Too late, Dennis noticed the group gathering around him. "Stay back," he called out, his gun moving closer to Trey's chest. "Get back," he said again. Trey could hear more footfalls, this time as everyone moved away.

Trey prayed that Dylan was safe. He could hear her crying and begging for his life.

"No, Rice never told us anything. Why don't you tell me now?"

"Not Rice," Dennis screamed, spit flying from his mouth. The man looked thinner than the last time Trey had seen him. There were dark circles under his eyes and he had a wild look as he stared directly at Trey. The man's eyes never left him.

"Who then?" Trey asked, as he tried to steady his heart rate. It wouldn't do him any good to freak out, so he tried to take a few deep breaths, even knowing they may be his last.

"The McGowans with their stupid family rules. Who the hell makes it so that the youngest son gets all the rewards?"

"I don't understand." Trey settled on his butt, so now he was sitting facing the man. "Maybe you can enlighten me."

"Three sons. For three generations there's been three sons," Dennis spat at him.

"My brothers..." He wasn't making any sense, and Trey was having a hard time trying to stall him further.

"No!" he shouted, interrupting him as he pointed the gun directly between Trey's eyes. Trey heard several cries from behind him. "I'm not talking about you three brats. I'm talking about me."

"You?" Trey took a breath.

"I'm the third." The man laughed. "Which means, I should have gotten the name, the inheritance. I should be in control of everything."

Everything was silent for a moment. Dennis's last words hung in the air.

"You... you're a McGowan?"

"Finally! It's funny, you and your stupid brothers were too dumb to see it. But not your old man, no, my dearly departed brother caught on early on. It's the eyes." Dennis sneered, the gun wavering between Trey's chest and his head.

Trey looked beyond the barrel pointed at him to Dennis's eyes. Sure enough, for the first time in his life, he saw the resemblance between Dennis, Carl, and his father.

"You're the youngest?" Trey asked.

"Your grandfather, Thurston the first, fell in love with my mother, Norine. He was in the process of leaving his wife, June, when he died in that crash. He never got to acknowledge my birth, but someone did." Dennis smiled. "Someone did."

"Denny." A new voice broke in.

Trey glanced over as Uncle Carl stepped forward. Seeing the two men standing side by side, Trey wondered how no one in town or in his family had ever suspected it before.

"Denny, this isn't the way. The kid can't give you

322

what you want." Carl McGowan looked so frail, Trey wondered how the man was standing up. His hands were out as he continued to walk towards them.

"Of course, he can. Rice filed the new will. When he's gone, we finally have a chance again."

"Not like this, we never planned this," Carl said.

"Maybe you didn't." Dennis chuckled. "Of course, you were all gung-ho when it's blowing up an empty trailer or skinning a few animals, but I knew you'd never get your hands dirty. I'm the one that had to stop the deal between McGowan and JB Holding. I'm the one who had to snatch and feed that bitch in the cave." Dennis was screaming at this point. Trey heard a few gasps behind him, but his eyes didn't move from the gun pointing at him. "I'm the one who had to break in and try to delete those emails that Rice sent, but the new bitch secretary had changed Rea's passwords. I'm the one who had the balls to try it. I've always been prepared to go the distance. I'm the one who's suffered the most. I lost everything."

"Denny, it can't end like this. I never meant any harm to the boys." Carl was almost standing between them, when Dennis shouted.

"Stop making excuses!" The gun moved for a moment to Carl. "You can't fix this like you've been doing all these years. I can't keep hiding who I am. I'm a McGowan!"

It happened so quickly, yet the next few seconds seemed to stretch on forever.

Dennis's arm turned, the gun sliding between

Carl and Trey. Trey's eyes focused on the barrel as it pointed directly at his chest. Dennis' fingers twitched, and he saw a slight puff of air burst as the bullet flew out of the muzzle.

He'd been so focused on the gun that he hadn't seen the old man throw his body in front of his to shield him. Carl landed on top of him, knocking him back to the asphalt as he flew back and caught the man. Trey instantly recognized the warmth from Carl's blood flowing from the hole in his chest as it washed over him. All sound had ceased to exist until after he had caught his breath.

"Carl?" He held the man close to him. It was too late. The man stared back at him with empty eyes that eerily matched his own, his father's, and those of his other uncle, Dennis.

Several people tackled Dennis. His brothers held the man down, and the gun was kicked away. They waited for the other police to arrive.

"Trey!" Dylan broke free from someone's hold and rushed over to him. She knelt beside him, tears rolling down her face.

"He…saved me." He looked over at her, understanding finally catching him.

"Trey," Dylan cried again, her hands running over his body, mixing in Carl's blood. "Are you hurt?"

"No," he answered without really knowing if it was the truth. "He jumped in front of me and saved me." Trey looked down at the old man who he and his brothers had spent so many years fearing and hating. "Why?" he asked. "Why?" He shook his head.

"Hey."

Trey looked over as his brother's face came into view. Tyler gently moved Carl's body from covering Trey.

"Why?" he asked again, this time pointing the question to his brother.

"I don't know, but we need to check you out." Tyler's hands ran over him. Trey hissed when they found a tender spot in his side.

"Yeah, thought so. You may be fire, explosive, and freezer proof, but you're not bulletproof." Tyler turned and waved at someone. "Over here, he's been shot."

"No, I haven't." He frowned down at his blood-soaked shirt. "Well, look at that." He chuckled, then met Dylan's eyes. "I've been shot." Then everything went dark.

Jill Sanders

Chapter Twenty-Three

*D*ylan was once again sitting in the clinic watching Trey sleep. This time, the room was quiet and dark. He'd spent two hours in surgery to dig out the bullet that had passed through his uncle and embedded into one of his ribs, shattering the bone.

She sat in the dark room listening to Trey's labored breathing mixed with the machine sounds. His family had been by her side every moment of the way. When the doctors had described what was in store for him, she had held strong and listened to every detail, every instruction and concern.

Now, almost eight hours later, things were looking up, but she wondered why Trey still hadn't opened his eyes. His family had left a few hours ago to go shower and change. She hadn't moved from her spot and still wore the jeans and hiking boots from before. They were still covered in his dried blood, but she didn't care. She wasn't leaving his side until his eyes opened.

Tyler had taken Dopey home with him and was taking care of the dog until she could go home.

She'd been surprised by a phone call from her brother. He wanted to leave North Dakota and come back to be with her, but she told him that there wasn't anything he could do and to plan a visit for later when he had built up some more paid leave.

She must have fallen asleep for a while. She woke to voices in the hallway and, after checking on Trey, stepped outside.

Tyler, Trent, and Gail stood in the hallway, talking quietly with Mike.

"What's up?" she asked, tucking the flannel jacket around her.

"Sorry, sweetie, we didn't mean to wake you." Gail walked over and gave her a hug.

"What's going on?" She looked to Mike.

"I needed to ask you about an email you forwarded to Tyler."

"I forward a lot of emails to Tyler, anything I can't deal with myself," she answered.

"I had her start that practice shortly after she came on," Tyler jumped in.

"These were from Steven Rice."

She thought about it. "Sure, there were several. Why?"

"Did you read any of these?" Mike held up a stack of papers.

"No, why?"

"Dylan, there is a copy of Dad's new will in these. Rice had changed his will. In the email he said he was forced into it by Dennis. That Dennis was the one pulling his strings. Rice confessed to having an affair with someone in town." Tyler

328

glanced over at Mike. "For her privacy, we shall keep her name out of this." He turned back to her. "Dennis blackmailed him, told him that once he had his hands on McGowan Enterprises that he would throw away the proof he had of their relationship."

"So, it was Dennis, not Carl?" she asked.

"It appears so. When Carl found out about the new will, he hired Don Hathaway to contest it."

"Hathaway came in after hearing about Carl's death and clued us in that Carl never thought that everything should go just to Trey. He'd known about Dennis since long before you three were born. He'd been hiding his father's secret since he was in high school." Mike leaned against the doorway. "We were able to piece most of it together. Carl didn't lose most of his money to drinking. He'd started R&R Enterprises with Dennis. All of the money from his portion of McGowan Enterprises went into starting that business."

"So it wasn't Steven Rice who was the other R in R&R Enterprises," Trent said.

"Royce and Rodgers," Tyler broke in and glanced around. "Carl Royce McGowan," Tyler said softly. He turned the emails around to show the full name of the business. "They spent the last few years buying up sinking businesses. Looks like it cost them dearly." His eyebrows drew up. "They're broke."

"Dennis pulled out what little money they had left in the business to pay for his legal fees," Mike told them. "Apparently Kristen's kidnapping and Dennis's embezzling from NewField was the cause of a major dispute between the two of them. It could be the reason your uncle tried his last-ditch effort to get his hands on McGowan Enterprises."

"What else do you expect from a drunk and a psycho?" Trent said, earning him a scolding look from Gail. "Sorry."

"No," Tyler added. "He's right. The duo was doomed to fail."

Tyler started reading the email out loud.

McGowan boys,

I find myself in a deep hole that I dug long before any of you were born. For years I have been forced to cover up the lies and deception of a man I at one point looked up to. Now, however, I can no longer go along with his malicious intents.

Dennis Rodgers has crossed a line, and I can no longer keep his secret.

Dennis hired me when I was fresh out of law school and long before I knew better than to be picky about who I took on as a client.

Carl had sold his shares of McGowan Enterprises and, with that money, I helped them start a business, R&R Enterprises.

At the beginning, the business seemed legit. They bought up small businesses that were going under. After your father's death, things changed. They had me draw up an offer for McGowan Enterprises, and when you turned it down, strange things started happening around town. When I confronted the pair, they quickly denied any wrongdoing. I could see the strain between the pair and on several occasions, they fought in my presence.

It wasn't until after Kristen Howell's kidnapping that I realized who was behind it all. Once again, I confronted Dennis and was threatened to remain silent or they would release several secrets about me that would ruin someone else's life.

I'm sorry I didn't come out sooner with this information. I'm heading over to meet with Dennis now. I'm going to dissolve our professional relationship. I can no longer represent R&R Enterprises, or your uncles, Carl and Dennis Rodgers.

-My best,
*   Steven*

"Why did Dennis come after Trey then?" Dylan asked.

Everyone turned to her. "Rice had filed the new will in a last-ditch effort, and Dennis hoped the new will would stick. When Trey died uncontested, they could fight in court for their share of the business. After all, they were both McGowan," Mike added. "He even outlined his plans to Rice." He waved another page of emails.

"Who killed Rice?" Tyler asked.

"We're waiting for forensics to come back on the gun Dennis used to shoot Carl and Trey with, but my guess is they'll be a match with the bullet we found in Rice."

"Dennis?" Gail shook her head. "I never knew or suspected. We've known him all our lives."

"Dad never talked about his father leaving his wife before his death?" Tyler asked.

"I mean, sure, there were rumors about an affair.

331

But the woman left town shortly after your grandfather passed. We were only kids, in grade school I think." She frowned trying to remember. "I had already fallen in love with your father by then." She smiled at her two sons.

"Mushy." Trent chuckled and Gail playfully slapped at him.

Just then, a nurse entered Trey's room. Everyone followed her into the room.

Dylan was surprised to see Trey's eyes wide open.

"I thought I heard gossip," he said as they walked in.

"You're awake." Dylan rushed to his side.

"How could I sleep with all that racket outside," he joked, then he winced and held his side. "Okay, who's going to tell me what the hell happened?"

***

Trey stood on his land, looking out at the stream as the summer wind blew softly through the trees. The sound of the water trickling by and the leaves blowing caused his entire body to relax.

"Happy?" Dylan walked over to his side and wrapped her arms around him.

"More than I ever thought possible." He pulled her close. His rib was still tender, but he'd gained most of his strength back. Turning slightly, he looked over to where the cabin was taking shape. "It'll be ready to move in soon."

Dylan nodded. "Of course, you know what that means."

"What?" He turned his attention back to her.

"Furniture shopping." She smiled as he groaned.

"I'd rather be shot again," he said, making her smile.

"Don't worry, Addy and I are going to take care of most of it."

"Good." He leaned down and kissed her just as a truck pulled up. "That's my brothers."

"Go, enjoy your first day back working on the place." She dropped her arms.

"It's going to feel good actually working instead of just supervising my brothers."

Dylan followed him up to where the house stood. Over the past month, while he'd watched, his brothers had pretty much built the entire place. They had just installed all the windows and doors last week, before he'd finally gotten the sign-off from his doctor to start doing some heavy lifting again.

The plan was to install the kitchen cabinets so that the marble countertops could be installed by Monday. They hoped to also get most of the hardwood floor installed. The electrician and plumber were already working inside with the estimate that they'd be finished by midweek.

"Have you thought about my question?" He turned and stopped her from walking into the building.

Her dark eyebrows rose up slightly. "Which question is that?" she asked, a small smile on her lips.

"Two or three?" He pulled her close, his brothers making kissing noises from across the parking area.

333

He threw a glare in their direction and they stopped. "So?" he asked.

Dylan chuckled. "What if I say four?"

His smile grew. "Then I'd say we have a deal." He leaned in to place a kiss on her lips.

"Damn it, Trey, that damn pig is out again," Tyler yelled at him.

"Hold that thought." He dropped his arms and took off as Dylan laughed. The three brothers chased Porky around the yard. The little potbelly pig was faster than any other animal he'd ever owned.

It took over an hour for him and his brothers to corner the beast against the shed that was the makeshift barn at the moment. When Trey jumped on the beast, he was sure the pig's squeals could be heard clear to his mother's place.

"Damn it, we lost an entire hour on that pig," Tyler complained, but the smile on his face told everyone he hadn't minded. "Kristen's going to be here with lunch soon."

"Then let's get some work done." Trey slapped his brother on his shoulder. Dylan watched the three men walk towards her, then held up her hands.

"The three of you are dreaming if you think I'm going to let you step one foot in my house like that." She pointed to their muddy jeans and shirts.

"You'll have to head on down to the stream and jump in and wash off first." She motioned to the brook.

"Yes, ma'am," Tyler and Trent said at the same time and moved to do just that.

Trey walked over to Dylan, a frown on his lips.

"Go." She nudged him softly. "You've got this."

He took a deep breath. "Only if you come with." He wrapped his arms around her and muddied up her T-shirt and jeans as she laughed. Then he hoisted her up in his arms and walked down to the water. He walked right into it up to his waist with her still in his arms, laughing.

When he dunked them under the water, her lips found his and he knew that he could conquer anything with her by his side, or even better, with her in his arms.

Jill Sanders

Epilogue

As the fall leaves fell around the seated crowd, the warm autumn heat was soothed away by the crisp breeze that floated over the dancing brook only feet away.

The wood archway was decorated with white flowers that matched the bouquet in the arms of the bridesmaids that walked down the cut grass towards the group of men standing at the front of the altar.

When the music changed, guests stood and turned towards the bride.

Dylan's hair had grown past her shoulders. Her short spiky bangs still accented her beautiful brown eyes. Her dress was lace, showing off most of the tattoos on her arms and back. The front was low cut, and her hair fell over her shoulders in perfect curls. The veil covered her smiling face as she walked towards her handsome groom.

His classic black tux was accented with a bright blue cummerbund and bowtie that matched the bridesmaid's dresses.

Brent walked her down the aisle. When they stopped next to Trey, her brother leaned over and whispered.

"Take care of her. I can still kick your ass even though you're my brother-in-law now."

Trey chuckled and nodded, then took her hand in his and pulled her close. Before the preacher could

337

say a word, he was kissing her. The crowd laughed and clapped.

"You're supposed to wait until this is over to do that." She smiled and held onto him.

"Says who?" he asked, holding her close.

"I do." The preacher chuckled.

"Sorry." Trey smiled, then leaned in and whispered, "Not sorry," which made her laugh even more. "I love you. I just couldn't wait until the end to kiss you one more time." The entire crowd sighed before the preacher even started the ceremony.

Other books by Jill Sanders

The Pride Series
Finding Pride
Discovering Pride
Returning Pride
Lasting Pride
Serving Pride
Red Hot Christmas
My Sweet Valentine
Return To Me
Rescue Me

The Secret Series
Secret Seduction
Secret Pleasure
Secret Guardian
Secret Passions
Secret Identity
Secret Sauce

The West Series
Loving Lauren
Taming Alex
Holding Haley
Missy's Moment
Breaking Travis
Roping Ryan
Wild Bride
Corey's Catch
Tessa's Turn

The Grayton Series
Last Resort
Someday Beach
Rip Current
In Too Deep
Swept Away
High Tide

Lucky Series
Unlucky In Love
Sweet Resolve
Best of Luck
A Little Luck

Silver Cove Series
Silver Lining
French Kiss
Happy Accident
Hidden Charm
A Silver Cove Christmas

Entangled Series–
Paranormal Romance
The Awakening
The Beckoning
The Ascension

Haven Montana Series
Closer to You
Never Let Go

Pride Oregon Series
A Dash of Love

Follow Jill
Web: http://JillSanders.com
Twitter: @JillM Sanders
FB: JillSandersBooks

Jill Sanders

About the Author

Jill Sanders is *The New York Times* and *USA Today* bestselling author of the Pride Series, Secret Series, West Series, Grayton Series, Lucky Series, and Silver Cove romance novels. She continues to lure new readers with her sweet and sexy stories. Her books are available in every English-speaking country and in audiobooks and have been translated into several languages.

Born as an identical twin to a large family, she was raised in the Pacific Northwest and later relocated to Colorado for college and a successful IT career before discovering her talent as a writer. She now makes her home along the Emerald Coast in Florida where she enjoys the beach, hiking, swimming, wine tasting and, of course, writing.

Connect with Jill
Facebook: http://fb.com/JillSandersBooks
Twitter: @JillMSanders
Website: http://JillSanders.com

Made in the USA
Lexington, KY
05 April 2019